Undercover Thief

By

H.T.King

Copyright

First Edition August 2015.

ISBN-13: 978-1516914005

ISBN-10: 1516914007

Copyright © 2015 by H. T. King.

Cover design done by mnsartstudio

All Rights reserved in all media.

No part of this book may be used or reproduced without written permission, except in the case of brief quotations embodied in critical articles and reviews.

The moral right of H. T. King as the author of this work has been asserted by her in accordance with the Copyright, Designs and Patents Act 1988.

This is a work of fiction. All names, characters, incidents and locales are products of the author's imagination and any resemblance to actual people, places or events is coincidental or fictionalised.

Editing done by Alice May and Rose King

For my mother. Without all of your love and support throughout my life, I may never have fulfilled my lifelong dream. Thank you.

Acknowledgements

Thank you to my mother and my sister for all of your hours of editing and the early morning starts to help me get this done. I cannot tell you how much it meant to me. I love you both so much.

Contents

CHAPTER ONE	6
CHAPTER TWO	24
CHAPTER THREE	43
CHAPTER FOUR	61
CHAPTER FIVE	87
CHAPTER SIX	108
CHAPTER SEVEN	126
CHAPTER EIGHT	145
CHAPTER NINE	164
CHAPTER TEN	186
CHAPTER ELEVEN	202
CHAPTER TWELVE	220
CHAPTER THIRTEEN	234
CHAPTER FOURTEEN	254
CHAPTER FIFTEEN	276
CHAPTER SIXTEEN	290
CHAPTER SEVENTEEN	308
CHAPTER EIGHTEEN	317
CHAPTER NINETEEN	326
CHAPTER TWENTY	346
CHAPTER TWENTY ONE	371
CHAPTER TWENTY-TWO	380

CHAPTER TWENTY-THREE	**395**
CHAPTER TWENTY FOUR	**406**
CHAPTER TWENTY-FIVE	**421**
CHAPTER TWENTY-SIX	**428**

Chapter One

I pushed open the door in front of me, and surveyed the scene. There were a laser grid, sensor pad and infrared cameras, guarding the room. And in the centre was a small plinth, bearing my prize. Possibly the largest ruby I had ever seen. I smiled at the sight.

This was going to be fun.

"Ok, now," I said.

The lasers snapped off. Perfect. I shot the cord and grappling hook out of my gun and watched it smashed into the plaster of the ceiling, gripping into the thick beam behind it with metal claws. I tugged on it hard to make sure that it was secure. It didn't move an inch.

I tugged on the rope three times in a pre-arranged pattern. Then slowly, the mechanism kicked in and it lifted me off the floor. As I swung towards the ruby, I snatched it off of its silk cushion.

"Did the trip work?" I asked. There was a moment of silence before Leah responded.

Undercover Thief

"Oh yeah. You've done it girl," she crowed over our state of the art communication devices. I could almost hear her celebration dance.

"No, we did it," I corrected her as I slowly crawled closer and closer to the ceiling.

"And the suit is working perfectly. Infrared isn't picking you up at all."

"You're a genius Leah. To think of making a suit out of the same stuff as the tape."

"Well, I'm not disputing the genius part."

"Where's Jerry?" I asked checking my watch for the time. I was on time, but I wasn't alone in the building tonight.

"Still picking up a few souvenirs."

"Well tell him to hurry up. I'm dying for a cup of tea," I said putting the ruby into one of my pockets and zipping it up tight.

"Oh to be British," said Leah with a laugh.

"Um, Leah, you're technically British too."

"A small technicality. I have Thai blood."

"And the fact that you can't remember a single thing about Thailand doesn't matter?"

"Nope," she said defiantly and I snorted.

I reached the top of the rope. I was so close to the ceiling, I could reach out with my hand and touch the plaster if I wanted to. I let out the rope slowly, inch by inch and began to swing on it. I kept lowering it as I swung. Soon I got to what I felt was the right length. I fastened the rope tightly and swung, reaching out. My fingers closed around a small ledge, jutting out from just under a vent. I ripped off the covering, untied the rope from around me and crawled inside.

I wriggled my way along as fast as I could.

"Ok, turn left," Leah instructed in my ear piece.

"Gotcha," I said and wriggled left next turning.

"So you know our next target?" asked Leah.

"I'm trying to get through this one at the moment Leah."

"Aw come on, you always have something in store."

"Alright, I have a few ideas," I admitted. Leah let out a laugh.

"Oh, good! Can we go somewhere with some sun? Maybe a trip to Las Vegas?"

"To cheat casinos? How cliché you are Leah."

"Oh fine. Oh, and Micah is itching to practise his Mandarin. China is sunny, like always."

Undercover Thief

"I'll bear that in mind," I promised, "But if we get a job in Italy, we're taking it."

"Oooh, Italy. They have nice weather too. I'm in," she said and I laughed, "Ok, turn right here and then go straight, that should lead you to a corridor and you can walk from there. I'll keep all eyes blind."

"Thanks Leah," I said.

"So what are you getting him for his birthday?"

"Micah? His birthday isn't for three months."

"I'm talking about Jerry, obviously."

"Oh!"

"He's turning seventeen."

"I almost forgot about that, I was thinking some more military grade cable," I joked and she humoured me with a small laugh.

"And really?"

"I have no idea. What does he want?"

"Like I have a clue! He talks more to you than he does to me, his own sister."

"You know what, whatever you decide to get him, I'll pitch in. So think big."

"See, this is the problem with shopping for a thief. They just take everything they want."

"Indeed it is," I said with a sigh, "but we can think of something. What about that new iPhone? That's supposed to be good."

"Yeah, if we get it with three weeks to spare I can fix all the bugs and upload my software," said Leah thinking it through.

"I'm sure we can manage that, what else? That new iPad while we're in the Apple shop?"

"You know he's not much of a computer guy, but I would love one."

"You could build one yourself," I teased.

"True."

"What else, a phone isn't really enough?"

"I don't know, you know my brother, he's a bit of a closed book about things like that," she said.

"I know, annoyingly closed," I grumbled.

"Hey, I built you a new phone."

"Oh?"

"Yeah, works through jammers and stuff. Nothing can stop it, not even military stuff."

Undercover Thief

"Do I want to know how you tested that?"

"I know a guy," she said and I gave a small laugh.

"Well thanks; that will come in useful, I think."

"It should," she said proudly, "I'm working on wiring it to an ear piece at the moment. That's proving difficult."

"You're eleven years old and you understand more computer stuff than most professionals. Something is bound to trip you now and again."

"Oh I can do it, it is just taking a while for me to fix the bugs," she said.

"Of course," said Jerry, coming onto the coms.

"How long have you been listening?" I demanded.

"The new phone would be nice, thanks for the thought," he teased and I growled.

"Great, our one idea is completely wrecked," huffed Leah.

"Are you done collecting mementos?" I asked coming to the corridor that Leah mentioned and dropping down easily. I landed, knees bent looking around me for some kind of alarm. There wasn't one. I waved at the cameras.

"Hi Pam, I can see you," said Leah. I grinned and headed towards the door.

"I bet I have more money in my hands than you do in yours," said Jerry casually.

"Ooh!" I said smiling with interest, "anything in the form of jewellery?"

"Several."

I had first met Jerry, Leah and their younger brother Micah when I was ten years old. They were the Sklar family – a last name I had adopted when I was with them.

My parents were always away on business. They left me at home with my grandmother to look after me and money in an account to help pay for me. I don't really remember them all that well; I know their faces from pictures my nana used to show me, and the ones stood on the mantle above the fire place and around the home.

I had special education from an early age, as soon as my nana was told it was clear that I was incredibly bright. My grandmother had gotten me a number of special tutors, and I loved learning. Soon she pulled me out of regular school all together; with me so far ahead there didn't seem to be any point continuing in the state system.

And then, when I was nine, my grandmother died and my whole world stopped.

She had a heart attack while I was out at the shop. I called an ambulance – but they proclaimed her dead at the scene. My parents had only gone back to work thirteen days earlier. It was a shock to everyone – Nana had seemed so healthy.

Then money ran out. I spent what little there was left burying her. The tutors stopped coming when they stopped getting paid.

I was left alone. Broken hearted.

Most people would expect that to be the time for parents to come home. Or at least call. Or arrange for someone to take care of their nine year old daughter.

But they didn't.

I was nine years old, with no money, in a large empty house with nobody to help me. The food ran out and the money to buy more dried up, but I waited.

I waited for someone to come for a very long time.

I was smart. I soon realised that no one was coming to save me. So, I gave up crying and accepted that I was on my own, and that I had no one left to care for me. I needed to care for myself.

I needed food. So I began to steal. I stole only food at first, then clothes, and books so I wasn't bored. Then the power to the house was cut off.

I got more and more ambitious with my theft, as I became more and more experienced. Then I lifted a laptop. I had lifted it in the hopes that I could sell it, perhaps use the money to buy myself a hot meal. It was a desperately cold winter.

Only the guy had seen me as I stowed it in my back pack. So I was running away. They were going to catch me. That's when a boy grabbed my hand and pulled me into an alley way. I followed him blindly, not knowing where we were going, but glad that someone was there to help me. This was scary, it was the first time I'd ever been almost-caught. It was not long before we lost them. We stopped at the corner of an empty car park.

I could remember it like it was only yesterday.

He was about my age, coffee coloured skin and hair as black as night. Taller than me, he bent over his knees, taking several deep breaths as we recovered from our running.

"Hey," he said.

"Hi, thanks for that."

"No problem. What'd you get?"

"I didn't-"

"Cause I got a phone," he said holding up two iPhones. I shared his grin.

"Laptop," I said.

"Nice," he said holding out his hand, "I'm Jerimiah."

"Pamela," I answered, taking his hand and shaking it, "really, thanks for the help. I thought I was a goner."

"Got to be a bit more careful there Pammie," he said with a laugh, "kids like us don't do so well in correctional facilities."

"Who knows, perhaps that would get my parents' attention?" I muttered with a sniff, "So why'd you nab the phones?"

"To sell," he said, "you steal a lot?"

"Um...."

"Hey, don't be embarrassed about it," he said, "You're in like-minded company here."

"Well yeah. I need to."

"Need to?"

"I don't have any money, and I need to eat," I said with a sigh, kicking the concrete floor, embarrassed about voicing my financial worries.

"Yeah," he said nodding his head in understanding, "that's why we have to do it too."

"We?"

"Me and my family. Ain't you got a family?"

"No."

"Oh! You're alone?"

"Yes," I said blushing bright red, staring at my interlocked fingers, sort of ashamed to admit that my family had abandoned me.

"Well....." he said tilting his head sideways to study me for a minute, "why don't you come and meet my family? They haven't met anyone new in a while, and you seem nice."

"Won't your parents mind you just bringing random girls home from the street? I could be a thief you know," I joked and he laughed.

"Hey, you're funny Pammie. And no, it's just my brother and sister and me. We don't have any parents," he said, "so you're good."

"Really?"

"Of course, they're younger than us though," he warned.

"Well.....great. Thanks! I'd love to meet them."

"Cool."

And that was it. I met Leah and Micah. I loved them in an instant, they were kind and fun and always joking around. I ended up hanging out there all the time. We started working together, sharing profits, and in the end, I was living there with them.

Undercover Thief

So it was the four of us. Leah, Jerry, Micah and Pamela. The perfect, underage criminal team.

"Ok," I said getting to my planned exit point, "I'm out."

I walked calmly out into the street along to the end and around the corner. A van drove beside me and pulled up, throwing open the door.

"Need a ride?" asked Leah. I climbed inside.

"Hold it!" called Jerry jogging over, swinging in behind me. We closed the door and drove away. That's when we pulled off our masks.

"So, let's see the ruby then!" said Leah. I pulled it out of my pocket for them to see.

"Ooh, shiny," said Jerry taking it in his hands and holding it up to the light.

"Hey, trade!" I said holding out my hands. He pulled a few necklaces from his pocket and tossed them into my hand with his trademark grin.

"You approve?" he asked as I examined them.

"Oh yes," I said holding them up to the light.

"You star Jerry!"

"I need a cup of tea!" I announced, feeling good about a job well done.

"Ok! We're headed back the attic now!" said Leah with a laugh. We drove all the way back to the attic, through the semi-empty streets of London.

"Oooh," I said inspecting the pile of jewellery that Jerry had stolen, picking up one of them I found particularly lovely.

"You want to keep it?" asked Jerry, "It would look good with your blue dress."

"Yes, it would wouldn't it," I said picturing the two together. For a really macho man, Jerry had such a good eye for colour, and he wasn't afraid to admit it either.

"How's the cash flow looking?" I asked.

"We're stable," said Leah.

"When's Micah's next bill due?"

"Three weeks, I've already put money aside," said Jerry.

Whenever we stole or did anything illegal, all of the money that we made we split into two, and that was before we factored in things like running costs. Fifty percent of the profit we kept divided between the four of us equally after all costs had been paid for.

The other fifty percent went to charity. When we had hit the big leagues, we started making a lot more money than we actually needed. Lots more money. Having all that money, after struggling and having so little for so long....it felt almost wrong to me. Leaving aside the little fact that stealing is, of course, wrong. Whenever I walked down a street in London, I would see poverty and homelessness all around. It brought back the memories of when I had been like that. I had managed to pick myself out of the dirt, but some people couldn't do that. So, fifty percent of all the money we earned went to soup kitchens, food banks and towards charities devoted to getting people off the street and giving them a fresh shot at life.

I turned my gaze back to the necklace.

"Go on Pammie, it can be your cut," said Jerry, "You know you want it. Besides, when we run a con, first impressions count and nothing says first impression like that amount of money around your neck."

"Ok, then I think I can give these diamonds and sapphires a new home," I said, claiming the necklace that I loved. I really didn't need that much persuasion.

Leah and I swapped who was driving. I took a firm hold of the wheel and watched as Leah picked through the jewels, doing some mental calculations about the money we had left and trying to decide if this really was more than my fair cut — because if that was the case I wouldn't accept it.

"You don't worry about it Leah," said Jerry, "it's not at all the most expensive one I swiped. You'll like this one, look at the size of this Emerald."

"I didn't like it for the expensive-ness.....if that's even a word," Leah laughed as my argument fizzled out.

"It probably isn't," she said, "It looks good Pam."

"So, what do you think about our next target Pammie," asked Jerry.

I was the one who decided our targets, our plan. I just had a better head for strategy than they did. They didn't mind though, and if they had ideas, then I happily listened to them. But Jerry was definitely the head of the family, he and I were sort of the collective leaders. But Jerry was the one who made all final decisions. However, we were a family, and everyone got a say in how things were run and the decisions that were made.

"Well....I'm not sure. I need to check with Milo, see if anyone is hiring at the moment. If not, there is a lovely museum in Italy that could really use a visit."

"Oh dear, are they getting too bogged down by material possession?" joked Jerry.

"Yeah, it's only fair that we help them out, it'll give them more storage space," I said playing along with his joke.

"Well, it sounds good to me," nodded Jerry stowing the ruby in one of our brief cases as I drove into our warehouse and parked the van.

This was where we lived. The warehouse had been abandoned when we had found it. We lived upstairs, in the attic space, hence called our home an attic. We had bought the attic legally a few years ago, so it was a safe haven for us to come and live.

"Micah, we're back!" called Jerry as we piled through the door into our living space. I kicked off my work heels (you would be surprised how many times sharp, glass cutting heels could come in handy) and pulled my hair out of its tight ponytail.

"How was it?" asked a voice from the sofa. Micah's face turned towards us. Micah's face was shocking to most people. There was a mass of red scars and buckled skin where his eyes had healed badly – after an attack when he was small. He was completely blind, and simply turned his head in the direction of the noise.

The truth for all of us was that, if we could, we would walk away from this life of crime and never look back. We all had plans about how we'd get out if we chose to, as a family. Jerry would get a job at an apprenticeship that paid well; I was going to get a job at a firm.

The problem with that was it wouldn't pay for Micah's treatment. He needed constant checks for his eyes, they were at risk from infection almost constantly due to the way they had healed – half open. The damage was extensive, and all the appointments cost a lot.

It wasn't like we could take him to a traditional doctor on the NHS. People would ask about his parents and then take him away when they realised we were living alone. So we had to go private but not just any kind of private. Most doctors that did private work would also argue about needing to see his parents. We had to go through illegal channels to find doctors – doctors that didn't ask questions, and they cost a lot more money.

"We did well," I said immediately, going over to him and wrapping my arms around the small seven year old boy and giving him a tight squeeze.

"Yay!" he said yawning.

"Are you tired sweetheart?" I asked gently and he nodded.

"Yeah," he mumbled leaning back against the sofa and my arm, snuggling up to me, raising his hand to my jaw. I closed my eyes as his hands ran over my face for a minute, his version of seeing me.

"You could go to bed," I told him.

"No thanks," he sighed, "I want to listen to what we do now."

"We're going to celebrate," said Jerry.

"With a cup of tea?" I hinted and Leah let out a huge bark of laughter, switching on the kettle.

When we had moved into the attic part of the warehouse (purely for security reasons and the view) we had slowly kitted it out to make it homey and comfortable. We had decent furniture and everything was done nicely and decorated as well, like a proper apartment. There was no reason not to live in a bit of comfort, now we could afford it.

Undercover Thief

Over time we had made a lot of acquaintances. A lot of less than legal people. The kind of people who ignored the law and laughed in its face.

Our kind of people.

Some were nice and we remained in touch with them, and others we said good bye to as soon as possible. But they were able to hook us up with people in the Underground who could get us what we need without asking questions.

This included doctors for Micah.

"Ok, time for cake!" said Jerry producing it from the fridge.

This here was my family. This here, in this moment, was when I was happiest. Everyone was in a good mood, everyone was smiling. Nothing could touch us. We were walking on air.

But good things never last very long.

Chapter Two

That morning I woke up early. Very early. It couldn't even be two in the morning, and I felt slow and sluggish. Then I realised I had been woken up by a persistent beeping sound.

"Pam! Shut it up!" yelled Jerry grumpily from his room.

"On it!" I yelled back, dragging myself from the warm embrace of my bed and over to my laptop. I sat down with a plop on the seat, yawning and wiggling the mouse simultaneously. The black screen vanished and it popped up with an alert. The security at my parents' place had been tripped. And not just once either.

Someone was in my house.

Annoyed I brought up the cameras I had installed there. I couldn't see anyone. Just because I didn't live there anymore didn't mean I didn't keep watch over it. I did, because it was somewhere to run just in case we needed it.

There wasn't anything on any of the cameras that I could see. I groaned, rubbing my eyes. That was annoying.

Undercover Thief

This meant I had to go and check it out. I didn't really care if someone stole from the house. I mean, everything I wanted from it was here already. But it could be someone investigating me, in which case I needed to know that. And if they were a thief, I would stop them. It was the principle really. It wouldn't do to have a thief steal from me. With our family's growing respect and name in the Underground, we didn't need an event like this spoiling everything.

I got up and dragged myself to my dresser. I pulled on black jeans, a blue lace top and a black leather jacket. I pulled on some comfortable boots, lacing them up while all the time throwing glances at the monitor of my laptop. Still no movement that I could see.

I pulled my hair up into a pony tail to keep it out of my face. I threw a small glance in the mirror and sighed when I saw that my purple eyes were framed by dark, sleep deprived shadows. Never mind, I could sleep when I got back.

Then I grabbed my phone and my keys from my bedside table and shoved them into my jacket pockets before leaving my room.

"Going to my parents' place," I called to anyone that was awake.

"Why?" came a muffled sound from Jerry.

"Security was tripped. Be back in a short while," I called. All I got in response was a tired sounding groan escaping from Jerry's room. He had heard and that was all he could be bothered to respond with.

"I'll get bacon too!" I called, walking out the front door. I closed it behind me and started down the twisting metal stairs to the warehouse below.

This was where we kept a majority of our gear, the large computers where we monitored security feeds and carried out our hacks. There was military cable and high spec climbing equipment on various shelves. There were boxes of various kit, and on hangers were the specialised outfits that we'd use when we were stealing. A lot of thought had been put into their design, making them perfect for each specific purpose – depending on the type of place we were going to rob.

But what we also kept down here were the cars. We owned three cars, all of which were bought legally, with money obtained less legally and they were driven with very illegal driving licences. There was the van, for surveillance on buildings that we were planning to case. Inside was a state of the art computer system, or at least that's what Leah told me.

We also had two other cars. They were high end, expensive and very fast. They were incredible to drive....even though I was fourteen and I wasn't supposed to drive, I did anyway. I was a master thief; of course I could get my hands on fake driving licences and ID!

Undercover Thief

We normally used the cars when we ran a con. First impressions counted, and often a big expensive car did the job nicely. After all, the people we were tricking were most often materialistic douche-bags. Only Jerry and I were allowed to drive them however. The van had tinted windows so no one could see in. But these cars did not, and Leah did not look old enough to pass for seventeen. And Micah couldn't for an obvious reason.

I got into my favourite white sports car and started the engine, pulling on my seat belt. I rubbed my fingers together trying to warm up a little. I turned up the heating and plugged in my phone to the dashboard of the car. It was abnormally cold for late July.

I pulled up the security camera feeds onto my phone, so that I could keep watching as the car de-misted. Nothing new. No more security had been tripped, telling me they hadn't left. Whoever it was, they were still there.

I put the car into first gear and was off, driving comfortably through the streets of London at the dead of night. I switched on the radio, listening to the club music for two reasons. First was because I liked it, and the other was because I was hoping the heavy beat would wake me up. I tapped along to the base rhythm as I drove.

It was a thirty minute drive to my parents' house, in a nice area of town, on the outskirts of the city. Rather scrawny looking trees were planted at intervals along the pavement; the street was illuminated by green energy lamps. Every house looked a lot like the last, perfectly kept lawn with a people carrier car in the drive. Except my parents' place. The lawn was brown and un-kept, popping up with weeds. The windows needed washing, the dark bricks on the outside were crumbling, no car in the drive.

I drove past it, not wanting to stop right outside. I parked two blocks away deciding to walk back. I fished the forgotten house key out of my car door and headed to my destination. I walked, tossing the key up in the air and catching it absentmindedly, humming to myself. I avoided the few puddles there were littering the pavement, the result of a brief shower I hadn't heard in my sleep. In the background there were the usual city noises, dogs barking and cars sounding horns. Oh, the joys of London.

I got to the front door and opened it carefully. It wasn't locked. Interesting, so they had picked the lock. Some thought had gone into this, maybe they weren't run of the mill thieves after all. I bent down to look at it properly, running my fingers across the mechanisms and frowning. There wasn't any sign of locking picking, none of the usual scrapes and lines that went with an amateur. This was either a professional job (in which case why were they in my house?) or they had a key.....even more interesting. I closed the door quietly behind me as I walked in.

I silently walked a little way down the wooden corridor. I paused as I got to two doors and the stairs. I had three directions to choose from. Where did I check first? Then I heard a large bang and some muffled voices, talking intensely but quietly.

Undercover Thief

The kitchen.

I looked around me; grabbing a dusty cricket bat from the place I had hidden it in the hall. I didn't know who or what I would face in there, and it didn't hurt to be prepared to defend myself, just in case.

"Then where are they? Hmm?" came a male voice, he was angry and stressed. And it sounded like whoever was in there was waiting for someone. And it was more than one person.

"Calm down."

"No! I will not calm down! What if something has happened?"

"We can't think like that! We have to be positive."

"I'm trying, but it's been such a long time."

"I know that."

"Where are they? Where could they be, I mean look at the time!"

"I trust them, don't worry."

It sounded like just the two of them. I knew exactly where they were by where their voices were coming from through the door. They were sat at the breakfast bar. Weird. Who broke into a house to sit at a breakfast bar?

I decided now was the time to announce my presence. I burst through, knocking one of them off their seat, sending them sprawling over the floor. Then the world was flying as I was thrown into the cabinet with a loud shattering of glass as I made contact and my arm went through. I hit the floor and looked up to see the cabinet about to fall onto me. I rolled out of the way as it crashed to the floor. There was a stinging on my face and my left hand was sore and had a warm liquid on it.

That was close.

"Ella!" gasped a voice.

That was a name I hadn't heard in a long time. No one had called me Ella since I was little....Jerry had called my Pam and that had stuck. I liked it; it fit who I was now more than Ella ever had. I looked up at the two people and finally recognised who they were.

"Oh. It's you," I said rolling my eyes. I looked at my hand, a couple of cuts and some blood. But it didn't look like it had glass in it.

"Oh my goodness, are you ok?" asked my mother picking herself off the floor from where I had thrown her and hurrying to my side. She knelt next to me, trying to look at my wrist. I tore it from her hand like she burned.

"Urgh, what are you doing here?" I asked brushing shards of glass off my clothes and being careful that they didn't fall into my boots.

"We live here. Ella, why were you rushing through the door with a cricket bat?" asked my father, who offered me a hand to my feet which I ignored. He had thrown me into a cabinet after all. And he looked angry and ashamed.....both. Good.

"I thought you were here to steal stuff," I said getting up easily, "what are you two even doing here?"

"What do you mean Ella? We live here."

"You haven't been here in almost six years," I retorted going to the tap and inspecting the cuts on my hand again, double checking for glass before I washed the blood off of it. They were superficial wounds.

"Sorry darling," said my mother.

"Well, good to know you aren't stealing from me," I said, "And that I don't have to keep watching this place anymore. It's so annoying to keep doing. I was going to sell it, but now you're back I'll leave it to you."

"What?"

"Deeds are on the desk, but this place might need a spruce up if you're going to sell it too. I wasn't so worried about the capital but you might be."

"What do you mean sell it?"

"I mean sell it. There isn't really a double meaning there. I changed the deeds to my name about six months ago," I rolled my eyes.

"You don't live here?"

"Course not, look at this place. If I lived here I'd keep better house."

"And what does Nana think about you selling the house?" demanded my mother. I gave a short bark of humourless laughter.

"Oh, that's a funny joke," I said sarcastically as I snapped off the water from the tap and dried my hands with a tea towel.

"I'm serious. Where is she?" asked my mother.

"Same place she's been for the last six years. The cemetery," I answered sharply, walking out of the kitchen.

"What?" she gasped in a quiet voice. I went into the sitting room and used the mirror to wipe some of my blood off of my sleeve.

"Ella, have you been living here alone?" asked my father, "for the last six years?"

"You can drop the surprised act," I said fixing my hair.

"Act? This isn't an act Ella!"

"Oh come on, you knew," I said walking into the study. They followed me like lost puppies. I scooped the deeds off of the desk and handed them to my father. He took them and put them back on the desk.

Undercover Thief

"No, we didn't!" exclaimed my mother, hand clutched to her mouth and tears streaming down her face. She was crying. My father put an arm around her and tried to comfort her.

"Didn't what?"

"We didn't know your grandmother had passed away," said my father seriously.

"Wow.....I mean.....wow.....I called so many times I lost count. I left you so many messages on your answerphones until they ran out of room. And you couldn't be bothered to listen to them? Any of them? I mean, I knew you didn't care but that is a new level," I said stung slightly by this new revelation. I pushed past them and headed out into the hall.

"We never got the messages. Oh darling, we're so sorry!" sobbed my mother, rushing towards me, clearly looking to embrace me. I side stepped her neatly.

"You know what, it's really doesn't matter. Like I said, I don't live here. Excuse me, I gotta go home. Nice to see you again. See you again in another six years....or not. I really don't care," I said making my way back to the front door.

"Pamela!" said my father, grabbing my arm to stop me walking.

"Ow!" I said yanking my arm free, "this thing went through glass you know!"

"Sorry, where do you live?"

33

"What?"

"You said you don't live here, so where do you live?"

"With my family, now I have to get home or they'll worry. Bye," I said turning around and freezing as I caught a glimpse out of the window. There were people outside, and I knew that stance. I had the stance.

Damn.

"Ella, you did-what's wrong?" asked my father sensing there was a problem.

"There are three non-descript black vans outside," I said with a groan, "and they weren't there two minutes ago."

"What?" he demanded, about to storm over to the window to see for himself.

"Oh don't go over you idiot! We currently have the advantage! We've don't want them to know we've spotted them genius!" I snapped walking back into the study.

I turned on the old computer and plugged in my phone, bringing up my cameras so I could see the images more clearly, looking for some kind of detail.

"I didn't install those cameras," sniffed my mother, wiping her eyes with a hanky.

"No, I did," I said without think about it. I brought up the camera that was most relevant and enhanced the image. A gun.

Undercover Thief

"Shoot!" I said at the same time as my mother.

"Sorry, I didn't mean to drag you into this," I said quickly, unplugging my phone and going back out into the hall way.

"Wait a minute, you think you caused this?" asked my father.

"You think you did...." I realised, narrowing my eyes to inspect the two of them. Now I looked, they had the stance too. A stance that was ready for action....my parents? Really?

"They're on the move Gordon," said my mother looking at the computer screen.

"Right," said my father producing a gun from the waist band of his jeans.

"Whoa," I said taking a couple of steps back. My parents had guns? Oh no, no way were they sales representatives. The little liars! But I had a rule, one I didn't want to break. And it was simple really, a rule that a majority of thieves stuck to – or the good ones did anyway.

Breaking the law was fine; doing what it took to get the job done was ok. But no one should ever get hurt or die. Nothing materialistic was worth a life. So no guns.

"Pamela, you need to stay with us darling, and do exactly what we tell you too." My mother's face meant business.

"Well....you guys seem to have a plan. I think I'll just leave you to it."

"Pamela, where are you going?"

"As far away as possible from the guns," I said.

"Pamela! You need to come back here and do what we say! We can protect you!"

"Are you kidding me? You plan to fight them! Six bullets against.....twenty men on average? For goodness's sake it's like I'm the only one with a brain!" I turned and ran up the stairs.

"Pamela! Ella!" yelled my mother chasing me.

I didn't care that they were following. If they wanted to use the escape route I was using then go ahead. They were my parents after all, and I probably should look after them. I threw open the window at the end of the corridor and climbed easily up, onto the roof. I turned back and looked at them, and saw them about to try and follow me.

"Keep a good grip," I called, "and the third brick from the right is loose."

I found the cable I had left there, disguised as a power cable, about three years ago. I had left it there just in case I ever needed an escape. I was a thief, and a good thief always had an exit strategy, and tonight it more than paid off. I pulled it tight, tying it through a purpose built bracket (also installed by me for just such a time) attached to the chimney.

"Ella!" gasped my mother, "where did you get military grade cable?"

"How do you know its military grade?" I shot back, tugging on it to make sure it was done up tight.

"How do you-"

"Keep up if you're coming," I said breaking into a sprint. I sprinted towards the edge of the roof and threw myself off. I caught the cable, swinging my legs in front of my and wrapping them around the wire. I pushed myself, feet first, along to the other end of the wire, which was tied to the roof of another house over the road, and most importantly, away from the men with guns.

I pulled myself onto the second roof and looked down. Nobody saw me making my speedy escape. That was good. I looked back at the cable and saw both my parents following me. I waited impatiently at the other end of the cable.

The moment they touched the roof I was untying the cable. I attached it to a launcher to get rid of this end of the cable.

"Pamela!" said my father, snatching the launcher from my hands, "where on earth did you get this stuff?"

"Around, I don't know. How about once we're out of danger you can ask stupid questions?" I snapped, taking the launcher back, and sending this end of the cable far away. If they found it, they wouldn't know which direction we had gone.

I threw the launcher aside and went over to the other side of the building where I knew I could climb down easily.

"Pamela, where did you learn to do this?" asked my mother.

"I have a few hobbies," I said vaguely. I didn't stop at the edge of the roof, hoping off easily, and spinning so my fingers caught the edge of the re-enforced gutters. My feet were dangling over the window ledge and I dropped on it, and started systematically working my way down the side of the house using previously scouted finger and toe holds. I had come up with several routes of escape from my house over the years, and I knew all of them like the back of my hand.

At the end, I jumped onto a large waste bin and then onto the concrete floor. I brushed off my hands and took my phone out of my pocket. I needed to talk to Jerry and tell him what was going on. This was a huge development that no one could have seen coming.

"Pamela!" yelled my father angrily; they hadn't started their way down yet.

"Yeah?"

Undercover Thief

"Wait there, we're coming down!"

"Nah, I have a better plan," I said, pausing before I hit call, "I suggest we separate. If they are after you and not me, then I won't have to deal with it. And vice versa. Win-win for everyone."

"Pamela!"

"Bye! This was fun, let's do it again in six years!" I called.

"Don't walk away from us!" snapped my mother, "why do you have military equipment? Why are you able to do that? Why are there infrared triggers and secret cameras in our house? And why on earth would men with guns be after you?"

"You know what," I called up, "Figure it out!"

"Ella!"

"I'm not Ella! I'm Pam!" I shouted not looking back as I walked away, "I hope we don't meet again."

I rounded the corner and kept walking, moving fast. I didn't know how fast they would reach the bottom and I didn't want them to come after me. I walked all the way back to my car, reconnected my phone to my dash and phoned Jerry.

"It's early Pam," protested Jerry, sleep thick in his voice.

"Well wake up, we might have a problem."

"What? Hang on; is this to do with why you went to your parents' place?"

"Oh yeah," I said starting the engine, "my parents came back."

"Oh, nice of them to show their faces after so long. So, why is this a problem?"

"Because they're the real deal,"

"Huh? Hang on, parents?" he definitely sounded more awake now.

"Yeah, I know. I'm still trying to process it."

"Hold your horses there Pam, run it by me again. What happened?"

"I just had to out-run men with guns. And my father had a gun."

"Guns? Damn, you're alright?"

"Nothing a band aid won't fix, there was an incident with a cabinet. But whatever my parents are, they aren't sales representatives," I said pulling on my seat belt.

"Leah! Get over here," yelled Jerry.

"What?" I heard her mumble sleepily.

"Parents are back," I said.

Undercover Thief

"Wow! Are you alright?" that woke her up.

"Eh, I knew they had to come back at some point. The thing that counts is that they brought a truck load of gun men with them."

"You say what?"

"I know right? Actually, three truck loads. Are we certain that no one like that is after us?"

"No one," said Jerry certainly.

"That's just more evidence to my 'not sales representatives' theory."

"You have more evidence?"

"I used an escape route over the roof," I explained, "They followed and they didn't even break a sweat."

"The one with the cables and the climbing?"

"Yep,"

"And the window drop?"

"Yep,"

"And nothing? Like, not even hesitation?"

"Nada," I agreed.

"I am beginning to support Pamela's theory about them not being sales reps," said Leah.

"Yeah, me too," piped up Jerry.

"Yeah, so Leah, think you can do some digging for me."

"Of course. By the sounds of it, they shouldn't be too hard to find," said Leah, "What are their names again?"

"Isabell and Gordon Torres,"

"By the sounds of it, you're parents have some secrets of their own."

"Let's find out what they are," I said as I accelerated hard away from the scene of my escape.

Chapter Three

The summer fell away to the beginnings of fall, and two months later we had heard neither hide nor hair of my parents. And to top off good news, we hadn't had truckloads of men with guns around the attic. So I assumed that those men had been after my parents rather than me.

It was business as usual after a week of being on alert.

In the two months that had passed, we hadn't been able to dig up a single thing about where my parents were, what they did or who they had seen. We went through all the normal channels and to all the people we could think off. It left us with the conclusion that they had to be very bad people, not to be a part of the Underground. And that meant I wanted to stay as far away from them as possible.

The mid-September sun beat down on me as I walked to my usual newspaper stand. I put my sunglasses on top of my head as I reached for one of the newspapers in front of me and flicked through the headlines, hoping to be struck with inspiration.

"Why hello there Pammie," said the stall owner with a familiar smile.

"Hey there Milo," I said grinning at my friend, "how's business?"

"Can't go complaining,"

"And how is Lola?"

"She's alright, we're alright," he said nodding as I handed him a pound coin for the paper.

"Oh good. I do like her. She's a keeper Milo."

"I'll bare that in mind there Pam," he said with a chuckle.

"You know you should, I'm excellent at judging a person's character," I said with a wink, "Plus that apple crumble she made Leah for her birthday was divine."

"She says thank you for the note."

"See, she's a keeper," I said with a smile.

"Want change?" he asked waving the coin.

"Nah, you probably get some thieves here," I said flicking back through my paper and he cackled with good humoured laughter.

"You don't say," he wheezed.

Undercover Thief

Milo was a man who knew everything. He knew everyone in the law-ignoring world that was of any good, and could get us anything we needed, as long as we gave him notice and cash. If we needed equipment or even actors for our con jobs, he could get them for us. He was our source of gossip for the Underground.

"So, anyone in town that I might like to meet?" I asked as I scanned the headlines for a new job. He shrugged.

"You like rich American Senators?"

"How rich?" I asked instantly interested. He gave a wicked smile.

"Very."

"Oh, my favourite kind,"

"Aren't they everyone's?"

"Shouldn't be hard to find a dirty secret or two to exploit," I said turning to read the newspaper article announcing to the world that he had travelled to London.

"A simple blackmail? Can't you kids come up with something a little more ingenious?"

"Oh, I'm sure we will. Simply a contingency,"

"I still love the job you pulled on that actor's wife. Pure genius,"

"Why thank you."

"And Peru......now that was a way to make a name for yourself,"

"That was eighteen months ago."

"People haven't forgotten," he said with a wide smile, "You kids are up and comers, I've said it all along."

"Thanks Milo."

"So how's little Micah doing?"

Micah had lost his eyes the night the three siblings had run away from their home. Their father used to get drunk and then get violent. That night, the violence was directed towards the two year old. Jerry and Leah fought with their father; managing to pull him away, but not before Micah had been blinded.

They hadn't been home since, point blank refused to go back and I never pushed. I understood disappointing parents well, but I couldn't image the horror of what they went through. My parents had never scarred me like that. They were just absent.

And when Milo had heard that little Micah needed a doctor, he had been able to put us in contact with the best people. People who didn't ask questions. He helped get us on our feet and able to make enough money to pay them. He kept us away from the bad crowds, giving us a few pointers and steering us into the direction he thought we should go. Kept us out of a lot of trouble, our world wasn't always a safe one after all.

Undercover Thief

He kept us the 'good' kind of criminal. The kind that never did any serious damage to anyone except leave holes in people's bank accounts. He had a good heart and we could count on him, a true friend.

"Another doctor is coming to check his eyes," I said with a sigh, "it's more and more complicated than they originally thought."

"Poor kid. It ain't right what some folk do to their own blood."

"To right. Yet, given half a chance it's us they'd put in prison. Shows you how twisted the world really is."

"You said it," he agreed, taking a swig from his costa coffee. He scratched his grey beard and sat on his stool again thinking.

"You ever need something for Micah, you just let me know alright?" he said with a serious nod in my direction.

"Thanks Milo."

"I know your team prefer to target guys who have dirty pasts, and you all have dreams of going straight one day, but remember that eating and your health are more important than a few materialistic items."

"We aren't struggling at the moment," I said smiling at this repetitive lesson, "but thanks for the advice."

"Not at all. You team are quite the little illegal vigilantes."

"Aww, I'm touched," I said smiling and flicking over on the next page of my paper. Then I froze, looking at his mirror.

"How's Leah's education anyway?"

"Milo, do you see that?" I asked pretending to go back to my newspaper like nothing happened, waiting for his response anxiously. He scanned the crowd casually and nodded.

"The guy in the blue cap,"

"And the four others. The woman by the buggy not checking on the baby. The two men having coffee not talking or looking at each other. The man sat by the bus stop, phone in his hand but not checking his texts."

"Oh yeah. Good spots. I told you that you were good," he said grimly.

I glanced to my left as thought something banal had simply caught my eye for a moment. There was an escape over the road. Nobody was blocking that exit.

"Need a distraction?" he offered casually.

"Think you can muster one up for me?"

"No problem," he said with a good natured wink. Then he gave a loud whistle. A boy who was playing with a cheap plastic bubble blower stood up and walked down to the other end of the street.

Undercover Thief

"Milo?"

"Ready?"

"Yep,"

Milo tapped the newspaper desk three times. Then the kid collapsed to the floor screaming. The noise was like he'd been shot. Everyone instantly turned their head, looking his way. Which meant no one was looking at me.

Giving me an escape.

In the two seconds that everyone looked, I moved away. I ditched my jacket in the bin and took down my hair and walked around the corner. I saw them all get up at once, realising I was gone. That was not very smooth at all.

I watched them all, in the reflections of shop windows, casually so they didn't know that I had clocked them. I stopped, pretending to be admiring a dress, and then look at my reflection, checking my hair. I knew the instant they spotted me again. Damn, they were after me as I had feared; they were all communicating and getting back into their bad covers.

"Ok," I muttered to myself, "Let's see how good you are at following a thief."

I finished pretending to inspect my non-existent make up and moved on, keeping to an easy walking pace. As I walked, I assessed the people tailing me. They were good tails, very casual. Not as bumbling and stupid as I had first thought. I was just very good at picking up on threats.

I rounded a corner, and there was a load of traffic, a very busy road with several lanes. And I ran, breaking into an instant sprint, racing through the moving cars. I slid smoothly over the bonnet of a car that didn't stop in time, and continued running again. The whole action flowed naturally and didn't for a moment decrease my speed.

It didn't take them long to start chasing me. I pegged it through the crowd. Sure I was wearing heals, but that didn't stop or hinder me in any way. All my heels were as comfortable as my flats and I could always work in them.

"Stop her!" they yelled, some talking frantically into ear pieces as they moved. I banked a hard left and ended up in a huge shopping centre.

I ran into the first store I saw. It was a clothes store. I hid behind a rail of clothes as they ran in. They didn't see me and decided to split up and look. I smiled.

Then I realised I was in Zara, nice. I needed a change of clothes; it would make it easier for me to ditch the people chasing me. I grabbed a dress, a bag and a wig off the head of a manikin as I passed by, and headed straight for the dressing rooms.

I transferred the contents of my old bag into the new one; easily taking off the price tags and security labels (stealing clothes was nothing compared to lifting items from the Tate Modern). I walked out in the pretty yellow dress, wearing white heals and the white bag over my shoulder. I pulled on the wig and some sunglasses. I caught a reflection of myself in the mirror.

Wow, I was gorgeous in this dress.

I walked out of the store casually. I noticed that two men were guarding the door I had entered in and instantly decided to find another exit. In a place like this, there had to be a few. As I walked, I passed a lady sat at a table outside a coffee shop. She was so caught up in her conversation with the waiter she didn't even notice when I stole her phone.

I called Jerry, each ring that went unanswered made me want to throw the phone into the wall with frustration.

"Hello?" said Jerry finally picking up.

"We have a problem."

"What is it?"

"I have four....no, more than that. I have tails. I can see five of them.....make that six. Not your average cop either, they're good."

"How good?"

"I may have just ditched them, but I wouldn't count on it yet."

"Struggling?"

"I might be."

"Interpol?"

"I don't know," I said. I saw one heading back, looking for me still. I switched my sunglasses so they hid more of my face.

"Where are you? I'll drive out and give you a hand."

"No, you don't need to get involved. Steer clear."

"No way!"

"Don't leave Micah and Leah. If we both get caught how does that help anyone?" I hissed as I found and exit. That raised my mood significantly. I walked out onto the street.

"But-"

"You don't even know where I am Jerry," I pointed out, "I bet you aren't tracing my call, I'll hang up before you have time."

"Pam, please just let me help you!"

"Listen, don't you worry about me. I'll let you know what happens either way. Bye," I hung up. I didn't want them getting mixed up in this mess, but they needed to know why I didn't come home.....if I didn't come home. I took the sim out of the phone and then the battery, snapping them both in half and threw the pieces in a convenient bin.

I kept walking, and it wasn't long before I saw some new tails. Three of them. They were systematically scanning the area. One of them narrowed his eyes as he looked at me and then yelled at the others as he set off towards me. Oh great!

I started running again, racing down the steps to the underground, ditching the wig and acquiring a cap and hoodie. I threw myself in between the escalators, sliding down the long metal section in the middle. I hit the bottom, having slid almost vertically down, and rolled, landing on my feet and sprinted off again.

"Who the hell trained this girl? She's nuts!" one yelled as they followed me. I threw away the hoodie when I was out of sight and pulled on a coat that was left lying around. I literally stole the hat off of a woman's head and moved on swiftly. I looked completely different again.

I walked onto a platform and got straight onto a train. I sat down, and watched and waited. I saw them run onto the platform. I grabbed a spare metro paper holding it up to cover my face.

Then they got on the train and started checking people's faces. I threw the paper aside and got off the train, blending with the crowd on the platform moving away. The doors closed and the train sped off, carrying the people following me with it.

I smiled.

Turning back to the exit I saw one man still there, searching through the sea of people trying to find me.

Well, I suppose it wasn't the only exit, but it was certainly the safest. There was a service hatch just up the tunnel that I could see. I jumped down onto the track and hurried over to the door. No one spotted me.

I easily bypassed the feeble and rusted lock and closed the door firmly behind me. Looking up at the long ladder to the to the surface, which was nothing more than a tiny dot of light that was so far away and only just visible, I sighed, gripped the filthy ladder and started climbing up the tiny tunnel.

Now was a good time to remind myself that claustrophobia was for wimps.

I finally got to the top and pushed the cover to one side, climbing up onto the tarmac of the street. I stood up and looked around. I saw two sleek black, non-descript black cars a little way off, in front of the entrance to the underground. No one was watching me.

There was a woman, leaning against one of the car bonnets, talking furiously into a small hand set, clearly angry. She was obviously organising this search. She had shoulder length, thick and shiny, dark blond hair and was wearing a professional looking trouser-suit.

I turned and walked away, smiling to myself. I had done it.

"I see her! How did she slip by you?" I heard her say and internally groaned. Idiot! I should never congratulate

Undercover Thief

myself too soon! I should know that by now! It was just asking for trouble.

"No! Stop her!" She yelled out, running after me. I smashed through a group of people and down the road. I lost the hat somewhere.

My hair streamed out behind me as I ran. I heard her yelling into the radio as she followed me. I ran and ran, and managed to cut through one of the back alleys. I knew my way around here like the back of my hand. I ran, pushing off a large box and easily jumping over a fence. I looked back to see she was following me easily.

She was better than I was used to. Damn.

"Pamela!" she yelled.

She knew my name? Oh no, that really wasn't good.

I decided I needed a more inventive approach as she wasn't slowing down, even for a moment. I jumped through an open window and into a house.

"Sorry," I said as I ran through a dining room where a family was about to enjoy a meal. I sprinted up the stairs to an attic, threw open a dormer window and climbing out onto the roof. Time to test this woman's commitment.

She followed without hesitation. I ran straight at the edge of the roof, not slowing down. I jumped, landing easily on the flat roof of the building over and kept moving like this, jumping from roof to roof, hoping that this might now daunt my chaser.

No such luck.

I skidded to a stop at the edge of a roof, my mouth going dry. I knew I couldn't make this jump and the woman finally caught up.

"Stand down Torres!" she yelled. I turned to face her. There was a gun trained on me, she was panting fiercely and so was I. We had both been through quite a work out.

"Seriously? A gun? I'm a fourteen year old girl!" I protested.

"It's merely a precaution. It's to stop you doing anything stupid."

"What? Like carry a gun! You know a funny thing, if a group of people don't have guns they are less likely to be shot!"

"Interesting theory Miss Torres. Now you're going to walk over here, slowly, and come with me."

"Where?"

"I can't tell you that."

"Then I refuse to come with you."

"Remember the gun?"

"You're willing to shoot a fourteen year old girl?"

"If I have to."

"You're bluffing."

"Are you sure?"

"Pretty sure."

"Then test me," she said slowly walking closer. I raised my hands in a gesture of surrender.

"Oh, you don't want to issue a challenge like that in a neighbourhood like this. It'll get you beaten up."

"You live in this neighbourhood?"

"No, but I know people who do."

"Are you going to beat me up?"

"Like I have pointed out, I'm little more than a fourteen year old girl. I prefer flight over fight."

"That's probably a sensible policy to have."

"Worked for me so far," I said. Then she was close enough.

I shot out my leg; a swift inner crescent kick knocking the gun from her hand with precision followed immediately by a spin and then smashed my elbow into her temple. She fell to one side. I made to run while she was stunned. But she grabbed my ankle, pulling me down to the roof tiles with her. Her hands scrambled for the gun, which I kicked further away.

I managed to get to my feet, but she grabbed me. She tried to pin my arms together, so I smashed my knee into her ribs and stamped on her foot. I shoved her away violently. But she didn't let go. She just pushed me back against a large, oblong chimney. I yelped as I hit my head. That was going to bruise.

"Come with us Pamela."

"Stranger danger," I spat in her face.

I used her momentary distraction to get out of her vice like grip, and the move was an obvious shock for her. I was a thief and I wasn't stupid. I knew there were some nasty people in this world, and playing the game that I did, I was bound to run into them occasionally. I knew how to defend myself. I side-kicked her sharply in the stomach, and followed it with another, sharper kick to her legs and she fell backwards, landing on the roof with a smack.

Right next to the gun.

Not good. Then I spotted something. My exit.

"There is nowhere to run Miss Torres!" she shouted, breathing heavily as she stood and raised the gun, it trained on my heart. I smiled.

"There is always somewhere to run," I said and jumped off the roof.

"NO!" I heard her shout in horror, as I slid down the handy builders rubbish chute and landed at the bottom awkwardly on my ankle. Not a terribly stylish way to travel, but it was better than nothing.

The woman looked over the roof, the relief evident on her face as she brought out her radio. I waved, giving her a rude hand gesture as I started running again. I rounded a corner and ran straight into a man.

That man happened to be my father.

He grabbed me, his grip inescapable.

"No! Let me go!" I screamed and struggled wildly. My father simply altered his grip, no way out.

"Ella? What the hell!"

"I said let go of me!"

"Stop fighting me Pamela!"

"Gordon!" called the woman from the roof, bursting out of the door of the building we were just on top of.

"Your men said she was on a tube train!" he accused, "how did she slip them and get all the way over here?"

"She slipped them, climbed up the service shaft."

"Slipped them?" he demanded, "She's a fourteen year old girl with no training! Pamela, stop squirming," he snapped.

"Go to hell!" I got one hand free, striking him across the face. He staggered back, stunned but not from the blow but rather the action itself.

The woman grabbed me, a steely grip around my throat, and a needle in her hands.

"No! No!" I screamed in panic trying to stop her.

"It's just a sedative," she shouted as she held me tighter to stop me moving away.

No no no, this was really not good.

"No! Please! I'm allergic!" I screamed as she sank the needle into my arm. I felt my entire world begin to spin as the cold drug entered my blood stream.

"I'm allergic," I murmured as my entire world faded to black.

Chapter Four

The first thing I felt, was nausea. It ripped through my like lightning through air, there was no stopping it. My eyes flew open and I rolled over, grabbing the nearest object to hand and was violently sick into it. It happened to be someone's bag. Luckily, not mine.

I was sick, again and again. My torso ached, my throat burned and my eyes watered and leaked big fat tears. I could barely breathe; my heart racing faster than I thought was even possible. The acid burned my throat, my stomach convulsed.

I heard a door open five minutes later.

"Ella? Oh my word, are you sick?" asked my mother. I was prevented from answering as another crippling wave of nausea followed. I had to be empty, but that didn't stop my body from going through all the motions.

"Oh my poor baby," she said walking over and rubbing my back as I choked and heaved into the bag. She stroked my hair. I had had enough.

"I'm allergic to sedatives and anaesthetics!" I yelled at her, throwing off her hands from my head and back. She meant it to be soothing but to me it just felt patronising. I didn't want sympathy from a woman who had abandoned me.

She sat, arms raised in the air where I had thrown them off, trying to process a little bit as I returned to being violently sick.

"I had no idea! Oh god, I'm so sorry Pamela," said my mother, putting her hands on her lap, but still leaning over me, trying to be all mothering. I didn't want any of it.

"Oh be quiet," I moaned.

The nausea was slowly beginning to fade away. I must have been asleep for a long time; it usually had that effect. I wiped my mouth on the back of my hand and pushed the bag away from me. I wiped my tears from my cheeks with my fingers.

I looked up and around me. And I realised we were in a plane, because outside the windows there were fluffy white clouds. We were in a small relaxing area with a few comfortable sofas, the longest of which I had been lying on.

"And now I'm flying. I'm on a damn plane!" I groaned annoyed.

Where on earth were they taking me? It had to be across the world, no point flying otherwise. It only meant that it would take that much longer to get back home to the others. They were probably worried sick.

"You don't like flying?" enquired my mother.

"No, I don't mind flying. I need a bathroom. Where?" I said standing up and looking at her expectantly. A little stunned she raised her hand and pointed to a door.

"There."

I walked off without another word and into the bathroom, locking the door with a quick snap of my wrist and started trying to clean myself up a little bit. I splashed water onto my face to try and cool the skin; I washed my mouth out as best I could. But try as I might, the redness in my skin was still very apparent and obvious.

I sighed. I looked like I was either sick or had been crying, which I kind of had been. Throwing up like that is not nice.

This was why I hated anaesthetics. That and the fact I don't like other people knocking me out. I liked to be in control of my body at all times.

I took a deep breath and tried not to think about my appearance or about just how fragile my stomach was feeling at this moment in time. That wouldn't help anyone, and if I thought about my gut then I knew I would start being sick all over again.

"Pamela sweetheart, are you alright in there?" called my mother through the thin plastic door.

"Yeah, some privacy please!" I shouted back. Were parents always this annoying and nosey? I had no idea.

I needed to think logically about the situation I was in now. I needed to come up with a plan of action. Ok, so where was I right now? Well, obviously in the sky somewhere. That didn't help me much. So, perhaps I should focus more on the people rather than the place.

They were some form of official body; that much was apparent to me immediately. Another important fact was, as I had realised before, my parents obviously weren't sales representative. That was only too clear. So it was logical to assume that everything I thought I knew about them (other the fact that they were my parents and they were married) was also complete rubbish too.

Ok, so I was on a plane filled with strangers that were connected to a form of official body somewhere. And all I wanted to do was get home.

This was not perhaps the best situation to be in. Obviously they wanted me for something. So I should probably expect some questions.

As if on cue, there was a knock at the door.

"It's occupied," I called back.

Undercover Thief

"Miss Torres, when you're ready we have a few questions for you," came a female voice. It was the woman who had followed me onto the roof.

I looked at my reflection in the mirror. I ran my fingers through my hair and pulled it around my shoulders so it framed my face prettily. The redness had faded a little as I had thought. I wiped the residual water off my skin gently and flashed my best smile.

Time to work.

"Alright," I said walking out of the bathroom.

"Follow me Miss Torres," she said.

"We going somewhere special?" I asked as I followed here.

It was a small corridor on a plane, and on the way there I ran into several people. I made a quick mental calculation. As I passed, I knocked into as many people as possible deftly picking pockets whilst simultaneously apologising and generally giving the appearance of being a little bit of a clumsy air head.

I realised I was still dressed in that business like yellow dress (the one that Zara had unknowingly donated to my collection) with a huge blue hoodie with helpfully large pockets (I couldn't begin to remember where I had picked this up), and some gorgeous white heels I had every intention of keeping.

She ushered me into a room and I stopped, rolling my eyes and supressing the laugh that bubbled up to my lips.

It was an interrogation room. I knew the style. The walls were grey. In front of me was a table, a place to chain handcuffs, and I would have bet the table was welded to the floor. This was government stuff by the style of it, it never really varied.

I turned around the room bored, scanning over everything with my eyes for the briefest of moments. They had seven different cameras at all angles and nine mics. Every single breath taken in this room was being recorded. Clearly, it wasn't built for me but something a lot more serious. We were only borrowing it.

The woman shut the door behind me, a file in her hands.

"Please, have a seat," she said gesturing to the table.

I walked over, falling into the seat easily, putting my feet on the table and leaned back on my chair, just looking at her, waiting with my head tilted to one side.

"So, Miss Torres, you're a hard girl to find," she started, lacing her fingers on top of the file in front of her.

"Are you sure we were looking properly?" I asked innocently. She gave me a look which could only be described as a 'don't-be-stupid' look.

Undercover Thief

"It's not often we can't find people."

"That's embarrassing, considering I'm only a teenager and all," I said with a small chuckle and inspecting my finger nails, bored, "I'm supposed to take your word for that?"

"Miss Torres, how old are you?"

"Oh don't give me that," I said rolling my eyes, "You know how old I am. I'm fifteen in a couple of weeks."

"And how have you survived this long without any money? For two and a half months. We have monitored activity on your parents account, and you didn't touch it."

"Who said I didn't have money?"

"You did have money?"

"What do you think?"

"It wasn't your parents' money."

"I never said this fictional money was their money."

"Then whose?"

"Why can't it be mine?"

"You have money? You don't have a job and we can't find a back account for you."

"Ahh.....a girl must have a few secrets," I said with a wink, grinning widely and crossing my arms.

"Why not tell me where this money came from?"

"Oh you know....around," I said easily.

"Where were you staying?"

"London."

"Where in London?"

"Around," I said again, still smiling. She sat forwards annoyed.

"Are you deliberately avoiding my questions?"

"What on earth would give you that idea?" I asked innocently.

"Because you haven't given me a single straight answer,"

"I thought I was answering your questions. I can stop if you like," I said. She pressed her lips together in a thin line and was clearly trying to think.

Bored, I felt around in my large pockets and fished out a tube of mints. Oh that's good, my breath no doubt stank. I started crunching through them easily.

"Thanks for the mints by the way, whoever you were. Really takes away the bitter after taste of poison," I said waving at one of the cameras.

The woman in front of my started talking again.

"Miss Torres, you do know that you're safe on this plane don't you?" she said gently.

"Am I?"

"Yes, of course," she said, a kindly and nurturing look on her face, "We only wish to help you. We only want to understand. If there is a reason why you're holding your tongue, if you're afraid of someone, we can protect you."

"Oh?" I asked slightly humoured. She'd really gotten the wrong end of the stick.

"No one will ever find you or hurt you. I promise. You can trust us."

"Trust you? Not likely darling. I'm not afraid of anyone."

"No?"

"Nope. And I'm not holding my tongue. I'm talking aren't I?"

"A lot of words, but you are not saying anything useful."

"We'll have to agree to disagree."

"Well then, if you're really not afraid, tell us why we couldn't find you."

"You know, you're also hard people to find," I said spinning the tube of mints around my thumb for something to do.

"You were looking?"

"I wasn't so much looking as learning where to avoid."

"Why were you trying to avoid us?"

"Well, there seem to be a lot of guns with you people. And that really isn't my idea of good company."

"So you were actively running from us?"

"I don't know. Define us," I said, "and I'll tell you whether my running was intentional or not."

"The government,"

"Which one and which section?" I asked again. She nodded.

"That's classified."

"Oh, now that is a shame," I said with a sigh, "I suppose I'll just have to read it off of your ID." I took it out of my pocket and her face fell.

"So, Special Agent Sally Price. Works for the CIA. Oh, so you *are* American, I thought the accent fit."

"How on earth did you get your hands on that!" she practically shrieked.

"Oh, 'inside the plane voice' please," I reprimanded brightly, pressing a finger to my lips, as she glared at me, "it's a nice picture of you, but I think I prefer your hair shorter, like it is now."

She reached across the table and snatched it back. I looked indifferent in any case.

"Mint?" I offered.

"No."

"Can I call you Sally?"

"No. You can call me Miss Price."

"Whatever floats your boat," I said popping another mint in my mouth. She sat back and pressed her lips together again trying to think. I could see her annoyance with me building up. It was fun to watch, I wondered how long I could push before she exploded.

"Quite clearly you have had some training, and I want to know where you got it."

"Training?" I asked genuinely confused, "I'm not following."

"It's not rocket science Miss Torres, just answer the question."

"I can't."

"Why not?"

"Because I don't understand the question,"

"I want to know where you were trained!"

"What training?"

"Don't play silly buggers with me!' she snapped. 'I am not an idiot Miss Torres, and my patience with you is running dangerously thin."

And there it was, the volcano had exploded. Shame, I was hoping she'd hold out a little longer.

"I'm terrified," I said sarcastically.

"Answer the question."

"I can't. I could tell you everything you're waiting to hear. I could tell you that I had training in Uruguay or Wales or wherever you think I am supposed to have had training. Problem is it wouldn't be the truth. And the truth is this, I haven't had any training and I don't understand what I'm supposed to have had training in!"

I gave her a steady stare as she watched my face, trying to decide if I was telling the truth. The silence was beginning to bug me.

Right. Enough of this. I had questions too.

"Ok, my turn then," I said, "Who are you? Interpol?"

"Why would you assume that?" she asked immediately. I nodded slowly.

"I see.....so you're not Interpol," I said, "You're good."

Undercover Thief

"Why thank you."

"Or a psychopath," I said shrugging. I watched that annoyance flare up in her eyes as she puffed a little short breath.

"I am not a psychopath."

"Are you sure? Have you been tested?"

"No," she replied, grinding her teeth together.

"You should get yourself tested."

"I'm not Interpol."

"I figured," I said with a dazzling smile.

"Miss Torres, we have that little boy who screamed in custody. He blabbed."

"I'm certain he did," I said without missing a step, "six year olds don't take much intimidation."

"So you knew he would?"

"You offer a kid a tenner to scream, he will."

"You didn't give him a tenner."

"Darling, I got your badge. Apparently you don't see a lot," I said. I crunched through some more mints, and bored I pulled out a phone I had stolen.

"How did you get your hands on that?" demanded Miss Price.

73

"Same way as your badge," I said, "Now please, I'm busy."

"What do you think you're doing?"

"GPS, oooh, we're heading to America. Why are we doing that?"

"Hand it over Miss Torres, it doesn't belong to you."

"Doesn't belong to you either. How do I know you won't keep it?"

"Because stealing is wrong, and as you have already pointed out, I'm part of the CIA. We have a code."

"Right," I said sarcastically with a snort, "and the CIA isn't corrupt in the slightest."

"Give that here."

"You know what, no. I won't. I don't trust you," I said moving it as her hand came around to snatch it, "you did kidnap me and poison me."

"It was an anaesthetic."

"Which caused me to throw up in my mother's purse. I'd say you owe her a new one."

"You're the one who threw up in it."

"Well next time don't poison me."

"I didn't! And we didn't kidnap you! We had parental consent."

"You do realise that they signed the papers giving away their rights to me when I was eleven don't you?"

"They didn't do that."

"Ok, they weren't there and didn't realise it was happening, true. But their signatures are on the documents and they're all officially on file," I said.

She sat back in her chair and studied me. Not finding anything she dropped the tough woman act.

"What are you?"

"Excuse me?"

"You heard. What are you?"

"A girl."

"Seriously."

"You don't think I'm a girl?"

"I think you're being deliberately obtuse."

"I think you're getting your knickers in a twist love. Watch that or you'll go grey early."

"Let's try something new."

"New? Oh now I'm excited," I joked, wiggling my shoulders.

"We found some things at the house," she said.

"You did?" I said. She pulled out a few pictured and flicked through them.

"Oh yeah, I forgot about these. Mine, mine, not mine," I said showing her a picture of a gun, "that is my parents'."

"You seem certain."

"I don't use guns," I said, "Ugly things."

"Out of preference?"

"Why would I have need for gun?"

"You tell me?"

Hang on. Since when did thieves need guns?

"Wait a minute, you don't know do you?" I said sitting forward, taking my feet off the table.

"Don't know what?" she asked staring at me.

They didn't know I was a thief.

"I thought you knew," I said sitting back and smiling with realisation, "I thought you people were chasing me because you knew."

"Knew what?" she pressed.

"My goodness," I muttered and giggled. The giggle grew into full blown laughter, laughter of relief as well as the hilarity of the situation. They weren't after me because I was a thief. My parents had simply asked them to locate me.

"What's so funny?"

"You haven't got a clue!" I said, "Oh my goodness, what did you set the tail team on me for if you didn't have a clue?"

"You were a hard girl to find, and we didn't want to lose you."

"So you set them on me, preparing them for me to be what? Did you tell them I was just a school girl? What do you think I am?"

"I have no idea," she said honestly.

"I see," I said with glee, still laughing a little, "I wasn't sloppy on the job then. That makes me feel so much better."

"Good to know we haven't bruised your ego."

"Out of interest, how long had they been tailing me before I spotted them?" I asked and she just smiled in return.

"Long enough,"

"Trying for obtuse?" I asked innocently.

"Perhaps,"

"So, why did they follow me? I mean, why are you even looking for me?"

"Because your mother asked me to,"

"Oh for goodness sake. That woman ruins all my plans," I joked. Miss Price took a deep breath and started speaking again.

"So far all I have learned about you Miss Torres is that you are a very rude, very annoying and secretive young lady."

"Thank you," I said without missing a beat and grinning.

"You are seriously irritating."

"Stop it, I'm blushing."

"What must your parents' think?"

"Who cares?"

"Pardon?"

"Don't care," I said tapping the table and smiled at her, "why should I?"

"You know they can hear you."

"Of course I do. Seven cameras and nine microphones in this room, and I bet they're watching them. Do you think I am an idiot?"

"No, that is something I don't think you are," she said sitting back and studying me again, it seemed that her curiosity got the better of her.

"Why don't you care what they hear or think?" she asked quietly, I could hear genuine confusion and interest in her voice.

"Why should I?"

"Most people care about what their family think of them."

"I do. They aren't my family."

"What? Of course they are?"

"I haven't seen them in the better part of six years. So no, I don't think they are."

"Harsh words,"

"Doesn't make them any less true."

"Really? Are you sure?"

"Really," I said waiting for her response. There wasn't one for a while. So I smiled and stood up.

"I think we're done here."

"I'm not finished."

"But I am, and I have a phone call to make. Thank you for your cooperation, you've been most helpful," I said taking a phone out of my pocket and dialling. I hit call, as I left the room, walking back to where I had woken up from the anaesthetic.

"Hello?"

"Hey Leah," I said.

"Oh my goodness, you're alive!"

"I know right," I said with a laugh, "though considering the amount of guns in this place, that might be an uncertainty."

"Why? Are you in trouble?"

"Nah, not trouble. Just dealing with the parents,"

"You found them?"

"Other way around," I said with a sigh.

"So why will you get shot?"

"It's me."

"What have you done?"

"I've been awake all of twenty minutes and I've been called, rude, annoying and irritating among other things."

"Awake?"

"Yeah, anaesthetic,"

"Ouch!" she said knowing full well about my unfortunate allergy.

I was tapped on the shoulder. I turned around to see Miss Price holding out her hand for the phone with an expectant expression. My parents were stood behind her, watching.

"One moment Leah," I said putting my hand over the receiver and looked at Miss Price, "yeah, I'm on the phone at the moment. Can it wait? Great," I didn't wait for her answer, but I could have sworn I saw my father crack a small smile. I put the phone back to my ear.

"Listen, I haven't got a clue how long this is going to take, so you need to go ahead and do the Washington job without me. Call Milo, give him my thanks and apologise to Micah for me. I promise we'll do China next time, kay?"

"You got it," said Leah, "Just let us know what's happening yeah? And let us know if you need us to break in and steal you."

"Will do Leah. I shouldn't be away long, I hope." I said lowering my voice.

"You just stay ok, yeah?"

"You got it hon. Give the other's my love, alright?"

"Will do,"

"I'll be home before you know it."

"I'll hold you too that."

"Ok. Love you. Bye."

"Love you too," she said and hung up. I sighed and fished the sim card and battery out of the phone and snapped them. Then I dropped everything into the bag filled with sick.

"Oh great," said my mother wrinkling her nose.

"Well, my vomit is good for something," I said brushing my hair over my shoulder with a flick of my fingers. Then I spotted my own bag on the side and picked it up, looking through it.

"So," I said sitting on the couch and crossing my legs, "where are we going?"

"Miss Torres, who was on the other end of the phone?" asked Miss Price.

"Oh, you know, people," I said with a smile, "so, where are we going?"

"America," said my father from the corner with a small smile.

"Well I know that. America is rather big, and I'd like to know which bit of the country. And how long to I have to be there? I promised my friend I'd take him to China to practice his Mandarin."

"You aren't going back to England Pamela," said my mother walking over and sitting next to me, trying to put a reassuring and authoritative look on her face.

"You what?" I asked and she gave me a small smile.

Undercover Thief

"You're going to spend the next school year at a special facility where you'll be safe and receive an excellent education," she said.

"A year?" I gasped, horrified.

A whole year? They needed me! My family needed me! Micah would be heartbroken! They would survive no problem, but I couldn't be away from them for that long. It would hurt them and me!

"Yes," continued my mother, apparently oblivious to the pain the idea caused me, "every year until you finish studying."

"No! No!" I said jumping up, needing to express my horror, "You can't be serious! Now you want to take an interest in my education? Now?"

"Pam-"

"You can't do this to me!"

"Pamela, sweetie, you'll like it there."

"No!" I shouted sharply, pulling away like she was a viper as she tried to put a hand on my arm. I turned to look at Miss Price, hoping she was more understanding, "You can't do this. I'm needed at home."

"We are you family Pamela, and this place will become your home. You'll be happy," tried my father.

"How dare you! Don't make assumptions! I was very happy with my home the way it was! I don't need another one!"

"This is what's best for you."

"You don't have the right to make that decision! Only I do!"

"Pam-"

"I am not talking to you right now so shut up!" I snapped, holding a hand up to him and turning my head to look straight at Miss Price.

"I have to go home. People need me," I said.

"I.....I'm sorry Miss Torres," she said, and she seemed genuinely sorry that that was her answer. I turned away from them all, eyes closed and hands over my eyes.

No! Why? Why did they have to come back and ruin my life! Things were good! We were happy! And they come back and screwed everything up again.

"Pamela, we know this is very sudden and will be hard, but you'll make some new friends and-"

"Don't," I spat, my voice was low and held all the venom I could muster.

There was a long pause of silence before my mother tried again.

"Pamela, I know you must be feeling a little confus-"

Undercover Thief

"Shut up!" I snapped spinning around to look at her, her face was one of shock, "I've been dragged into it again! Into your mess again! Why? Why do I have to keep paying the price for being related to you? I don't even know you!"

"Pamela, please darling-"

"I thought I was finally rid of your influence, and then you sweep back in and screw everything up! News flash sunshine, I'll be damned if I let the two of your drag me back down into the gutter!"

"Pam-"

"No! Just shut up! I don't want to hear your ready-made excuse!"

"P-"

"I need some time to myself. Get out of my way," I said pushing past my father and walking into the bathroom and locking the door. I wasn't coming out any time soon.

I leant over the sink as fresh tears bubbled up in my eyes. I might never see any of them again. What about little Micah? Jerry and Leah would pay for his education by any means; they could easily manage without me. But I would miss them.

And they would look for me and they might get hurt doing it. Micah was only seven years old. The thought I was never going to see them again made me cry and cry. Silently. So no one could hear me. I was sat on the closed lid of the toilet, hunched over and sobbing helplessly – feeling all alone. I didn't know what I could do.

I knew hours passed, but I didn't care. I wasn't coming out. Eventually I ran out of tears and after a long time someone came and knocked on the door.

"What?" I snapped.

"We're going to land in a few minutes," my mother's sad voice drifted through the door.

"Fine," I said with a deep breath. I washed and dried my face then went outside. I threw off the hoodie, feeling warm, walked over to a seat and strapped myself in. I sat as far away from my parents as possible, staring at my shoes as I tried to think.

I would get home. I'd do whatever it took to go home. If this was a school, all I needed to do was get thrown out.

I could manage that.

Chapter Five

I pulled on my shades and tossed my hair over my shoulder as I descended the plane stairs. At the bottom Miss Price was met with three people who were all talking to her at once. She was trying to get them to shut up, no one was listening. I let off a high pitched whistle. Everyone looked at me.

"One at a time please, I feel a headache coming on," I said inspecting my nail polish. I would need to re-do that.

Miss Price completely ignored my involvement and went back to dealing with them, although it was considerably more organised now. My parents were talking to each other in hushed voices. I turned my face towards the sun and closed my eyes, soaking in the rays. It was warm. I took a deep breath and allowed myself a brief smile. Maybe I could get a tan while I was here, that was a hard thing to do in London.

It was early September now. In London it had already started turning cold. I wondered where exactly in America we were. The sunshine was just wonderful.

"Miss Torres?" asked Miss Price. I snapped my eyes open and turned easily to look at her.

"Finished?" I asked politely and she gestured.

"Ok, time for a tour of the school," she said.

"Sure, whatever,"

"Now Miss Torres, I have no idea what you know. We couldn't find any school records for you. So tell me, do you speak any languages?"

"Are we counting the various forms of braille and sign languages?" I asked bored. She gave me a look that could only be intrigue.

"Alright then, yes. So tell me, which ones do you speak?"

"Ok, so there are the basic European ones, English, French, Italian, German and Spanish. Then Mandarin and Thai. My Japanese is a little rusty and my Polish is laughable. I also know various forms of Braille and British Sign language."

"That is quite the list," said my mother, sounding pleasantly surprised.

"I guess. I pick up languages quickly. And I meet a lot of people who don't speak any English, so learning languages is sort of compulsory."

"Are you fluent?" asked Miss Price.

Undercover Thief

"All but Polish and it's only on the finer tunings of Japanese grammar where I get out of my depth," I said shrugging.

"How do you know if you're fluent?"

"Well, for example, I went to Germany for four months."

"When did you go to Germany?"

"Um......almost two years ago?" I said, "I turned thirteen over there so, you know, I guess you could say I'm fluent enough to get by."

"I see, well we teach twenty languages here," said Miss Price proudly, "braille and sign language aren't included I'm afraid but perhaps that should be added as a course here."

"Which ones?" I asked vaguely interested despite myself. I had to do something while I was here after all.

"Oh, French, Spanish, Italian, German, in the first year, so you're already ahead there. Then in the second year, they take Russian, Arabic and Mandarin Chinese in the second year. The third year, you pick up Portuguese, Turkish and Japanese."

"What about the other ten?" I asked.

"Well, you pick one of the others to study if you want to, for extra credit."

"Oh, right, it's an American education system," I said, "So, which ones?"

"Cantonese, Polish, Albanian, Farsi, Korean, Dutch, Thai, Hindi, Vietnamese and Urdu."

"Wow, so those last are optional."

"Yes, though many of our students pick up a couple of them," she said.

"Could you pick up all?" I asked. She stopped and looked at me.

"If you really wanted," she said, "but I don't recommend it. You missed the first two weeks of school, so you'll need to catch up."

"Oh honey, I'm not picking up any of them, I was wondering if that was possible," I said with a laugh, "gives me an idea of the free time on my schedule."

"Like I said, you have a lot to catch up on."

"It's only two weeks' worth of lessons? Not exactly a challenge."

"And keep up with all homework assignments."

"I would just like to bring something rather obvious to your attention," I said stopping short to look at her. She frowned at me.

"What?"

Undercover Thief

"I don't want to be here," I said slowly, "so why on earth would I do my homework?"

"Because you've been told to," she said like it wasn't up for question.

I laughed, throwing my head back, amused.

"Try again," I said through my chuckling, "I'm going to need a better reason than that."

"Perhaps you arrived here against your knowledge or will. But I am sure in time the resentment at being brought here will pass. But you will obey the rules of the school, there are other students here and I will make an example of you if needed."

"An example? I'm shaking in my gorgeous new shoes," I said with a snort. She gave me a steady and serious look, not impressed. Damn, that was really creepy and good. I really was a little bit frightened. I held up my hands in mock surrender.

"Alright, alright, I'll consider doing my homework."

"This way," she said briskly, obviously slightly pleased she had won that little fight. I struggled to keep up with her a little bit as she marched off, but no way would I let her know that. My parents followed on behind, obviously carefully watching me for another outburst. We walked into a gorgeous main hall way. It had huge glass doors that opened out onto big stone steps leading down to a huge drive and immaculately kept gardens. The floors were made of two types of marble, the walls of old orange stone and panelled woods with old and probably priceless artefacts decorating the halls. There were two enormous staircases that spiralled up and away to places I couldn't see. I was on a third set of stairs, walking down.

"So, this is your new home. The Victoria Institute. We train you to be the best. You can be whatever you want to be," she said proudly and with a satisfied smile.

"Really? So this is the Victoria," I said remembering the name. I looked through one of the windows and saw a huge dance hall where people were obviously having lessons.

"Wait, you've heard of it?" she asked sharply and kind of horrified. She was shocked and angry.

"Yeah, calm down. Rumours. Only rumours," I said quickly, not wanting to ruffle any feathers just yet. I needed the information first, "well, that and I met someone who went to the Lincoln."

"What do you know then?" She asked folding her arms unhappily.

"It's....for lack of a better and less cringe worthy way of putting it, a spy school," I said hating the cheesy way it sounded as I said the words, "there are three that work for the allied Britain and US, the Victoria, The King George and the Lincoln."

"Do you know where they are?"

Undercover Thief

"I'm assuming you mean more specific that somewhere in Britain and America?" I assumed. Miss Price nodded shortly.

"Afraid not," I said. She processed that for a moment and then smiled. Apparently that answer was satisfactory.

"Hang on a minute……you want me to be a spy?" I said incredulously as that little fact sank in. They had to be kidding.

"As I said, you can be whatever you want to be. But if that's your calling……" said Miss Price not bothering to finish the sentence because I doubled over laughing.

"Me? Me? A spy? Oh that's so funny! Imagine me? With a badge! Good lord that's hilarious!" I said wiping the hysterical tears from my cheeks.

"No, it's not," said Miss Price, "you can be whatever you want to be here."

"You keep saying that. You're deadly serious about this aren't you?"

"Yes," she said.

"Well darling, you are in for one hell of a shock."

"How so?"

"You'll see. I don't want to ruin the surprise," I said shaking my head and sniggering slightly.

"Well, come this way. That dancing you see is part of our etiquette lessons," said Miss Price as we moved on like we'd never had the previous conversation.

I followed her along the gorgeous halls of the magnificent complex. Everything was expensive and protected by a state of the art security system that had me a little breathless (after all, security systems were sort of my thing!)

"This is our library," she said and we walked into a huge room, three stories high with floor to ceiling shelves as far as the eye could see in organised rows with desks and chairs scattered everywhere. Huge windows lined one wall letting in the American sunlight.

"Wow," I said, feeling she wanted me to say something in response. To be fair, this was very impressive...but I had seen a lot of impressive rooms. She moved on quickly and I followed, taking it in as quickly as possible.

She called out rooms and I memorised the layout.

"This is the main hall. The rec room. Study halls." I managed to keep up with this quick whirl wind tour. She rattled off rules that I ignored. I noticed all the security. It was excellent. Top model. Very good stuff. Very, very hard to fault.

"Is that a Malikam Mark 6?" I asked pointing to the top corner.

Undercover Thief

"Why yes. It controls the entire system, although there are some wonderful modifications for our particularly exclusive needs," said Miss Price with a small smile, "So you see, this place is really very secure. No one gets in or out."

"The flaw in that particular system is the power. You cut the power, and it does down. Wouldn't work here though, as you have multiple backup generators," I said firmly and Miss Price raised an eyebrow.

"You seem certain of that fact."

"You keep assuming I'm an idiot," I said passing her up the stairs, "I'm not."

"Why do you know so much about security systems?" asked my father.

"Oh, a hobby," I said with a shrug.

"Right! Of course," he said, "Along with your multiple languages,"

"What can I say? I'm smart," I said, more than happy to own that little fact.

"There are from ten to thirty students in each year. Your year I believe is a small one, including you there are just fourteen," said Miss Price continuing along with the tour.

"Right," I said, "And we stay here for four years?"

"Correct."

"Right,"

"You will be given a full and extensive timetable. You will study things such as advanced science, math, English, computing and ICT, languages obviously, home economics, religious education, history, geography, etiquette and culture, economics and advanced politics. They are all situated in the outer perimeter. There is more relaxed security in those areas of the building, but do not think they are not there."

"Trust me, I can see it," I said.

"And then there are the more specific lessons we provide here, such as code class, communications, advanced technology, PE, manipulation, operation studies, covert history, and law."

"You're going to teach me the law?" I asked, but she continued like she hadn't even heard me.

"All of these lessons are in the inner perimeter. The security there is of the highest standard. So, do as you are told and you won't die."

"Right," I laughed. I laughed because I knew she was lying out of her backside. There was no way these security systems were deadly.

"There are strict rules here Miss Torres. Everyone is in their rooms at ten o'clock. There is to be no loud music, or disruption to the studies of the students here. And as such, there are strict punishments such as detentions."

"Oooh," I said with a laugh, "sounds scary."

Undercover Thief

"Are you mocking me Miss Torres?"

"Take it how you like, but detention is not what I call strict. Every school has it."

"I know you are not exactly excited about coming here Miss Torres, but I promise, you will learn to like it here," she said seriously.

"We'll wait and see shall we?" I said looking around. The bell went and people started to fill the once empty corridors. People started staring at me.

"Well, you've been noticed," said my mother.

"Yeah, I tend to have that effect," I said taking off my shades and throwing them into my bag as I continued to walk down the stairs, wiggling my fingers at a few people who were looking at me. They hurried on quickly, blushing furiously.

That was so cute.

"Ah! There is Ronnie," said Miss Price.

A tall girl with the same dark blond hair as Miss Price walked over. Her eyes were the same colour as well. She was gorgeous in a word. She was slightly taller than me, nicely proportioned. She looked strong and healthy and her skin seemed to almost glow gold next to my china white.

"Hey Mum, when did you get back?"

"About half an hour ago," said Miss Price hugging her daughter briefly. That was nice. Miss Price immediately earned a little bit more respect from me. She clearly loved her daughter a lot.

"Hi Mr and Mrs Torres," said the girl with a bright smile at my parents.

"Hello Ronnie dear. My you look lovely," said my mother fondly, walking over and hugging her too.

"Ronnie, this is your new roommate," said Miss Price gesturing to me.

"They found you then," said Ronnie with a laugh.

"I swear, you step outside go to get a copy of the paper and you end up drugged and on a plane," I said with a wave of my fingers and she laughed.

"So typical," she joked with me, "I'm Ronnie."

"Pam, you snore?"

"Not that I'm aware."

"Then we'll get on just fine," I said.

"I look forward to it Pam."

"Ronnie, why don't you show Pamela to her room? I'll see you for dinner tonight."

"Sure thing Mum," she said, "Come on Pam," I walked away with her.

"Pam, sweetheart," called my mother. I paused turning back.

"What?"

"Be good, ok?"

"Don't worry, I won't be good but I won't get caught," I called back in response as we continued to walk away. That made Ronnie laugh.

"So, you're their daughter. Mum said that Isabell and Gordon had a daughter."

"You know my parents well?"

"Your mum and mine are best friends, so I've seen them occasionally over the years."

"Well, that's more than I have," I muttered.

"But you are their daughter?"

"Unfortunately. Though I think they're about to disown me," I said.

"Why?"

"Well, I tick a lot of people off," I said. She snorted.

"That's a good skill to have. I am sure it will come in useful."

"You know, you'd be surprised how often," I agreed.

"I'll take your word for it. The dorm is this way. You and I were assigned a room together. I hope you don't mind but I already picked a bed, you're kind of late to the start of term."

"So I gathered. And don't worry, I don't mind."

"That's great."

"We got the biggest room though. And the largest bathroom. Benefit of being the headmistress's daughter."

"I think your mum doesn't like me either."

"Why?"

"I ticked her off," I said and Ronnie grinned.

"How did you do that? My mother is usually such a calm person. She is pretty hard to rattle."

"I'm very good at annoying people. It's a gift," I said with a cheeky grin.

"Well don't worry. I don't have any kind of problem with that. Any opinion my mother has of you won't affect my view of you, I promise. This is our room just up here," she said. We were on the third floor now, at the end of the corridor. She opened the door.

It wasn't extraordinary. The room was painted a soft cream colour with a thick brown carpet. There was a large window in the wall, overlooking an Olympic sized swimming pool, some outside areas with training mats (clearly for some kind of contact sport) that had a transparent cover over it, and an intense looking assault course.

There were two beds and two desks, two wardrobes and a bookshelf. Everything fit in easily, nothing cramped, which was nice. The beds were slightly larger than average in size. One was made up perfectly with thick white sheets. The other had patterned sheets, a couple of brightly coloured, odd shaped cushions on it as well as pillows. At the foot of the bed was a large pink circular carpet. There were some posters and photos on one half of the wall, and one of the desks was littered with books, papers, pencils and pens. I guess those were the ones that Ronnie had claimed as her own.

"So, this bed it mine," she said sitting on the patterned duvet and picking up one of the cushions, tossing it up to the head of the bed.

"Cool," I said walking over, dumping my hand bag on the other bed and looking out the window. I leant against the soft cream coloured curtains and looked down at my feet.

"So," she said, "you're British?"

"Yeah," I said, "I warn you, this room is getting a kettle. I need my tea."

"That's cool."

"I'm not kidding. It's almost an addiction. I need it."

"That's fine. I like the smell," she said with a laugh, "though where you'll get a kettle from is the question."

"Oh trust me, I'll find one," I said with a laugh.

"I like your confidence in yourself. It's so.....great. Not many people are that self-confident."

"Do you put yourself in that bracket?"

"Nah, I mean, I'm not as confident as you but I'm not shy."

"Good, so I don't need to help you out with that."

"Thanks for the thought."

"No problem love," I said with a wink.

"Ok, so I have to ask. I know my mum has been looking for you for the past two months. I have to know how you managed to hide from her. I mean, our parents have serious connections, and they're...well...really, really good at what they do," she said.

"Oh, that! I know some people."

"You know some people?" she said folding her arms and giving me a look.

"Yeah. Let's just say if you ever need an escape or somewhere to hide, give me a shout."

"Alright then, I'll remember that," she chuckled and then something seemed to bug her so she added, "Just so you know, I won't tell my mother a word you've said. I'm not a snitch or anything like that."

"I'm sure you won't," I said smiling at her, "but I haven't scanned the room for microphones yet."

"There aren't any allowed in the dorms."

"You believe that?" I asked. She frowned.

"Hmm," she said, looking thoughtful.

"So you lived here all your life?" I said moving on. No need to break her perfect ideas about the government. It wasn't fair.

"Well, pretty much. My mum took the position here as headmistress when I was one and a half. Gave up normal spy work so she could stay home and take care of me. Enrolled me in the local schools until I got kicked out."

"Kicked out? Why did you get kicked out?"

She sniggered about something in her head and shrugged.

"Well, what can I say? Eleven year old girls can be so mean. I had to sort a situation out."

"Alright then...vague and mysterious. I like it," I laughed, "So it's just you and your mum?"

"Well, pretty much. I mean technically have an older brother too, half-brother mind because we have different dad's."

"Technically?"

"We don't speak at all. My mum and her ex-husband got a really nasty divorce and aren't on speaking terms. He's a civilian and didn't like that my mother was never around. You know, when she was on spy missions. And she couldn't tell him about them because he wasn't a spy and didn't have clearance. Anyway he got custody of my brother in the divorce because of that fact mum was always away. But my brother got a place here because of mum and when he found out why mum was away all the time, he got angry, particularly when he learned that she gave it all up for me. That was when he refused to speak to me, but we never really got on very well before. He transferred to Lincoln to carry out the rest of his studies there."

"Wow, sorry to hear that. That was a lot heavier than I was expecting. You didn't have to say it if you didn't want to. I really didn't mean to pry," I said a little bit stunned that she just came out with something so personal.

"Nah, it doesn't bother me, at all. I don't need anyone but mum. The divorce and stuff happened years before I was born. My brother is four years older than us. Just don't bring it up around my mother, obviously it bothers her a lot more than it bothers me."

"Understandably, no problem." Wow. It was definitely time to move on to lighter topics, hopefully!

"So, percentage wise, how bad is the boy to girl balance?"

"Not terrible at all for our year!" she said smiling, "six girls including you in our year that's now up to fourteen students."

"Oh, so not at all bad. I was expecting worse."

"It normally is a lot worse," said Ronnie nodding, "there are more boys than girls, and some years are entirely full of guys."

"Men are just more suited to this type of work I guess."

"Exactly," she said rolling her eyes, hearing the sarcasm in my voice. Good. I liked someone who knew the value of girl power.

"So what do people do for fun around here?"

"We have a common room, a separate one for each year. That's where everyone hangs out."

"They keep the years separate?"

"No, not deliberately," she said shaking her head, "It's just easier numbers wise. There are no rules that say one year can't go into another's common room or anything,"

"Good to know. So where is this common room?"

"At the end of the hall, each year has its own level in this dormitory, and that level stays with you for as long as you're in the school, so we'll be spending the next four or more years here."

"More than four years?"

"Well, if you don't want to be a spy, after four years you get kicked out or if you want to stop training and just get a job. However you can spend a maximum of three more years here training before they send you out into the field, if you want to specialise or do research or whatever."

"Wow, so it's like a secondary school and a university rolled into one."

"Huh, guess so."

"So, you got many friends?" I asked.

"Not really. I have a friend is named Gwyneth Olsen-Jones. She's a tech girl though, and has the hand eye co-ordination of a baby. It's embarrassing."

"No one else?"

"I'm friendly with everyone else. We've only been here two weeks; it's not long to make friends" she said defensively, "But Gwen seems to be the only one who sees past the 'headmistress's daughter' part," she didn't say it in a 'please-feel-bad-for-me' kind of way, it was more a 'that's-just-how-it-is' kind of way.

"Shame. I find most people don't take me seriously because I'm a kid,"

"That has to suck."

"It really does.

Undercover Thief

"So? When does school start?"

"For you? At nine o'clock sharp tomorrow."

Chapter Six

So, it didn't take me long to realise that I had no clothes with me. No one had thought that part through apparently. So, I managed to persuade Miss Price to let me make one phone call to Jerry. I knew they were tracing the call, so I kept it short and sweet so there wasn't enough time to track it. They sent my stuff over express mail.

I woke up this morning to find three suitcases at the end of my bed, all addressed to me. I smiled and went over to them opening up the first. Inside was a white envelope with my name on it. I tore it open and pulled out a letter.

Hey there Pam,

Sucks that you're going to be away for so long. I was looking forward to us having some fun in Washington. You'll be home before you know it, don't worry. We didn't know what you would come across at this new school, so we sent a load of the normal stuff just in case (you know).

See you soon. Micah asked me to tell you that he misses you and that he'll keep reading that book you got him so that the two of you can talk about it when you get back.

All our love,

Jerry, Leah and Micah.

That almost broke me down right then and there. I was awash with a feeling of home sickness.

"Hey Pam, what you got there?" asked Ronnie. I held up the envelope without really speaking.

"Can I read it?"

"Sure," I said shrugging. Why not?

I opened up my case to see all of my favourite clothes. I could tell it was Leah who packed, because it was all folded neatly and completely organised. I doubted whether Jerry would have bothered with even taking them off the hangers.

"What do they mean 'you know'?" asked Ronnie.

I laughed and opened up all the secret compartments and brought out the various pieces of gear. Ronnie watched in astonishment as I produced the component parts for and iPad and a phone from sections of the case. Apparently we usually had to get all electronic equipment signed off before we brought them in. I bet that was so they could ensure it could all be monitored. She promised not to rat me out to the teachers.

I walked into the cafeteria for breakfast, iPod on, listening to Daughtry. I got an apple and a cup of tea and sat on my own. Eating, listening, watching. I had on my favourite blue denim shorts, black combat boots, studded leather jacket and tight black lace crop top. My nails were painted a shiny, deep red.

"Wow," said Ronnie sitting opposite me, a huge tray filled with food.

"What?"

"You look incredible," she said. I looked her up and down. Sensible trousers and a plain long sleeved top. She looked comfortable, casual and made it look completely couture, even if it really was Tesco Value.....or whatever the American equivalent was.

"Ta muchly," I said with a smile, "oh, just so you know. I might be a bit more annoying than usual today....and by a bit, I probably mean a lot."

"Why?"

"Eh, I'm feeling irritable," I said with a wicked grin and a wink. She snorted.

"Whatever Pam. It's your life."

"I promise to give you all a show."

"I look forwards to it."

Undercover Thief

"Hey Ron....." said a girl behind me. I looked over my shoulder at her.

She was tiny and very thin, almost skin a bone. She had short cut black hair, and obviously had Latin American roots. She had brilliant brown eyes that almost shone. She was cute, with a small button nose and lips that seemed to naturally rest in a smile.

"Hey, Pam this is Gwen. Gwen, meet Pam."

"Hi," said Gwen putting the tray down. I smiled at her.

"Hey," I said. She was wearing a knee length pink dress with a white long sleeve shirt underneath. It was kind of childish, but she made it work, giving off an aura of sweet naivety and innocence.

So, you're just late starting?" asked Gwen nicely.

"Yep."

"I have all the notes if you want to borrow them and catch up."

"You know what honey, that sounds wonderful. But I think I'll just go to classes and see if I can't just wing it," I said. She looked horrified by the idea.

"But you're *two weeks* behind!" she gasped. Ronnie snorted and put more food into her mouth.

"Yes, I know," I said with a chuckle, "I like to get a feel for a subject before I start to memorise it."

"Gwen is our resident smarty-pants, it's only too obvious already," said Ronnie patting the small girl's head.

"I just have a photographic and eidetic memory

"You don't say? That's a talent and a half to have."

"Thanks," said Gwen blushing bright red.

"That apple all you had for breakfast?" asked Ronnie.

"Yeah."

"That's not going to be enough," said Gwen seriously.

"I've gone days without eating. I'll live."

"Have you done school on an empty stomach?" asked Ronnie.

"Haven't been to school for a few years," I said honestly.

"How many?" asked Gwen, again completely dumbfounded that this was the case.

"Six, roughly," I answered truthfully.

"Six! Why?"

"Didn't really feel like it," I said with a sly smile.

"I like you," Ronnie said grinning, "You're full of strange things like that. Odd stuff."

"Yeah well, I'm a bit rules optional. Trust me, I wear off quickly."

"Nah, I don't think so," she said smiling.

"Here, have some toast," said Gwen handing me the toast that was dripping butter. I took it and smiled.

"Thanks."

"No problem. So what are you best at? You know, subject wise?"

"Who knows? Probably languages, I already speak a fair few."

"Well, we have manipulation class first thing," said Ronnie as the bell went.

"Oh yeah? What's that?"

"We learn to manipulate people," said Gwen, "I'm awful at it. I can barely hold one sentence together before it falls apart." That sounded like that would be like pulling off a con. Huh, perhaps I wouldn't stink at everything after all. I had a lot of experience there.

"Honey, it's all about confidence," I said as we got up. I walked with them over to where they put their dirty plates.

"How would you know? You haven't had a class yet?"

I just winked at her.

"I have some experience with manipulation" I teased as we left the main hall. I followed them along the corridors to the 'inner perimeter'. Apparently to get inside required a retinal scan. To my surprise, mine was already uploaded.

"They must have taken them while I was out of it," I muttered feeling uncomfortable knowing that.

What else had they taken? Wasn't that against the law? I mean, I know I had complete disregard for the law but weren't they supposed to follow it? Or was that something else that they felt was their decision because they were my parents? The idea made anger bubble inside me. There was going to be a serious conversation with my parents about my privacy sometime very soon!

We walked into the classroom. I had a look around. It was a bog standard class room, tables lined up in rows and columns. The teacher was already scribbling away at a black board covered in white chalk diagrams. A bit old school for me but never mind.

I waited for everyone else to sit down; leaning against the door, watching for a vacant seat to become apparent. There was one towards the back. That suited me fine. Out of obvious line of sight, easy to be forgotten about.

Undercover Thief

"You must be Miss Torres," said the teacher pulling me out of my thought.

"Yeah," I said taking some gum out of my pocket and popping it into my mouth.

"Well, please take a seat; you have a lot of work to catch up on."

"Gotcha," I said walking over to my chosen seat and sitting down, facing sideways. I took my iPod out of my pocket and skipped through a few songs I really wasn't in the mood for.

"I'm Mr Compton," he said looking at me expectantly.

"Right."

"You look at a teacher when they address you," he said sharply. I turned to look at him.

"Happy now?" I asked, putting my feet on my desk.

"Feet off your desk," he said narrowing his eyes. The whole class was watching.

"Sure," I said chewing.

"Are you being deliberately rude Miss Torres?"

"I don't know sir. You're supposed to be the manipulation expert. You tell me. Better yet, try to manipulate me," I said snorting. He glared at me, and could almost see him deciding what he was going to do about the situation.

Then he frowned and gave me a face that I was not prepared for.

Pity.

That was something I was completely not expecting.

"Alright then, let's move on. Class, today we are doing spot manipulation. That is when you see someone, without any prior background, and you have to get the information you want," he said turning back. He turned on a projection. It was blank.

"You are going to have exactly a minute to tell me what you see and what you'd do," he said. He pressed the button. I took out my iPod again.

"Miss Torres," he said. I looked up.

"What?"

"You're going to answer my question. Giving you don't feel the need to pay attention to my class you must be an expert."

"Fine," I said smiling. He didn't know just how right he was, "Where do you want me to start?"

"I want you to tell me what you know about this man? And then how you'd manipulate him....if you think you can." his tone made it obvious he didn't think I could.

Undercover Thief

Perhaps this wasn't sensible and it was goaded by pride but he was in for one hell of a shock.

"He's divorced, newly by the looks of things. He's stressed and has a tan line on his fourth finger. He had two dogs, one larger than the other, you can tell because of the hair on his trousers. He has kids, and he probably only sees them at the weekend, when he takes them out to fast food restaurants. This constant eating out has made him gain weight, you can tell by the belt – he's had to use another notch recently. His face also has a few blemishes. He's balding, so he'd probably sensitive about that. He is wearing a Rolex, he's very well off, but will be anxious of losing it all in the divorce settlement, a man like him probably has a highly demanding spouse or soon to be ex-spouse, and she will probably take him to the cleaners.

"If you're asking me how to get to him, then you need to be what he wants, and that's a friendly face. I'd be his friend, start by asking him about his children, tell him he's looking well under the circumstances. What am I trying to get him to do, because after that point my plan would change depending on the end goal? If it's as simple as steal his phone then I'd lift it and leave him. If I need information, then I buy him a drink or three and let him pour out his heart and soul on my shoulder."

Silence.

Shock.

Everyone was stunned, staring at me.

"Well.....you got that in one minute?" asked Mr Compton, wearing a pleasantly surprised expression, not outright shock like the rest of the class. He was much better at keeping his thoughts to himself and not written all over his face.

"Eh, five seconds, maybe six. I'm good at this kind of thing," I said sitting back with an innocent smile, tapping the desk with my red fingernails.

"How good?"

"Try me," I said opening up my arms, awaiting the challenge.

"So if I was telling you I needed to know the name of his stock broker?" He asked pressing deeper.

"I'd buy him a drink, probably a coffee. Start talking about his annoying ex-spouse, and how much she's going to cost. I'd work it into conversation."

"How?"

"Well I'd probably ask him how good his stock broker was, because he's going to need to make a lot of money to cover legal fees. So....yeah, get the name that way."

"And, from that point, I want to know the serial numbers on his ten dollar bills."

"Well, assuming I had known this from the start, when I hugged him on greeting, I would have already lifted his wallet. If I only just knew that I needed it now, I'd hug him on parting and get it then."

"And if he notices it's gone when he is with you?"

"Well, if that's the case, act as though he's lost it."

"He could catch you in a lift." he said. I snorted.

"Trust me that wouldn't happen" I said, "So we can skip that one."

"Say it did happen? What would you do then?"

"Pretend it fell out of his pocket; be startled that it fell into my hand."

"That's it?"

"It's simple and it works."

"Interesting," he said, nodding, "you seem to have an answer for everything."

"I'm good on the spot

I said inspecting my flawless nail paint, "but this subject might not bore me to death."

"I'll take that as a compliment," he said with a chuckle.

"You should," I said, "Because I'm pretty sure I'm going to snooze in French."

"I wouldn't want to encourage that kind of behaviour. French is an important subject in its own right," he said trying not to smile.

"Eh!" I said shrugging.

The lesson continued.

I didn't speak.

He ignored me.

I considered this a happy, working relationship. He set an essay for homework. Everyone was packing up and leaving for the next class; I slung my bag over my shoulder and headed for the door.

"Miss Torres," he said, "I'd like a word with you." Ronnie and Gwen stopped when I did.

"We'll wait outside," said Ronnie.

"Thanks, or else I'm hopelessly lost."

"Off you go Miss Olsen-Jones, Miss Price," said Mr Compton and they walked away.

"Take a seat Miss Torres," he said patting a desk and chair right at the front. I tossed my bag on the table part and sat down. He walked around to the front of the desk, leaned against it and looked at me.

"So, do you want to tell me?" he asked.

"Tell you what?"

"Where you learned to do that?"

"Nope."

"Ok." he said and I raised an eyebrow in surprise.

"I'm not here to interrogate you Miss Torres; I get the feeling that perhaps your parents ought to know."

"Ptf!" I scoffed, "they're lucky I'm even speaking to them."

"I did hear that you didn't get on with them," he said nodding, "Can I ask why? Again, merely curious – not meaning to pry."

"I'd rather not," I said folding my arms.

"Ok." he said nodding.

"Is that it?"

"You're sharp," he said, "Very, very good."

"Thanks," I said.

"But your attitude stinks."

I smiled.

"Listen," I said, "I'm going to go ahead and save you a lot of time trying to figure this out. Here's the thing: I don't care what people think of me. So tell me why I should care about your opinion of me?"

"I give you your grade," he offered. To be fair, that would be a good point, if I cared at all about grades. But I didn't.

"Ah, this is why I prefer England," I said "A teacher's opinion of you has no effect on your grades. Or it's not supposed to anyway."

"Miss Torres, at risk of repeating something you've already heard already, you could try here. I think you'll like it. You're obviously intelligent, capable and, even though you won't admit it the stuff here will interest you. I can see it; this is just up your street."

"Listen, I don't need another lecture," I said getting up, "Ever since my parents showed up again that's all I'm getting at the moment. I get people thinking they're better than me and that they know me and they all look down on me. Now, at this moment in time, I like you. Please don't do something to change my mind." I said slinging my bag over my shoulder.

"I didn't mean to lecture you Miss Torres. But I think if you paid attention in class, your extraordinary talent could become something rather special. Why don't you give it a go? You did say it might not bore you to death." I pressed my lips together.

"Alright, I'll think about it," I said turning to leave.

"That's all I ask. Homework is for next lesson," he called after me.

Undercover Thief

"Got it," I said walking out.

"So what did he want?" asked Gwen immediately.

"What do you think? To tell me that I have a sucky attitude."

"He's not wrong you know."

"Gwen!" hissed Ronnie.

"What? He isn't!"

"It's not our place to say anything about it."

"Well I'm going to," said Gwen stoutly, turning back to me, "you clearly know everything. But you don't have to be rude."

"I wasn't actively rude to him," I said, "I chose not to do what he commanded me to. I don't do well with orders."

"Pam, I only brought it up because you'll get in some serious trouble."

"Bring it on; I can handle anything this place throws at me!"

"Detention is not fun," said Ronnie.

"I won't go."

"You have to! Or you get more," Gwen said it like this was the worst thing possible. I laughed. These guys were such goodie-two-shoes. Had they never broken a rule before? Even a little one? I had to get them to loosen up while I was here.

"And I won't go to those either," I said, "Just chill you guys, it won't affect you."

"You know, what you did in there, it was pretty amazing," said Ronnie grinning from ear to ear like a Cheshire cat.

"Huh? Oh, answering his question?"

"That was so cool!" said Gwen bubbling, even jumping a little, "How did you do that? Photographic memory or something?"

"No, I've done that type of thing for years. Experience."

"You don't say," said Ronnie with an inquisitive edge to her voice as we walked up the stairs towards the languages department.

"Why?" asked Gwen bluntly.

"Sorry girls," I said, "That is kind of personal."

"Alright," said Ronnie with another wide grin, "but now I want to know more."

"Where are we heading now?" I asked, trying to shift the topic of conversation away from myself and my past.

"French," said Ronnie.

"So I can take my nap then. Time difference is really hitting me," I said.

"Either you hate the French, something I hear rumoured is an English tradition, or you already speak the language," said Gwen joking.

"I don't hate the French. I love their wine and food."

"So you speak French."

"Yep."

"Are you fluent?"

"Yep."

"Seriously?"

"I was taught French by a French man, while I was in France."

"What were you doing in France?"

"Um......" I said pulling a small face, kind of embarrassed, "that kind of crosses into the personal area. I don't want to lie to you girls, so I'm just going to say nothing."

"Sure," said Gwen shrugging her shoulders and smiling at me.

"Come on, I'm feeling a snooze coming on."

Chapter Seven

French had been a little bit of a rerun of manipulation. I had annoyed the teacher, and then passed a little test meant to try and prove to me and the rest of the class that I was stupid and didn't know what I was talking about. Only difference was, my French teacher got really annoyed when I passed, Mr Compton hadn't.

English, Maths and Geography had gone pretty much the same way. All of these teachers, unlike Mr Compton, seemed determined to not like me from the moment I started. I liked that about them. It was what made the game fun.

My goal was to annoy enough people to get kicked out of the school. I didn't want to be here, I wanted to get home and back to my life. I missed Jerry, Leah and Micah desperately. I knew that annoying people so much that I got kicked out would take work, but it would be quicker than trying to sit out the whole five years here.

It was lunch, and we were sat at the long tables with plates of food. The year group was split up into separate little groups and pairs. I didn't like that much. With so few of us there should be more cohesion, it made for a better team.

"Ready for PE?" asked Ronnie stabbing a chip – or fry as she called it – with her fork and putting it in her mouth.

"What? Do we do laps or something?" I asked looking down at my shorts and being thankful I wasn't wearing jeans – I was too tired to bother changing at the moment.

"Yep!" said Ronnie with a laugh, "And that's just part of it!" Gwen groaned.

"It's terrible. We have to fight."

"Wait, this school teaches us to fight?"

"Yep."

"They encourage fighting?"

"Inside PE lessons only."

"That should make the fights outside PE lessons more interesting," I said with a grin.

"You think there will be fights?" she asked frowning.

"Teenagers of a mainly male populous?" I said giving her a look. She tilted her head slightly thinking about that and nodded, agreeing with me.

"Yeah, so are you any good?" asked Ronnie.

"I hit your mother in the face, does that count?"

"You gave her that bruise?"

"You do not sound overly sympathetic towards your mother," I said picking through my pasta. It was really good food – not your average cafeteria rubbish.

"Well, the way I see it, you don't want to be here and she brought you here against your will. Of course you were going to fight back."

"How do you know that?" I asked quickly.

"What? That you didn't want to be here?"

"Yeah."

"That was easy," said Gwen, "I summed it up from your behaviour. You can be so nice to us but such an arse to the teachers."

"I like you more and more Gwen," I said. She beamed at me happily.

"I hear you threw up in your mother's purse and then blamed my mother for it," said Ronnie grinning.

"It was her fault! She poisoned me!"

"Poison?" asked Gwen alarmed.

"Sedatives aren't poison," said Ronnie.

Undercover Thief

"Most of them are to me. You don't have to deal with the vomiting and then stomach turning nausea and the headache and the inflamed throat- just trust me on this one. It's poison," I said shuddering at the thought, "And the dose she gave me wasn't small either. That was some nasty stuff!"

"Hang on, why does that happen when you're given a sedative?" asked Gwen.

"I get this bad allergic reaction to some of the most common main ingredients," I explained.

"No way! That must suck."

"Yeah, totally does," I agreed, "Although, I haven't had many occasions where I have been needed to be knocked out, so that's ok too."

"I guess...."

"When did you find out you were allergic?" asked Ronnie.

"I must have been about eleven...yeah, because I had appendicitis and when I woke up from the anaesthetic.....well, let's just say it wasn't pretty."

"Ew," said Gwen wrinkling her nose.

"Ron asked," I said in my rather feeble defence.

"Shouldn't they have made a medical record of that? This allergy? Why didn't my mum know?"

"I didn't go to the doctors on the NHS," I said.

"Which is the British free health service?" clarified Gwen quickly. I nodded.

"So you went private?"

"Yeah," I said, deciding to go with that, "but the notes were.....lost as it were."

"Why?"

"Bordering on personal again girls, sorry."

"A lot about your past is 'personal'," said Gwen, "Not complaining, just stating a fact."

"I know.....it's so much a part of who I am now."

"Everyone's past is Pam."

"Yeah....you're right."

"But we're off topic, are you good at fighting?"

"I can hold my own in a crisis. I have a few surprises. I managed to get away from your mum and the only reason she didn't grab me and haul my back down again was because we were on a roof and she thought I had nowhere to run to. She would have won easy."

"So you had somewhere to run on the roof?"

"I jumped off."

"What!"

"Down the rubbish chute."

Undercover Thief

"Oh, nice," said Ronnie sarcastically.

"Meh, I've been in worse situations," I said. I flicked my hair over my shoulder and then played with the pasta on my plate deep in thought.

"You tired?" asked Gwen sweetly.

"Yeah," I said, "I didn't sleep as much in French as I thought I would."

"Why?"

"Mainly because Madam kept yelling at me whenever I closed my eyes."

"I'm sure you'll get used to the time difference in no time."

"I hope you're right."

"Trust me, you'll sleep well tonight. I'll partner you in PE if you want," said Ronnie. Gwen looked dismayed.

"But who will I go with?"

"I don't know? Lydia? Marley? But this is Pam's first lesson, and I want to see just how good she is."

"I didn't say I was good," I protested, "I just have some emergency moves."

"Either way, this will be fun."

"Ronnie is really, really good. Her mother has been teaching her since she could walk," said Gwen.

"Just because it was her mother that taught her doesn't make Ronnie's accomplishment any less significant," I said, and that caused Ronnie to smile, "Besides, it wasn't like she learned it through osmosis. It took hard work."

"I know, I know, but the two of you have had a head start in things like that. I am going from zero."

"Honey, I am dead certain you will be tutoring the both of us through advanced science," I said and she smiled at the thought.

"Yeah. I guess that is sort of my niche isn't it?"

"Come on, we'll be late for PE," said Ronnie as we stood up. We dumped our plates and set off across the grass towards where our lesson would take place. We ambled slowly, and I looked ahead. There were a load of mats on the grass, our class mates were already sat around them, waiting for the lesson to begin. The bell had only gone minutes ago.

"So, you guys like being early for class," I muttered.

"Problem?" asked Ronnie confused.

"No, no, it'll will wear off soon enough."

"You think?" asked Gwen thoughtfully.

"I know," I said with a laugh, "I swear, I will turn you guys into normal teenagers even if it kills me!"

Undercover Thief

"And what would you know about being a normal teenager?" asked Ronnie, "From the sounds of it you really aren't."

"True, but do you have Facebook?"

"No."

"Twitter? Instagram? Snapchat?"

"Well I used to," inserted Gwen.

"Ok, let's try a different track. When was the last time you broke a rule – even a little one?"

Ronnie sniggered.

"Day I got expelled from middle school," She laughed.

"You got expelled?" Gwen gawked, "What did you do?"

"Well...one of the girls was always mean. Bullying me because I didn't have a dad. Anyway she started on this much younger kid one day and...I saw red. I might have over reacted a little but she deserved everything she got. Anyway she healed....eventually..." Ronnie blushed and looked like she really didn't regret it all that much but felt like she ought to pretend.

I burst out into fits of laughter while Gwen blinked trying to process that.

"Ah, well, remind me not to get on your bad side," I laughed, throwing an arm around her shoulders, "but that was the last time you broke a rule?"

"Yeah."

"Then I rest my case," I said with a mock bow, reaching the mats and dumping my bag down where the others had put theirs.

"All those websites are redundant here anyway. We have scramblers so no external signals can get in," said Ronnie, "I've wanted those things for years."

"What do you mean?"

"My mother has been the headmistress here since I was a baby remember. I've always lived here."

"So you have literally grown up here?"

"Yep."

"Wow....that has to suck," I said, "And if your mother is a spy, how do you get away with anything?"

"What do you mean?"

"Tell me you've broken a few rules before. Please? It would really make my day," I said with a wiggle of my shoulders.

"You're such a bad influence."

"I know. Own it and love it darling," I said with a laugh.

"Afternoon ladies and gentlemen," said a man, obviously our coach, walking over onto the padded area. Everyone scrambled to get in line and I fell in place beside Gwen, "I hope you ate early at lunch, because I do not want vomiting now."

"Sir," they all chorused. Ok. It was that kind of a lesson.

"Right, I need a volunteer." no one raised their hands.

"You," he said pointing to one of the larger boys who walked forwards without a word.

"Right, today you will be practising simple punches and kicks again. As I will demonstrate." he threw a punch it was so close to the boy's body for a moment I had thought he'd hit. But he hadn't. He had some amazing control there. The boy being used for demonstration stood like a statue, not daring to flinch.

"Everyone down! Ten press-ups," said the Coach. Ok. I could see I would use the free period next to take a shower. This looked like I was going to sweat a lot.

"You will take turns in throwing punches and someone else will defend. But first, warm up, I want three laps of this field. At the end of each lap I want ten push up and ten sit ups before you continue running. Right, pair up. Move!"

I was fit. Very fit. Ronnie, Gwen and I stuck together initially for the run, but Gwen tripped and stumbled a lot, falling behind. Ronnie and I performed the warm up with smooth efficiency.

Ronnie was clearly near the top of the class. Her punches were expert, and so were her defence. Every single move was calculated and precise and I could see a light in her eyes. She was good at it and enjoyed it.

I was not appalling. I was certainly above average. But being paired with Ronnie did make me look the weaker of the two of us. I didn't mind that. It was refreshing not being miles ahead or miles behind everyone else.

The coach was a man that obviously liked to make you sweat. Every few minutes we had to paused and do some stupid exercises before getting back on our feet and at it again. And as people got tired, they got sloppy. Gwen managed to punch her partner in the face by accident. That had been very funny, although not so funny for poor Lydia.

Ronnie was still bouncing with energy at the end of class. I was extremely tired, a mixture of the exhausting workout I had just had to do and the time difference. They were eight hours behind over here! That was just insane! I just wanted to curl up and go to sleep. I was sure if I looked in the mirror I would have heavy purple bags under my eyes. Note to self, change for PE in future.

Undercover Thief

After the lesson was over, we went up to our rooms to change. We split off from Gwen and headed into our room. Ronnie bagged the shower first, so I lounged on the floor, waiting for her to finish. I flicked through a couple of the text books, completely bored.

"Ok, all yours," said Ronnie coming out as she patted her hair dry.

"Ta," I said walking into the bathroom and showering. The hot water was so comforting against my skin; I could have dozed off right then and there. I immediately turned the water a lot colder in order to wake me up a little bit.

I hoped out and changed into my favourite black ripped jeans and blue lace crop top. I changed my shoes to a pair of gorgeous black heels, and pulled on my black leather jacket again and headed out of the bathroom brushing my hair. Ronnie was sat at her desk, writing some essay or other.

"What have we got next?" I asked yawning.

"Operation Studies," she said, "Apparently there is a new teacher this year."

"Alright, let's break them in," I said with a wicked grin.

"You don't really do rules do you?"

"They're more like guidelines than actual rules," I said doing my best Captain Barbosa impression. She just frowned.

"You have seen Pirates of the Caribbean right?"

"No."

"Oh my god, that is what we are doing with our evening for the next few days!" I grinned.

"Now I'm intrigued. Come on, the bell will go soon."

"Let's go," I said patting on some concealer to hide the bags under my eyes.

We headed down the stairs, busy with other students. A couple of people threw me strange looks, I didn't know why. So I turned to Ronnie.

"Why do people look at me weird?" I asked.

"Um, it's probably the way you're dressed," said Ronnie shrugging, "you looked great, don't get me wrong. It's just unusual for here....you know?"

"Alright," I said taking that in, "well now I know."

"You don't mind?"

"I don't care what other people think about me. These people are strangers to me. I need to be happy with myself."

"That's a really admirable thing. I'm not sure I could do it."

"Sure you can. Listen, are we allowed out into the town at weekends and things? To shop?"

"Sure, some weekends."

"Then I will take you shopping to all the right places and we will make you look amazing. Not that you don't rock the stretch cotton and sensible slacks, but there is so much more you can work with," I said.

"I look forwards to it," said Ronnie with a snort as we walked into Operations. People were already there, sat down at the desks. The teacher was absent.

"Guys!" waved Gwen, bobbing up and down a little.

"The front? Seriously?" I asked slinging my bag by the closet one and sitting down, kicking feet onto the table.

"What? Best seats!"

"Thanks for saving them Gwen," said Ronnie.

"So, what's do you think the teacher will be like?" I asked.

"We don't know yet, we've only had cover teachers so far this term. Not sure why," replied Ronnie with a shrug.

"Sorry I am late class," said my mother walking in, pushing my feet off the table as she passed me. I raised an eyebrow. You had got to be kidding me. My mother was now my teacher? Well, this could only end terribly.

"Right, well, I'm sorry for the delay in actually meeting you all this term. Let's see what your cover teacher has taught you," she said turning on the projector and flicking off the light switch.

"Right, now, these are some photos of locations just before an event – something is about to happen. I want you guys to tell me what will happen." She went to her computer and pulling up a power point presentation.

"Ok, here is the first picture," said my mother.

It was a busy market street, completely packed with people. Window reflections showed lots of people outside of the picture as well. And there were rooftops and balconies. There was so much happening on in the picture it took me a while to clock what was going on.

"Nobody got an answer for me?" she asked and someone must have raised their hand as she continued, "Mr Demarin?"

"Shots get fired?"

"Nope. Mr O'Heart?"

"Um...someone dies?"

"No. Anyone?" There was silence. I couldn't take it anymore.

Undercover Thief

"She steals from that stall," I sighed.

"Correct. How did you know?"

"The look on her face," I said, covering a yawn.

"That's not really enough evidence."

"In my world it would get you a conviction," I said with a snort.

"Well, now you live in my world. What else?"

"Stance, it's on edge and not natural. Eyes, not looking in front of her but around," I said shrugging.

"Alright, how about this next one?" she asked.

There was another busy scene, but this one I knew. I knew what was going to happen because I knew someone who had been there and told me the story.

"Miss Olsen-Jones?" my mother was picking on people.

"Another robbery?"

"No, anyone else?"

Again there was silence so I gave a large sigh.

"A bomb goes off," I answered bored.

"How did you know?" she asked, clearly a little more than surprised.

"Nothing majorly clever," I answered, shrugging, "You see that guy in the blue shirt, looking at the bag by that lamppost? He told me what happened last time I saw him."

"What?" she said, confused.

"He told me last time I went to visit him. He got put in prison for it, but he didn't plant the bomb. Teddy knows a bomb when he sees one, and he went over to the bag and opened it. He saw the timer and the wiring and threw it down into that sewer, saved a lot of lives doing so. But the idiots that investigated the case put him behind bars for it."

"You know this man?" she said, her face twisting with outrage at the thought, "You know Theodor Matiswel?"

"Yeah. Man is like an uncle to me. If you knew him, you'd know he'd never make and plant a bomb. That man is so kind he couldn't hurt a fly. He is one hell of a forger though," I conceded.

"The man is guilty Pamela."

"Not of this crime he's not," I said with stubborn certainty, "He told me so himself."

"He's a criminal!"

"And?" I scoffed, "What's your point? He's a nice guy."

"I know the person who put him away Pamela. I know he's guilty."

Undercover Thief

"He didn't plant the bomb," I said slowly, rolling my eyes, "Whoever you know is an idiot."

"Pamela, are you going to take the word of a criminal over me? Are you seriously telling me you believe him over a team of qualified agents?"

"Yes," I said certainly, "that man bought me my first bike. I was eleven."

"Your father and I bought you your first bike. You were six."

"I'm not talking pedal bike. I mean motor bike!"

"You're not old enough to drive a motor bike," she said with gritted teeth.

"Also not old enough to live alone," I said sharply, "but there you go."

She took a deep breath, visibly trying to calm herself down. The whole class was watching the exchange with fascination.

"Pamela, he is guilty of a long list of crimes, and therefore he is in jail. Where people who break the law belong."

"I'm not saying he didn't break the law! I'm just saying that the crime you put him away for he didn't actually do," I said with a laugh, "I wouldn't have been surprised if you'd put him away for cooking the books, for tax evasion or something like that, but nope. You guys locked him up for saving lives."

"Pamela, I refuse to let you speak to this man again."

"You can't do that!"

"He is dangerous."

"I told you he isn't! Are you deaf or something?"

"Pamela! You will not speak to me like that!"

"Hell if I won't!"

"Pamela, I will send you out."

"Go right ahead," I snapped.

"Pamela, go to the headmistress' office! Now! I will have a word with you later!"

"Oh I'm terrified!" I said sarcastically getting up, throwing my bag over my shoulder and leaving the room, really annoyed.

Who the hell was she to break into my life and start judging me and my friends?

Chapter Eight

I trudged my way up to the headmistress' office. I just about managed to remember the way from yesterday. I walked up the beautifully carved wooden stairs and along the hall until I came to the door bearing a plaque with her name on it. I knocked.

"Yes?"

I opened it and walked it. She set down her pen surprised.

"Miss Torres. Why are you here?" she asked.

"Had a fight."

"Oh?" she asked a little shocked.

"With my mum."

"Oh?"

"In class."

"Oh," She nodded understanding the situation.

She took a deep breath and smiled at me.

"I'm sorry to hear that Pamela; I guess I should have foreseen that this might happen. Sit down," she gestured to the chair in front of her desk. I walked over; my bag slipped off my shoulder and hit the floor with a quiet thud. I sat comfortably in the seat.

"May I ask what this fight was about?" she asked.

"My mother is an arrogant hypocrite that can't be told she's wrong," I grumbled with a sniff.

"That doesn't really help me," said Miss Price gently.

"She was bringing up photos of scenes before something happens, and she asked us to predict the next event. Baby stuff, you know. Anyway, she brought up a photo and I knew the story from my friend who was there. Only he got landed for the crime which he didn't commit and got put in prison for it. She flipped out when she heard I knew a criminal," I said laughing at the end with a shake of my head. Let's face it, if she knew the truth about me, she'd have kittens.

"Is that all?"

"I tried to tell her he was a nice guy and innocent. When she heard that I visit him in prison, she tried to make me not see him ever again. Like I'm going to do that!"

"What did you do?"

"Nothing really."

"Miss Torres," she said expectantly.

"I may have accused her of being deaf. But in my defence, she totally over reacted to me knowing him. It was almost as if I wasn't allowed to know other people, or people in general. And that may or may not have sparked my temper a little bit. So I guess I really didn't help the situation."

Miss Price sighed.

"So, you have a temper do you?" she asked.

"Oh honey, my mother ain't seen nothing yet," I said with a cackle.

"Ok, and how do you know this man that argument was over?"

"He's a good guy. Like an Uncle. He's a family friend really."

"Family friend implies he isn't part of the family."

"I'm not going to talk about my family Miss Price," I said flatly, shutting down that line of inquiry in one sentence.

She laced her fingers together and pressed her lips into a straight line, something I'd noticed she always did when she was trying to think. Probably looking for the most diplomatic phrasing for what she was trying to say.

"Miss Torres.....I understand that moving here has been difficult for you, and perhaps not as easy as it could have been. I also know you have a history that I hope one day to understand, and I see now that perhaps it's a little bit bigger that we thought originally. But this place is where you truly belong. I can tell just by talking to you now that you are an extremely smart and very talented girl; I have experienced your raw talent first hand. Here, you could truly excel."

"But I don't want to excel. I just want to go home," I said sitting back in the chair and tapping the arm with my fingernails.

"I'm afraid that just isn't possible Miss Torres."

"Why? Why don't I get a say in the matter?"

"Because you're a child in the eyes of the law."

"And why should that matter all of a sudden? Why, because I'm fourteen, do my desires and wants get brushed under the carpet and the big adults get to walk all over me? I've had to mature a hell of a lot faster than everyone else my age, and even then what I want should count for something and be seriously considered."

"What you want is considered Miss Torres, but sending you back to London alone is out of the question."

"Why?"

"Miss Torres, I can tell that you have perhaps experienced a lot more of life than most children your age. You've clearly dealt with a lot more. But that doesn't make you mature Miss Torres, not on its own anyway. I am yet to see if you are mature. However, exactly what you've dealt with I can't figure out. So rather than me making probably a large amount of wrong guesses, why don't you tell me?"

"No thanks."

"No? Why not? I promise what you say will be confidential."

"You and my mother are friends. And, despite my opinion of her as a person, I can tell she's good at reading people. And she'd get it out of you."

"I'm better than you give me credit for Miss Torres."

"I have no doubt," I said, "I have respect for you Miss Price. At the moment. But I only give people one chance. One chance and one alone. If you lose my respect you have no way of getting it back."

"That's rather dramatic."

"It's truth; call it an observation of experience. No one can ever really change. If someone lets you down once they will do it again."

"My professional obligation to you would come first. Not my friendship with your mother."

"No," I said shaking my head and running my fingers over the wood of the arm of the chair, "I don't want to give you split loyalties. You and my mother have been friends longer that I've been alive. There's no way that won't influence things."

"That's an odd stance for someone your age to take on the subject."

"I guess you could say I'm more aware of how the world actually works, if you don't want to use the word mature," I said with a smirk, "I'm a realist, and I'm not stupid, professional obligation means absolutely diddly-squat."

"But if I could understand your past, perhaps we could make your transition smoother-"

"I said no! I am allowed to have some parts of my life that are private you know," I snapped at her sharply, glaring at her and wishing she would just drop the subject.

"I just want to help you adjust! What is it? Cigarettes? Something else? Drugs? Do you need a few recovery days or something? Rehab perhaps."

"No! How dare you!" I exclaimed outraged.

"You look really rough Miss Torres-"

"I'm dealing with a huge time difference is all!" I said folding my arms crossly, "sleep deprivation is my only problem, I don't need rehab! I'm not addicted to anything, illegal or otherwise!"

"I didn't mean to offend you!"

"Yeah well it came out that way. I'm not stupid enough to take drugs."

"Ok. I'm sorry that was how it was received."

Undercover Thief

"How else did you think I would take it? You told me I look like a drug addict going through withdrawal! The only drug withdrawing from my system right now is that bloody sedative you pumped me full of. You're damn right I'm offended."

"I'm sorry about that; I didn't know that you would react like that. And I didn't mean to offend you."

"Well how would you take that?"

"I didn't mean to offend you, and quite clearly I have struck a nerve. I'm sorry." There was a pause as the two of us mentally recharged.

"What are you finding hardest? You've had twenty four hours here? What do you miss? Internet? Freedom?" She asked.

"My family," I said shortly.

My eyes went down to the desk, homing in on a tiny little chip in the wood. I bit back the wave of homesickness that came over me. I wanted more than anything, right then and there to call Jerry and Leah. Just to hear their voices.

"You keep mentioning them, but you refuse to tell me more about them. I have to wonder why."

"Like I said, some parts of my life are private."

"But if they're such a big part of your life, why try to hide it?"

"Because you're all strangers to me! Tell me, when you meet a stranger, a stranger that poisons you and carts you half way across the world to some random and insane school in another country, do you immediately tell them all about Ronnie?"

"Good point."

"I've got several."

"There have to be other things."

"Sure, but the other stuff is nothing compared to that."

"You know, all the students who come here miss their families at some point or another. It's not uncommon; they're away for such long periods of time."

"Yeah, but I've never gone a day without seeing mine."

"Can't you believe that it is the same for some of the students here?"

"It really isn't the same."

"Really? Explain it to me then. How is it so different?"

"You know what? Forget it. You wouldn't understand."

"I'm fairly sure I can keep up with however complicated it is."

"No. It's not complicated. But you would just laugh. I highly doubt you can understand because to understand you have to have been there."

"Where is that?"

"Like I said. You would laugh."

"No I wouldn't."

"Really? Because adults always have a knack for just telling me not to be so silly and to do as I'm told. Which I have a problem with, because almost all adults seem to be idiots with another agenda."

"Do you think I have another agenda?"

"Yes. This conversation we're having is certainly not for my sake. I already know what's going on in my life," I said.

"Is that why you are so reluctant to converse your parents? Because you feel they have another agenda, because I promise you they don't."

"That is not a topic that is open for discussion," I said coldly. She raised an eyebrow.

"It isn't?"

"No."

"Why not?"

"Because what's going on between me and my parents is none of your business."

"I am your teacher Miss Torres, please watch how you speak to me."

"I will speak to people in a manner I find appropriate," I said with a sniff.

"Being rude won't help you."

"Then people should stop kidnapping me and forcing me to go to secret government schools!"

"Your mother and father are just trying to help."

"I don't need their help!" I said seriously, "I was happy."

"Were you safe?"

"The majority of the time."

"Only the majority? That's worrying."

"No one is ever one-hundred percent safe."

"You are safe right now Miss Torres."

"I'll have to take your word for it," I said with a sniff. She sighed.

"Well, Miss Torres, if you refuse to tell me any more to help you, I suppose that we should return to your argument with your mother. Now, your mother may be a very good friend of mine but she is also one of my teachers. And she is very experienced in the field. We're lucky to have her here. You two must keep personal matters outside of the classroom."

"Then tell her to keep her hairnet on."

"Miss Torres, it takes two to have an argument."

"And yet I'm the only one who's being told off. Because I'm the minor."

"Not true."

"It is though. You're not going to tell my mother off are you?"

"No."

"See."

"Your mother did the right thing sending you here and out of that situation. She couldn't leave her class."

"But she started it by getting annoyed that I actually know a few people."

"Miss Torres, regardless of your former friends, I must ask that you refrain yourself from outbursts in class. Your mother took this job so she could be around you. However, she is a professional and her duty is to the class. Don't make this hard for her."

"Right," I said rolling my eyes, "Noted."

"I'm sensing a lot of anger."

"Anger? No! Really?" I said standing up, my voice heavy with sarcasm.

"Give yourself a chance Miss Torres."

"Spare me the speech. I am too tired to deal with it. You're beginning to sound like a shrink."

"I promise you Miss Torres, I am not a shrink."

"Good. I don't need one."

"Miss Torres, I have to ask. Is your other family connection the only reason you don't want to be here?"

"I have a life outside of this place you know. And you literally snatched me away from it with no warning and no choice in the matter."

"But this is a better life here."

"Says who?"

"Me. Most children are amazed by this place and love being here, no matter how much they miss things or people from home."

"I'm not most children."

"Evidently," she said studying me. I kept my face blank and completely expressionless. She couldn't read me.

"So what now? Do I have to wait here until my mother turns up or what?" I asked.

"No. I think you can go to your room for the rest of the hour. Oh, and you'll need one of these."

"What? A hall pass? You have those in America don't you?"

"You don't need a hall pass here. If you get sent out you have to attend detention."

"Oh you are actually joking with me aren't you? This was her fault!"

"Afraid not, and you will go to your detention."

"For goodness sake! Ok. I'll take it. As per bloody usual," I took the slip of pink paper from her hands and picked up my bag.

"What's that supposed to mean?" Asked Miss Price.

"What do you think? See you Miss. I have no doubt I'll be back again soon."

"At least try to make an effort here Pamela."

"I make no promises," I said as I closed the door.

I walked back to my room, reading the slip of pink paper. I had to attend detention with Mr Compton at six. Oh, so much fun!

I shoved it into my pocket and walked along to my room. The corridors were mainly empty; a few of the older year students were walking around with arms of books and worried expressions on their faces. Might only be the first few days back but important exams had already got them stressed out.

I guess it would look like that in any school.

Kicking the door open to my room, I threw my bag on my bed and opened up my laptop, pulling up my iTunes and hitting play.

I opened up my e-mails and started reading over one sent by Leah.

"Knock knock," I turned to see my father at the door.

"What are you doing here?"

"I saw you walking past and decided to come and see you. I thought your mother said you had lessons."

"I do. I got sent out."

"Why?"

"Because Mum had a paddy."

"Your mother sent you out?" he asked a little sceptically.

"That's what I said."

"Oh," he said and paused, "What did you do?"

"Have faith in a friend," I said with a sniff, closing my e-mails.

"What?"

"Mum had a flip because I know someone that is in prison. It's not my fault that the idiots investigating the bombings got the wrong guy."

"You know someone in prison? Pam, not good!"

"Why?"

"Because people in prison are bad people."

"Wow, that is such a stereotype! Totally not true!"

"Pam, I think I have a little bit more experience in the matter than you do."

"I highly doubt it," I said rolling my eyes, "Anyway, Mum freaked out when I said I knew him, like the idea of me knowing and talking to people like that was some massive crime."

"She only wants what is best for you Pam, and she and I both deal with bad people. He's a criminal!"

"Yes! I know that! A forger! Not a bomber!"

"Pam! If he's a criminal you shouldn't have been talking to him."

"Listen, if you've come here to judge me like this, can I ask that you leave? I don't want to listen to it."

"Pam....I'm not here to judge. I don't want to get in the middle of this fight, but I do think that perhaps you could try to see if from our point of view Pam."

"You say you don't want to get in the middle, but no, you'll pick her side!"

"She's my wife and your mother, and she is right about this."

"No, she isn't," I said slamming down the lid to my laptop, "and neither are you."

"Pamela! This is ridiculous!"

"Why? Because I have an opinion that isn't yours! Because I disagree with you? Because while you were gone I grew the hell up and formed my own thoughts about the world and made my own decisions? You realise we're fighting over the fact that somebody in prison is a friend of mine. What is wrong with having friends?"

"Nothing. Criminal friends, however, are not good for you," he said softly.

"Neither are absent parents! Anyway why can't I decide that for myself?" I asked at a much more level tone.

"You're fourteen, and you don't know people the way your mother and I do."

"You can't claim to know Teddy. Or any of my friends, because you haven't met them. Everyone is different Dad."

"Ok, I can see that this is an emotional topic and I think it would be good if we changed the subject."

"Because I'm right," I said rolling my eyes.

"No, Pamela, because I don't think we're ever going to agree, so there is no point to continue arguing. It isn't good."

"Fine," I said in a huff picking up my laptop and moving over to the desk, putting it back inside it's bag.

"So, what are you going to do with the rest of your hour?" asked my father.

"Probably not all that much as it's just about over," I said pointing to my clock.

"Ok, well, perhaps you should have a word with your mother this evening, try to smooth all this out."

"Can't, I have detention."

"She gave you detention as well?"

"No, but when a teacher sends you to see the headmistress, you get an automatic detention. So this is her fault, again."

"Oh. Well perhaps you can see her after that."

"Probably not."

"Why not?"

"I don't want to."

"Pamela," he said disapprovingly.

"What? I don't want to see you either," I said bluntly taking out my iPod and putting the ear phone back in.

"Pam, that wasn't very nice."

"I'm not a nice person."

"Are you mad at us?"

"Take a guess Einstein."

"No need to be rude Pam."

"This is me not caring," I said picking up my bag and slinging it over my shoulder.

"Pam, are you angry that we brought you here? Is that it?"

"One of an ever growing list," I said with a tilt of my head, "So please, just do me a favour and move out of my way so I can go to my next lesson."

"Pam, we're only trying to help you," said my father.

"Please move. I have a lesson to get to."

"Pam," he tried as I pushed past him and down the hall.

"Pam!"

"This is me going to a class like a good girl! Now leave me the hell alone!"

Chapter Nine

Detention was held in the evening, after dinner. Apparently every evening had a different subject teacher in charge, and today it was Manipulation. I knocked on the door, and Mr Compton looked up from his laptop screen slightly surprised.

"Miss Torres, what can I do for you?"

"I was told to come here," I said holding up my detention slip.

"On your first day? Already?" he asked. I shrugged.

"My mum isn't my biggest fan," I said by way of explanation.

"Well, alright. Take a seat. Leave those headphones on the desk if you don't mind."

"Sure," I said taking them out and putting them on the side.

"What did you do to get a detention?" he asked taking the pink piece of paper and signing it off.

"I really don't want to talk about it," I said sitting down.

"Ok. I'll leave it to you then," he said handing it back to me. I sat down at one of the tables and slumped forwards, resting my head on my arms.

"Have you got any work to do?" he asked.

"No."

"I set you an essay for homework. Are you telling me you've already done it?"

"No."

"Well you could do that," he prompted, "seeing as I'm here to ask questions."

"Alright, what was it on?"

"Weren't you listening?"

"I was but I forgot. Sorry. I was banking on getting the title off Gwen later," I said. He smiled at that, but mainly to himself.

"Alright. I wanted an essay on the everyday examples of manipulation, a basic outline, the good points and the bad points."

"Ok," I said pulling out paper and pens from my bag. I went to write and stopped.

"What is it?" asked Mr Compton, guessing something was wrong.

"I...."

"Yes?" he asked kindly.

"I've never written an essay before," I admitted.

"Really? What did you do at school before you came here?"

"Honestly? I didn't go to school."

"At all?"

"Not since I was nine."

"Why?"

"No time," I mumbled embarrassed. He then smiled at me and nodded.

"Alright. Well, I can help you with that."

Actually, Mr Compton was a really nice guy, he was obviously very intelligent. We moved off essay structure quickly and were debating some of the main points between ourselves. It was a really good conversation, because he really knew what he was talking about. And it was really nice to be able to talk about this with someone who knew as much about the subject as I did.

"No! No! That wouldn't work!" he protested.

"Yes it would! It has!" I said with a laugh.

"No! It wouldn't because you've already told him you're a vegetarian and that you are allergic to prawns."

"Ok, he picks up on the fact I'm not throwing up, so I say I have a delayed reaction and groan about how much I'm going to pay for that later."

"But you are a vegetarian, so why were you eating it anyway?"

"I don't eat meat. Some vegetarians eat fish, so shell fish is allowed."

"But if you knew the meat was shell fish why did you eat it?"

"I didn't know it was shell fish, I thought it was regular fish."

"And this is where they guy has to be stupid to believe you."

"No! You say it confidently with conviction and then move on."

"No! That wouldn't work! No!"

"My point is something you say is always never going to add up. When you are confronted with a guy like the one we're talking about, you shouldn't start worrying about every word that you say."

"But if he is picking holes in your- oh my goodness, look at the time," said Mr Compton. I looked up. Half eight. Detention finished an hour ago.

"Ooops," I said with a laugh, "I guess I can argue a point a bit too excessively."

"Me too, Miss Torres," he said laughing with me.

"Well, I won't take up any more of your evening."

"No, it was a really, really interesting conversation. The way you think about things is unusual. Tell me, where did you learn all of your...technique?"

"If I told you, you wouldn't believe me," I said, thinking that if I told him I was a con-artist then he would run for the hills. Or put me in handcuffs, neither of which were something I wanted.

"Really? How intriguing. Well, you are miles ahead of the syllabus."

"I don't know if that's good or bad."

"Not bad. Certainly not! Rarely have I been able to have a conversation in this much detail with a student, even during the final years."

"Learning the theory of something and putting it into practice are two very different things."

"Very true. Anyway, the problem is you'll probably find my lessons boring for a while as we're going to have to cover the basics....." he said thinking, "Ok, I'll tell you what. I have some third year books you can have a look at instead if you prefer."

"That would be great," I said thinking how I could apply that kind of knowledge in our cons back home with Jerry and Leah. Maybe invent a few new ones. It might make any time spent here, before I could get home, worth it.

He wandered over to his book shelf and picked up a volume.

"If you have any questions, do feel free to come and ask me about them," He said and handed it to me. I opened the page and flicked through it.

"Interrogation? I've never done any of that!"

"It's a fascinating topic," he said, "but if you don't get it, don't worry about it. It is a bit advanced for your year group at the moment."

"I can handle it," I said with a confident smile.

"Alright then. Well I'll lock up the classroom now."

"Right. Thanks for the help sir. See you Wednesday."

"See you then Pam," he said. During our conversation I had told him to call me that. Miss Torres was for people I didn't like. Mr Compton was someone I could respect. I headed for the common room.

There were fourteen of us in total sharing the common room. Eight boys. Six girls. Everyone was there and there was a cheerful fire burning in the grate.

I looked around people were sat on their own or in twos chatting quietly. The atmosphere was almost that of a library.

"So, how was detention?" asked Ronnie when I wandered over to her. She was playing and losing chess with Gwen on the floor by the fire.

"Not bad actually, Mr Compton and I got into this really interesting discussion about the different techniques that you can use to manipulate a person who is suspicious of you," I said folding myself onto the floor and watching their game.

"Because you know how to do that," Gwen said rolling her eyes.

"Well duh!" I teased. I looked around the room and sighed.

Nope, this was almost uncomfortable. I didn't know names – I had been too busy being sent to the headmistress's office to think of learning names. My eyes narrowed in on two girls who were sat together on a sofa reading magazines.

"Hi," I said going over. They looked up a little stunned.

Undercover Thief

"Um, hi," said the first.

"I'm Pam, and you two are?"

"I'm Cassidy, and this is Lydia," said the other girl. I thought back over the last day and tried to think about what I had learned about them. They were always together – already firm friends like Ronnie, Gwen and myself. They were a bit like ying and yang. Cassidy was blond, pale with blue eyes whereas Lydia had shimmering black hair and beautiful dark skin.

"It's nice to meet you," I said, "So, are you liking the school?"

"Um, yeah. Yeah, the school is really cool," smiled Lydia.

"How about you?" I asked a third girl sat reading quietly curled up in a window seat nearby. She looked across at me with a gaze of pure ice.

"Marley," she muttered and went straight back to her book.

"Yikes," I mouthed at Cassidy who sniggered with Lydia. Marley was fairly ordinary, short brown hair and brown eyes. I tried to think about what I had learned over the day and it wasn't much. She barely spoke to anyone, unless she was asked a direct question.

"I kind of have a question," said Lydia.

"Oh yeah?"

"How? Like, out of all the subjects, manipulation is the one you're ahead in?" she asked.

"I guess it just clicks, you know."

"That's what you're going to tell us? It clicks?" laughed Cassidy.

I shrugged, smiled and wandered back over to Gwen and Ronnie.

"And that thing with you mum?" added Lydia slyly.

"Isn't up for discussion," I said leaning down to make a chess move for Ronnie which won her the game, much to Gwen's dismay.

"Now I want to know!" said Lydia intrigued.

"Hey," I said getting ambling over to where three boys were sat at desks doing their homework. They all looked up and smiled politely, "I'm Pam. Who are you guys?"

"Ian," said the blond boy.

"I'm George and this is Allister," said another. I processed what I had observed about them. George and Allister too had formed a fast friendship; the two of them were a bit like Gwen with their amazing brains. Ian just happened to be sat with them this evening.

"What you up to?" I asked leaning over so I could have a look.

Undercover Thief

"We're doing our homework for your mother's class," said Allister.

I snorted.

"Well, that makes some of us. I'm not going to bother," I laughed.

"Why?"

"It's complicated. I thought that was made a little bit obvious by today's display," I said with a smile. I sat on the desk and swung my legs.

"Yeah, just a little bit," grinned Ian. I picked up a piece of his plain paper.

"Do you mind?" I asked and he shook his head. I crumpled it up and threw it across the room at one of the boys. He looked up a little stunned.

"Hey big guy, I'm Pam. Who are you?" I asked.

"Gavin," he said amused. Gavin was simply huge –a pure wall of muscle. He was definitely near the top of the class in PE. By a long shot.

"And who are you?" I said wiggling a finger at the two of them. They raised their heads from their books.

"Um, I'm Peter," said one. I remembered Peter; he was already fluent in French.

"I'm Adam," said the other. He was a maths whiz, and very interested in the more unique classes on offer here.

173

I smiled at him and continued my circuit of the room to where the two remaining boys were sat that I hadn't yet pestered this evening.

"What?" asked one looking warily up at me as I approached?

"Want to play a game?" I asked batting my eyelashes.

"Um...alright," He agreed cautiously.

"Yay! What's your name?"

"Trevor."

"And you?" I asked turning to the other one and picking up his book for him.

"Lucas," He muttered a little reluctantly.

"Hi Lucas, come play with us," I cajoled, "Please! We've studied all day, it's time to have some fun. Come on." I nodded over to the large table at the edge of the room, "That'll do, let's use that." Lucas and Trevor appeared a bit bemused but slowly stood up and followed me. Peter and Adam looked intrigued, "All welcome" I called out to them on my way passed, and they got to their feet too.

"Ah, there was go. Much more sociable. Easier to have a chat this way," I said smiling at the lads as they settled down at the table. Ronnie and Gwen immediately started their way over. Lydia and Cassidy seemed hesitant, so

Undercover Thief

I smiled encouragingly at them and said, "The more the merrier."

"What do you want to talk about?" asked Ronnie dragging out a chair to sit on.

"Well, let's start by saying how we each got here. Let's get to know each other a little better. It's obvious what I did to be here; I was born with the most unfortunate mother. You guys?"

"I'm an obvious one again," said Ronnie. Everyone conceded the point.

"Ok. I'll go first," said Lydia, "I got a letter saying to come for testing. So I turn up, thinking it's an audition to a sports scholarship. Must have done well."

"What sport?"

"Urban running."

"What's that?" I asked confused.

"Like cross country running but for us city folk," she said grinning.

"Oh!"

"I'm a bit like you guys. My father died in Iraq when I was thirteen. I was taken in by my Uncle. He works for the secret service," said Cassidy.

"My brain got me here," said Gwen, "my father is a brick layer and my mother is a cocktail waitress. I was always an academic freak, way beyond everyone else my age. One day I got a letter and it says there is the potential to come to a great school for free. My parents love me, even if they don't understand me and jumped at the opportunity."

"Aww. That's nice. I figured your brain was your route in," Ronnie said smiling.

"Marley?" I asked, she was the only one that had refused to move from her spot on the window seat. She just looked up from her book and shrugged dismissively.

"I know someone," was all she said on the subject.

"I'm with Gwen, I was always ahead in school, so I got tested," said Allister and George nodded to imply it was the same for him too.

"What about you boys?" I asked.

"I worked with the police for a while, you know, volunteering and stuff. So, one day, they bring a guy in for questioning. Only he gets lose. I manage to contain him," said Lucas, "apparently he was a serial killer and ex-marine. So I got a place here."

"Sweet," I said with a laugh.

"My dad works for the CIA," said Ian.

"I was training for the marines. But I was offered this instead. Dad's a marine," said Gavin.

Undercover Thief

"I got invited to testing. But I don't know why," said Peter. Trevor and Adam nodded. Obviously that was the same story for them too.

"Well. That's cool," I said sitting back, "better than being forced to come because of your lineage."

"Why don't you want to be here? It's amazing," said Lydia.

"You got a choice in the matter. I didn't. They literally poisoned me on the street of London to get me here."

"Poison? I heard it was a sedative," said Lydia.

"I'm allergic to most sedatives. Like deadly allergic," I said. Lydia's mouth formed a perfect 'O' in surprise.

"Did they know that?" Cassidy asked.

"They do now. I threw up in my mum's bag as a get back," I said and Lydia laughed.

"Now that is pay back," she agreed.

"Ok, so you guys got a preference on music?" I asked as I leaned over to a sideboard behind me and casually hooked up my iPod to a set of speakers I saw there.

"Not death metal," said Peter.

"Good to know. Who are you guy's favourite artists? I'm loving David Guetta at the moment," I said putting on 'Hey Mama'.

"David who?" Gwen asked.

"Oh come on, you have to have heard of David Guetta! Titanium?" I offered. I was met with looks of confusion.

"You know, the song they sing in the showers in Pitch Perfect."

"What's pitch perfect?" asked Cassidy.

"You haven't seen pitch perfect? Next you'll say you don't know how to play poker!" I gasped.

"Um......" said Lydia throwing a glance at Cassidy who shook her head.

"No way!" I gasped horrified, "that's just not right. I am teaching you all how to play poker, tonight."

"What? Now!"

"Yes now, why not now?" I asked, "I have a pack of cards."

"We don't have anything to bet with."

"We've got pen and paper. Tear up strips of paper and write values on them," I said pulling a pack of cards out of my pocket, "We don't need to bet to start with anyway, Ok, I'll be dealer. Who's in?"

"Sure, I'm up for it," said Ronnie.

"Yeah, why not" Cassidy grinned.

Undercover Thief

"Ian? Trevor? Adam? Poker?" I asked starting to shuffle.

"Um, sure," decided Trevor.

"How many am I dealing in? Everyone?" I asked as people looked up. I gave them all an expectant look and they all nodded. Marley ignored me.

"Sounds fun," said George who was genuinely interested in playing.

It didn't take long for me to explain the rules to them, I wrote out what every wining hand was in order on a piece of paper for them, laying it out for everyone to see. Soon everyone but Marley was either, joining in, watching and calling out or generally just having fun.

"It's mine! All mine!" said Ian after he won a hand on a pair of twos.

"That is a serious poker face," I said holding up my hand for him to high-five. He slapped it in fun.

"Ok, let's go again!"

"Hey Pam, you said you didn't want to come here," said Allister, "I don't understand why?"

"It's about choice; I didn't know they were even bringing me here. I found out about here as the plane touched down on the roof," I said. Cassidy laughed.

"That is not much of a head's up!" she agreed with me as she put in her own bet.

"Bets done? Plus, because I left so suddenly like that, there are a lot of loose ends to tie up that I haven't yet and my family will be going haywire. It's just one big mess."

"But now you're here, why don't you want to stay?" Gwen asked, "Just ask your parents for a week maximum, to sort things out and then come right back."

"Two reasons. One, my parents will never agree to that. Two, I have people at home to get back to."

"Your family?"

"Yeah."

"But your mum is here?"

"Blood means nothing. Its actions that bind a family, not DNA shared. If you pick your family based on mutual love for each other, you'll be much happier and safer. You know you can count on them."

"Sounds like more than an argument between you and your mum," Ian said hesitantly. I sighed.

"Way, way more than an argument, but let's not spoil a good evening with all that," I agreed, "It will probably come out one day. I promise to try and rain it in in her classes. I will resist the urge to hurl my pencil case at her."

Undercover Thief

"Today was rather funny. But are you going to do it all the time? It could get old quickly," said Adam.

"Listen, I will keep it to a maximum of one hiccup per morning and afternoon. Don't want your grades to suffer."

"Why can't you just follow the rules?"

"Because when you get to real life, rules literally mean nothing. If it's a choice between kill or be killed, it's an obvious answer. And if you have enough money and hire the right attorney you can get away with murder."

"Certainly seems that way sometimes doesn't it," said Lucas.

"My point is, is that I do what I like regardless of rules."

"Most rules have a good reason."

"And if someone can explain that reason and I agree, I will follow the rule," I said.

"You are a strange kid Pam," said Lydia.

"Yeah. You're certainly not boring. I like it," said Trevor.

"You'll never met another one like me. I promise," I said with a wicked grin, "Ok, bets over for this round."

"I raise three," said Peter throwing in some more paper.

"Why not?" said Cassidy, matching Peter.

"I'm out," said Trevor. Ronnie and Gwen agreed.

"So where did you learn to play poker?" asked George.

"An illegal casino in London," I said seriously. He started laughing and froze when he realised that I was serious.

"You've been to an illegal casino?" gasped Lydia.

"Honey, you'd be surprised the places I have been," I said with a laugh, "but yeah. I learned poker there. I wasn't in any danger. I know the guy who knows the guy who owns the place, so it was real safe."

"So, if you've been to an illegal casino, do you know how to card count?" asked Ian with a grin.

"That's more for when you're playing blackjack than poker."

"What's blackjack?"

"You want to play blackjack?"

"Sure do."

"Ok, anyone played twenty-ones?"

"Where you have to make twenty-one with your cards?"

Undercover Thief

"Yep, that's the game. Well, it's a bit like that," I said with a laugh.

The evening didn't go on for too much longer. It was a school night, and these guys wanted to sleep and be bright eyed and bushy tailed for the next day's lessons. It was good to get to know them, they were all nice people. Barriers were broken down and things were talked about.

Cassidy loved country music.

Peter could play the violin.

Gavin could paint, Lydia liked to sew, and Ian happily described his addiction to books and reading in general as unhealthy.

Ronnie and I went back to our room and prepared for bed. I brushed my hair as she lay on top of her covers, looking up at the ceiling.

"You know," she said, "that was really cool what you did back there."

"What?"

"Aw come on, you managed to get everyone playing together and talking.....bonding," said Ronnie looking at me.

"You could have done that."

"No, I wouldn't even know where to begin to do that," she said.

"I just gave you all something in common and we went from there."

"What did we have in common?"

"None of you knew how to play poker," I said, "I gave you something that was fun to do, but allowed people to talk at the same time."

"Pretty impressive stuff there. You really are a master of manipulation."

"Nah, I didn't manipulate anything. But I figured with such a small year group, you should bond. Be more of a team. Help each other out, you know."

"*We* should bond," she said, "You can't exclude yourself you know."

"Thanks," I said pausing and then sighed, "but, I don't belong here."

"You're wrong," said Ronnie, "I think perhaps you belong more than any of us. I mean, we're all social misfits. You saw us, none of us really know how to be friends. None of us completely comfortable where we were before."

"And you think I'm a social misfit?"

"Yeah, I do," said Ronnie with a small smile, "are you seriously telling me you have lots of friends? Friends that are our age, I mean, not fraudsters or mates of illegal casino owners?"

"No," I admitted. After all, apart from Jerry, Leah and Micah, no one else our age was into my particular line of work.

"You see, you are one of us," said Ronnie.

I put my hair brush on the side and climbed under the covers of my bed.

"Thanks Ronnie," I said, "If it makes you feel any better, I wish you were right."

"I am right," she said, "You just haven't seen it yet."

Chapter Ten

The next day, I went down to breakfast with Gwen and Ronnie. They had had to literally drag me out of bed this morning. I was so tired! I was almost falling sleep in the cup of tea Ronnie had poured me.

"Come on. You need to wake up. More lessons to go to," cajoled Ronnie cheerfully.

"On a good day I'm not generally a morning person. And this is not a good day," I moaned as I forced myself to sip at the tea. It burned my tongue slightly but the warmth and the caffeine helped wake me up. I so needed it.

"You'll be fine. You can have a snooze through history. I think everyone will," said Ronnie.

"What makes you say that?"

"We have Mr Marsh. He is the most boring teacher on the planet," she said with a sigh, "and we have him for a double. We can both sit at the back and take a snooze."

"Yay!" I said happily.

Undercover Thief

"Guys, you can't plan to deliberately go to sleep during a lesson! We should take notes and-"

"Yes we can. Come on Gwen. Are you always this serious with your studies? The term has barely begun!"

"Making a good start is important," she said taking a bite of her porridge.

"Whatever honey," I said patting her hand, "I like your enthusiasm."

"You could show a little more," she said.

"That's why we work so well together. We balance," I said smiling. Ronnie laughed.

"In coming," said Gwen.

"What?" I asked.

"Parents. Your five o'clock," said Ronnie seeming to take no more than a cursory glance around the room.

"Which one?" I groaned rubbing my eyes.

"Both," coughed Ronnie behind her hand as they approached.

"Hi Pam," said my father. I didn't bother looking up.

"What?" I asked taking a bite from my toast, my mood deteriorating rapidly.

"I wanted to talk to you, I went to find you in the common room after detention ended yesterday but you weren't there."

"Yeah, I got into a conversation, kind of got held up," I said.

"You sort of...gave your mother a bit of a shock in class yesterday."

"Right," I said sipping my tea.

"We realise that perhaps we have drifted apart a little bit," said my mother hesitantly. I snorted.

"You can't drift apart if you were never close."

"We were close when you were small."

"Well, I can't remember that so it doesn't count."

"We remember it so it does count."

I just sighed and took a swig off my tea.

"Listen, if you have something to say, would you please go ahead and say it. I have to save what little energy I have so I don't fall asleep in my lessons today."

"Why don't we do something this weekend?" she suggested, "We could go to the park for ice cream or something."

"Ice cream? I'm fourteen years old, almost fifteen," I said rolling my eyes.

"Which is sort of our point. We don't really know you."

"Well, I can't. I promised to take Ronnie and Gwen shopping," I said.

"I'm sure the girls won't mind if you go another weekend."

"I mind. Listen, mum, I was letting you down gently. I don't want to go for ice cream with you," I said quietly getting up as the bell went for class.

"Why not?"

"Because, you haven't apologised."

"For what? What happened in class yesterday? I think you'll find that you were at fault as well young lady."

"Don't call me young lady, and no. It's not over what happened in class yesterday."

"Then what?"

"If you don't know then I can't help you," I said simply.

I walked away, Gwen and Ronnie were hot on my heels.

"Hey, are you alright? That was intense."

"Oh yeah, fine. So what part of history are we supposed to be doing today?"

"Woah, no way are you changing the subject. Your mother was trying to bridge whatever happened between you," said Gwen, "She offered you an olive branch. Why did you turn it down?"

"Because, they still haven't apologised."

"For what?"

"Gwen," I said turning to her, "you have parents who love you yes? Who tucked you in at night and put a roof over your head and fed you. And I'm happy for you, I really am. I'm happy you had that level of security. I didn't and that is all I want to say on the matter."

"I....I'm sorry," said Gwen looking worried.

"It's alright Gwen. I know I'm not a normal case," I said putting a hand on the small girl's shoulder, "Good friends do ask questions. But please can we talk about something different now?"

"Ok. Well, apparently we're starting with World War One," said Gwen.

Ronnie was dead right about history. Mr Marsh was, in two words, incredibly dull. I liked history. And this was the First World War like I hadn't heard it before. It was all about the espionage techniques, stories that were classified and weren't open to the public for that very reason. If it had been someone else teaching, I am sure I would have been fascinating. But the man had a voice and a manner that just put you to sleep.

Undercover Thief

I rested my chin on my arms and watched him talk about various people who had tried to prevent the war and failed. Ronnie and I ended up playing a game of poking each other to stay awake while Gwen, sat in front of us, furiously scribbling down notes and throwing us dirty looks.

She knew what we were doing, and the moment we were outside the classroom she started to tell us off.

"You should have been paying attention!" she scolded.

"We tried Gwen," argued Ronnie.

"Not hard enough!"

"But it was so boring!" Ronnie complained.

"It's important."

"Why? Why do we need to know something that happened almost one hundred years ago? We've moved on so much more since then."

"Knowing our past is the only way we can avoid repeating those mistakes in the future," Gwen quoted Mr Marsh in her argument.

"Are you seriously telling me you weren't tempted to take a nap during that?" I asked as we walked towards our next lesson of the day, Etiquette.

"But this stuff could come up in our exams."

"Our exam is literally like nine months away!" I said with a laugh.

"You're aware that we have exams at Christmas right?"

"You what? What kind of twisted school is this?" I joked, Gwen didn't find it funny but Ronnie laughed with me.

"If we fail we're out of the school! That's it! Caput!" said Gwen making wild gestures with her hands to dramatize the point.

"Yeah," said Ronnie bored, "But December is ages away."

"Are you serious?" I asked happily, "we fail and we're out?"

"You and me are probably exceptions," said Ronnie, "you know, linage and all."

"Damn," I muttered to myself.

"Come in class," said a woman coming to the door and beckoning us into the classroom.

So Etiquette and Culture Studies class wasn't as boring as it sounded. Our teacher, Mrs Riley, was a tall lady in her late fifties. Her grey hair was softly curled and cut short. She was a very pleasing woman on the eye, but she was also very easy to annoy. I wasn't even really trying.

Undercover Thief

"No, you don't do it like that. You're supposed to sign a letter that you do not address with a name as yours sincerely, not yours faithfully."

"What's the difference?" I squeaked, "It's a letter, and a thank you letter. When I write mine I put lots of love and sign with a bunch of kisses."

"This is not home Miss Torres."

"Clearly! I also prefer to write in pink. Much more character."

"Miss Torres," she said with a resigned sigh, "just try to remember yours sincerely and yours faithfully.....there is a difference and it is important."

"Alright," I grumbled.

"For what it's worth, I totally get it," said Ian leaning over to talk to me.

"Right?" I whispered back, "what's wrong with pink?"

"I can hear you Miss Torres and Mr Mathews," she said writing on the board.

"Ears like a hawk," I muttered.

"Thank you Miss Torres, but the expression is eyes like a hawk or ears like a bat," she said.

She impressed me, I'll admit it. So I shut my trap after that and just got on with it. As a con, I had learned to blend in with the crowd, be it ordinary people or the rich and famous. So I was up to par on table manners in a whole selection of social situations.

However, some of the stuff I saw flicking through the curriculum notes, looked quite interesting. They did cultures around the world, a variety of traditional dance styles, different signs of respect and disregard. It would be fascinating, I was sure, once we got past calligraphy.

We headed to our next lesson, Gwen and Ronnie debating the ease of using of quill and ink verses normal ball point pens. It was really, really boring.

"Guys! Seriously? You're having an argument over biros!" I said rubbing the sides of my head as we headed towards Advanced Tech.

"No we're not! We're saying that the use of one form of pen over another is-" said Gwen, who was happy to debate her point to the end.

"They're just pens!" I said exasperated, "Compromise and use fountain pens already!"

"You alright Pam?" asked Ronnie with a laugh.

"Fine! But an argument about pens is where I draw the line at tolerable!" I said and Gwen laughed.

"Ok....so it might be a bit pointless."

"A bit?" I muttered.

Undercover Thief

"Come on, Advanced Tech will be fun," said Gwen happily. She was almost bouncing.

"Why are you so happy?"

"Advanced Tech is going to be great!" she said excitedly. Ronnie and I looked at each other and burst out into a fit of laughter.

"Miss Price, Miss Torres, please would you keep the noise down. This is a school, not a football stadium," said a teacher walking past.

"Sorry Miss Alson," said Ronnie as both she and I choked back our giggles.

"Who was that?"

"Miss Alson, she teaches law," said Ronnie.

"Right, I'm guessing that includes international laws then."

"Bingo."

"Alright. Might not die of boredom in her classes."

"Really? Law? You can't listen in history but you can listen in law?" said Gwen, "I would say law is more boring."

"It's always useful to know the law," I said and grinned, "So you know when you're breaking it."

"Right, you're Little Miss Rules Optional," said Ronnie.

"Back to the subject of Gwen's love for tech," I said as we leaned against the wall outside the classroom.

"How can you not love it?" she said, getting a dreamy expression across her face, "have you even read the syllabus here? It's going to be so much fun!"

"And this is where our different ideas of fun come into play again, isn't it?" I said looking at Ronnie who nodded.

"Completely," she agreed.

"Well I don't see what's fun about being beaten up and throwing other people on the floor, but you seem to enjoy that," said Gwen at Ronnie.

"It's the looks on their faces," smirked Ronnie.

"Well, I'll enjoy the looks on your faces when you need me to fix your computers and I say no," she said with a huff.

"Aw Gwen, come on. You know we're only teasing you. And let's face it, the world these days is definitely run by the techies," I tried to sooth.

"Yeah Gwen, we meant no harm," added Ronnie squeezing the small girl's shoulders.

"I know, I was just making a point," said Gwen.

Undercover Thief

"Come in class," said the teacher coming to the door. I read his name off the door, apparently he was Mr Berry.

We followed him into the class, and found high white work benches with grey plastic stools. Of course, it was just like a science lab. Except with a hell of a lot more plugs.

"Welcome to today's class. Get out your books, we're moving swiftly on from how electricity is generated and onto electrical circuit," he began as he started writing on a whiteboard, "this is an area of tech that is advancing at an impressive speed, so the syllabus changes on an almost monthly basis, so you need to get all of the basics straight from the beginning."

"Then why learn anything at all?" I asked. He narrowed his eyes at me.

"Miss Torres, I'll presume."

"Yeah, why?"

"You're reputation precedes you."

"Well thank you very much."

"That wasn't a compliment."

"I know," I said resting my chin on my hands, which were folded together nicely, elbows on the desk.

"The reason you have to learn, Miss Torres, is because the fundamentals never change? Have you ever disarmed a bomb? I highly doubt it."

"No, but a Hallmark ninety four with five back up and trip systems, a manual override that changes every thirty seconds and an alternating command control pattern comes pretty close, or so I'm told," I said twiddling my pen around my thumb.

"You've disarmed a hallmark ninety four? When?" He demanded.

"Let me think....two years ago....maybe three? I was in Uruguay at the time."

"What were you doing in Uruguay?" asked Peter.

"Friend asked me to help out with some business. So I did. Took a turn for the worst, which is where the hallmark ninety four came in to it. But let's not talk about me; sir was explaining that we're going to learn how to disarm bombs."

"Yes," said Mr Berry slightly disturbed, "well, although a hallmark ninety four is a nasty piece of equipment, it isn't a bomb. And once I teach you the basics, you can put them into all kinds of field work and uses. It isn't just bombs, we're talking computer coding of different languages, phone technology, how to make your own satellite." I looked at Gwen, her eyes were wide with anticipation.

"But, before we do that, let's cover some basics. Who can tell me the difference between conventional current and actually current flow?" Gwen's hand shot straight up, almost taking off Ronnie's ear, causing me to smother a laugh.

"Yes, Miss Olsen-Jones?"

"Conventional current was established before electrons were discovered, when it was believed current flowed from positive to negative. However, after the electron was discovered, and it was realised that it actually flowed from negative to positive the old system had already taken off worldwide and trying to change it would be too much hassle."

"Very good Miss Olsen-Jones. Now, this is called a circuit diagram."

The rest of the lesson was actually quite interesting. We built our own circuits, and learnt about how electricity was manufactured. Nevertheless I could tell though that I was successfully getting on Mr Berry's nerves. I kept yawning, or saying loudly that I didn't get it, or asking what we were doing moments after he had explained it. I knew I was on the edge of him sending me out.

I think the final straw was when I put the capacitor in the wrong way around and it exploded. There were squeals of surprise from Ronnie and Gwen, who were sat closest, and I fell of my stool, smacking my head on the floor in the process.

Funny thing was that it was actually a genuine accident. I would never have done something like that on purpose, it could have been dangerous.

"Miss Torres, I said you plug the positive side into the positive on your power source!" Mr Berry almost shouted.

"Sorry sir," I groaned, rolling to my knees and putting my hand to my head which was stinging like crazy.

"You're bleeding Pam," said Ronnie. I took my hand from my ear, she was right.

"Oh damn it, I can't see, how bad is it?" I asked Ronnie who had gotten next to me on the floor to check I was ok.

"It's pretty bad. We should get some tissue or something to try and stop it from bleeding," said Ronnie.

"Look in my bag, I have a med kit," I said.

"Got it," said Gwen handing it to Ronnie who began to patch me up.

"Any dizziness Miss Torres? Headache? Shortness of breath? Feeling faint?" asked Mr Berry.

"Nothing more than usual. My own damn fault – ow! Ron!"

"Sorry Pam, that should do it," she said offering me a hand up.

Undercover Thief

"Ok," said Mr Berry taking a deep breath, "Can we try again Miss Torres, the capacitor goes the other way around. For someone who supposedly disarmed a Hallmark ninety-four, you know very little about electronics."

"Well, what can I say? I break systems, I don't make systems."

"Miss Torres, please just try it again. Remember, it isn't safe to put a capacitor in the wrong way."

"I will remember that one, sorry Mr Berry," I said getting back up and looking at my lump of melted plastic.

"I'll get you another board Miss Torres, try not to set anything on fire while I'm away."

"I will do my best."

Chapter Eleven

It was the end of the week. And I had been sent to the headmistress's office four times. I got back on the Friday, after my detention with Miss Alson, a teacher who had me copying out law files for an hour, to the common room.

"So, how's detention with Alson?" asked Peter who was playing patience with a pack of cards I'd donated for the common room use.

"Well, it wasn't exactly a gas," I said sinking into one of the sofas, "Miss Alson makes you copy out old law files."

"Ah, and soon we will have a complete survey of detentions," said Trevor.

"Yes, I wonder what detentions on Wednesdays are like," I said with a laugh. That was the one day I didn't have a detention.

"I'm sure you'll find out next Wednesday."

"You know, at this rate you'll see more of my mother than I will," said Ronnie.

"Well, you know how I do it if you ever want to see her," I said with a grin and she gave a short laugh.

"I think my mother might have a heart attack if I got sent out of class."

"It would be kind of funny," I sniggered.

"Hey, so we made it to the weekend without anyone dying," said Cassidy.

"Um, we had a few close ones," said Peter and everyone looked at Gwen who had almost managed to kill herself in one of our PE lessons when the skipping rope got caught around her neck.

"Hey!" she protested, "That has only happened once! It wasn't intentional!"

"Gwen, we know you didn't try to take your own life," said Ronnie patting her on the head, "You just have no coordination at all. To the point it's a little scary. Never mind, we love you anyway."

"Good, because you need my history notes to write your homework," said Gwen. It was true. Our other lesson of history had gone similarly to the previous one, except we were even less productive.

"Speaking of which, are you going to actually do this one Pam?" asked Ronnie.

"I will probably throw something together. I think I'll try and avoid detentions on Tuesday's as much as possible.

Apparently my mother is supposed to take them over next week. And I don't want the drama," I answered.

"Fair enough," said Ronnie who was sat at a desk doing some sort of homework.

"Have you done any of your homework?"

"I did my law homework and my manipulation homework," I said pulling out my iPod and flicking through the songs.

"And you wrote your French homework at breakfast," said Gwen piping up.

"Right, so I did," I agreed nodding.

"I think you like detention," chuckled Trevor, "I can't understand why."

"I don't enjoy it. I think Miss Price is about to buy a rubber stamp with my name on it so she doesn't have to keep filling out the slips," I joked and Ronnie laughed.

"She's stronger than you give her credit for," disagreed Ronnie.

"I know. I know," I said, "Trust me. I'm the one that had to jump off a roof to get away from her."

"You jumped off a roof?" gaped Lydia.

"Before being poisoned, yeah," I said, "I spotted the tales they had posted on me. I slipped all of them but her mother managed to see though me."

Undercover Thief

"So, it's Friday night and we're all off tomorrow, what are people doing?" asked Lydia.

"Well, Pam says Gwen and I need new clothes," said Ronnie.

"Oooh, a shopping trip. Can we come?" asked Cassidy.

"Sure thing."

"Great to have you," I agreed smiling.

"What about you guys?"

"I think I'll skip shopping," said Ian with a laugh.

"Oh you spoil sport," I teased.

"Yeah, not really my scene either," agreed Trevor.

"I'm going into town to check out the local teams," said Gavin.

"Sports teams?"

"Yeah, support the local clubs."

"The school has a football team," said Ronnie.

"They don't take first years," said Gavin with a sigh.

"Start one," I suggested.

"I might think about that. You boys interested?"

"Sure," said Peter.

"I'm up for it," said Ian.

"Just to be clear, we're talking about American football right? The wusy version of Rugby," I said picking up my second pack of cards and messing around with a few tricks.

"It's not a wusy sport."

"You wear pads. They don't in rugby."

"Have you ever seen a proper game? It's not a wusy sport," answered Gavin.

"Alright, but you are talking American football."

"Yes."

"Ok, then."

"I plan on getting all my homework done tomorrow," said George.

"Oh come on, you have to have more things on your mind than the homework," I said, "Take up a hobby."

"Well, I'm going to see if I can go down to the science club. Mr Finch runs this club where we can conduct our own investigations and things," said Allister.

"Oh, that sounds fun," added George intrigued.

"I was looking at that!" said Gwen.

Undercover Thief

"And the nerd-off begins," I whispered to Ronnie who snorted.

"I was going to look at the swim team," said Lucas.

"Swimming....nice," I said, "I don't suppose they have gymnastics here?"

"They might do. I've never really checked," said Ronnie, "Have a look." She went over to the side and pulled out a small booklet of the clubs available. She tossed it too me.

"You should join the debate club, considering you love to argue," jabbed Gwen.

"No, I don't love to argue, I'm just always right," I said, with a grin, "But that does sound fun."

"Who knows, you might even enjoy yourself," said Ronnie.

"Urgh, I'm bored," said Adam throwing down his pen and rubbing his eyes.

"Well....we could play poker," suggested Cassidy.

"Yeah....some Friday night poker," grinned Lydia.

"I'm game," said Peter.

"I'm up for it," said Ian.

"I've corrupted you all!" I said and let off an evil laugh.

207

"You in or what Pam?"

"You bet your last dollar I am? So we playing for pennies or paper?" I asked.

"You what?"

"Money guys! What are the stakes? We should have a maximum bet," I said.

"Let's play for pennies," said Lydia, "Nothing huge."

"Sounds good to me," said Cassidy.

"Ok, pennies it is. I only have sterling," I said fishing out my purse, "Do people mind?"

"Nope," said Peter.

"Let's set them up," said Ronnie.

"I'll be right back," I said hoping up, "I'll go get rid of my bag."

"Ok, Gwen's bank!" said Ian as I walked out of the room.

It was only just getting dark out as I walked back to my room. I stopped at a window and looked up at the sky, which was painted pink and orange as the sun lazily dropped out of the sky. This was similar to home. I guess all sunsets look the same.

I took a deep breath and bit back the feeling of homesickness that had overwhelmed me. Tears were no good to anyone; they just gave you panda eyes and wasted water. I could imagine Jerry and Leah bent over plans around the kitchen table; Micah sat on the sofa with his iPad listening to a story or reading something in braille. Life would be going on as normal. It had too. They needed to pay for Micah's education after all.

I frowned and turned around. Was someone talking? I walked a little way down the stairs, towards where the noise was coming from. I spotted a little alcove that was away from view and went over. I paused at the corner, poking my head around. It was Marley. She was facing away from me and she was on the phone. My mouth dropped and I hid around the corner again before she could see me.

How had Marley got a phone? And how was she getting past the scramblers? I had internet access, sure, Leah had made it so that my phone and iPod automatically got onto any internet that was around so I always had it in spite of any jamming. It piggy backed off the internet that was already in place here, and was completely untraceable. Nevertheless even I didn't have phone service.

"I know, I know.....It's only been a week," I frowned. Perhaps she was calling home. Perhaps I wasn't the only one who was homesick. I poked my head around the corner again. She was still facing away from me. I saw a huge amplifier in the corner, on a chair with a cloth thrown over it. Really? That was how she was hiding it?

And the phone itself was absolutely huge, and looked more like an old fashioned brick. But still, she was communicating through the scramblers.

I leaned back.

"You need to give me more time. I'll find it." That made me frown. Find it? Find what? More importantly, who was she finding it for.

"We don't need to pull this off in haste. The more thought through this is the better."

Ok. This was not looking good. This sounded illegal, and that was ok by my standards. I wasn't exactly a hypocrite. However, I was pretty sure that something illegal that involved this place, which was so heavily connected to various intelligence agencies, would not be safe.

No, it was definitely not the kind of illegal I worked. This was a whole different kind of criminal. And it was very, very dangerous.

I heard that she was about to hang up so I slowly crept up the stairs again. I went to my door and pretended to fumble for my key. I watched as Marley walked up the stairs, saw me, said nothing and turn and go into the room she shared with Gwen.

I went into my room, slung my bag onto my bed. I kicked off my shoes and paced up and down, trying to think. What could I do? Should I do anything? I didn't want to be here, and whatever happened here was sure to set off something that allowed me to escape.

But what about the people that could get hurt?

My eyes drifted over to Ronnie's bed and lingered there a while. Despite what I knew was sensible, I had actually gotten to like some of the people here, including some of the teachers. And I had no way of knowing who would get hurt when this thing blew up.

Besides, in a place like this, it wouldn't take long in the aftermath to add up there was an inside man. As soon as all the teachers were cleared, they would look at students. And I was certain; if they dug hard enough they would uncover my secret life. And I could probably run...for a bit. But in the end they would catch me and I would be in a jail cell for the rest of my life, and probably get blamed for whatever this was too.

So I had to do something. It was too dangerous to just let this be.

But I didn't know what this was. I didn't even know something was happening. They could be stealing something really not that important, or get caught doing it. I didn't know anything about the operation that Marley was trying to pull off. I had no idea what she was trying to find? Some kind of override code or something perhaps? Maybe a file. Maybe something another student had.

Maybe even another student themselves.

I groaned and ran my hands through my hair. There was a knock at the door. I went over and answered it.

"Now is a really bad time," I said going to close the door. My father put his arm in the way.

"Your classmates said you were putting your bag away before going to play a card game."

"Yeah, I am," I said folding my arms. Mum and Dad walked into the room and sat down on Ronnie's bed.

"We hoped that we might be more important than a game of sevens."

"Sevens? That's what they told you?" I asked with a wry smile. Sly dogs.

"Did they lie?"

"No, but it's a bit of unnecessary over sharing," I lied.

"So, we haven't seen much of you," said my father.

"You do realise that you enrolled me in a school? And that it's not exactly a nine-to-three and running to catch the bus kind of place, right?"

"We know poppet," said my mother, "We were talking to my colleagues and just wanted to....come up and have a word."

"You've had more than a word," I muttered.

"Pamela....."

Undercover Thief

"What? What do you have to say then?" I said waiting.

"They say that you're obviously talented. And intelligent," said my father.

"And that you have a very charismatic personality," said my mother.

"I sense there's a 'but' coming," I said repressing the urge to roll my eyes at them.

"You've have four detentions in one week. Your first week," said my father.

"I knew it! You're here to tell me to buck my ideas up," I said with a sniff.

"Four detentions in five days Pamela, that's a lot!"

"Ha! You ain't seen nothing yet," I said with a laugh, "That's just me breaking the teachers in."

"Pamela, that really isn't the attitude. We were hoping that you were mature enough not to act out like this," said my mother.

"Hate to break it to you, but I've not even started yet."

"Why are you doing this?"

"I have a problem with rules," I said, "And being controlled."

"Pam, we realise that this place is overwhelming," said my mother quickly, "Also that the way you came here wasn't exactly ideal but-"

"Ideal? You drugged and kidnapped me."

"It's not kidnap if it's parental consent."

"That's not how the law works," I said rolling my eyes.

"How would you know? You were sent out of law class," said my father.

"Touché," I admitted, letting that one go, "But that's unimportant."

"Pam, how you got here is beside the point," said my mother.

"Really? Is it?"

"Yes! Because here, right here is what you are doing now. It's your future. It's one we thought that you'd appreciate."

"Why would you think that?"

"After our first run in at the house, the way you handled yourself," said my father.

"Ah....that.....next time I'll leave you with the guns if this is the end result," I said. My mother sighed and they both shared a look.

"Pamela, sweetheart, why don't you like it here? Why aren't you trying?"

"What?" I said with a laugh, "Did you even think it through when you decided to bring me here? I left you on a roof top after out running three truckloads of gunmen. I'm assuming you sorted that out by the way."

"Yes, we did. That's beside the point."

"It isn't! When you thought that it was a good idea to kidnap me off the street did you think that I would be happy? Did you think that I would just come here, forget my entire life back home that I had built for myself and conform to your will?"

"We.....we hoped," my mother stammered.

"We came here for another reason Pammie. It is obvious to everyone that you have had some kind of experience before you came here. Your teachers all keep complimenting us on how well we've taught you," said my father. I snorted.

"I got nothing from you," I said.

"We know that," agreed my mother, "Which is why we're here to ask you...what gave you this set of skills?"

"That's my business."

"I think it's ours as well."

"No. It's not. It in no way concerns you," I said.

"It's something that involved you, and you are our concern," said my father.

"Really? Now is the time you want to start playing parent?" I asked.

"What is that supposed to mean Pam?"

"What do you think it means Dad?"

"Let's not get into an argument!" said my mother loudly.

"Bit late for that," I said rolling my eyes.

"Pam, we are trying to take care of you here," said my mother walking over to me and looking at me seriously, "Trying to protect you."

"Well I don't need you too," I shot back taking her hands off my shoulders, "I can look after myself. I've been doing it for a very long time."

"We know," sighed my father, "You shouldn't have had to. We're proud that you are ok, and completely relieved. But now you do have someone to look out for you."

"I do have people looking out for me, you're right. They just aren't here," I said.

"Pam, whoever you met in London, whoever you say this alternative family is, they don't care about you. Not the way we do," said my father.

"You're wrong."

Undercover Thief

"Pam, they don't love you," my mother stated loudly.

"What the hell!" I shouted, "You don't know them! You can't tell me what they do and don't care about! And I know for a fact that they care about me!"

"Pam I-"

"No! You don't know them! You don't know me, so you are unfit to judge anything about that! And as for your 'caring' for me, if the last fifteen years has taught me anything about the way you care, I don't want any part of it! Its lead me into nothing but trouble and misery! Now get out! I have better things to do with my life than sit here and talk to you about this."

"Pam-"

"I said out!" I snapped opening the door wide and gesturing angrily for them to leave.

"Pam! We are trying to help you!" snapped my mother.

"You know what, why don't you just cut out the parent rubbish and stick to being my teacher," I snapped right back, "I don't want your life advice."

"You are a stubborn young lady and that is going to come and bite you in the backside!" snapped my mother, "And when it does, I look forward to saying I told you so."

"Mother, do I look like I'll be around long enough to hear you say those words? And if things do go wrong, you are not the person I am going to go to for help," I told her with steel in my voice.

"Then where are you going to go? Your so called family?"

"Yes. Because despite what you think you know about me, you actually know nothing at all. About me, my life, who I am. You know nothing."

"Not true."

"Really parents know that their children are allergic to things! And what those things are!"

"Pam, we were working."

"Then go back to work if it's so important. Just leave me out of it," I shouted, snagging my purse from the side and heading out of the door, "I expect you can find your own way out. If you want to have a snoop around my room before you leave, that's fine. You won't find anything." I kept anything important on me at all times. My lock picking equipment and other such items were on a belt that I could put around my arm, thigh or middle. My files on my computer were all encrypted to the highest level. I had nothing to worry about.

I marched angrily down the corridor and into the common room.

"Hey," said Gavin as I marched into the room fuming.

"A little heads up guys, please, if you are sending my parents my way!" I snapped.

"Sorry Pam," said Ronnie.

"Was it bad?" asked Gwen softly.

"Is murder illegal in America?"

"Yes, yes it is," said Ronnie.

"Damn!"

"Come on," smiled Gwen throwing an arm around my shoulders, "A game of cards will make you feel better."

"Yeah, it will. And sevens? You told them we were playing sevens?"

"They saw the cards," said Cass shrugging, "It seemed more acceptable than bridge."

"Why not just say poker?"

"Figured that they wouldn't approve," said Ronnie.

"That is a very good point," I said opening up my purse and fishing out coins to use in the game, "Ok. So are you all ready to lose your money, cause I could really use some dollars."

"Bring it on Torres," said Ian with a grin.

"You'll be crying when I'm done."

Chapter Twelve

I woke up late on Saturday. The girls didn't seem to mind that we were late heading out for our shopping trip. We got on one of the school organised buses into town and Ronnie explained that there were rules regarding town.

"Obviously, there's the 'don't show the town's folk we're spies' rule," she said.

"Ah, that one. Puts a spanner in all of my plans," I joked.

"Also, we have to be back up at the school before eight."

"Eight? That's good of them."

"Well, the older years can go out until ten."

"Huh, so we all have that to look forwards to, anything else?"

"Appropriate conduct basically."

"And what qualifies as appropriate?"

Undercover Thief

"Don't hotwire a car and go for a joyride," said Lydia.

"Oh, so we can't have any fun?" I only half joked.

"So, where are we going?" asked Cassidy.

"Where do you want to go first?" I asked as we got off the bus, "Is there a mall?"

"Yep, this way," said Ronnie.

We got to the mall, and it was filled with shops. My first stop was a gorgeous little underwear boutique.

"You're joking," said Ronnie as Gwen cringed.

"Nope! Start with the basic's ladies. Now, I can tell that Cass is wearing the wrong size bra, and I know you love your sports bras, but ever think about branching out a little?"

"I am?" asked Cass.

"Oh yeah."

"Is that bad? I suppose it's to be expected, I was raised by a single man."

"Come on. I'll show you how to shop properly," I said.

I grabbed the attention of one of the assistants and they whisked Cass away immediately to measure her. The others perused the racks. I looked around myself and then walked over to Lydia.

"That's the wrong colour for you," I said, "Try this one."

"It's yellow."

"It's pretty."

"Who cares what it looks like, only I'm going to see it."

"It will make you feel better and give you better shape than a Tesco Value pack. Just try it."

"Alright," she said taking it from me and marching off to the changing rooms.

I steered Gwen away from the plain, bog standard bras and towards the pretty flowery ones. I noticed Ronnie looking sceptically as some of the more risqué lingerie.

"Hey, you should try this one," I said walking over and picking up a lacy red one.

"No way," she said laughing.

"Oh go on, what's the harm?"

"Don't you think it's a little....you know....."

"I'm not following you."

"Slutty?"

Undercover Thief

"I don't believe in the word," I said simply, "I believe woman should be allowed as much freedom in that area as men. Besides it's only a bra, you'll be wearing other clothes."

"I still don't know."

"Listen, your underwear is as important as your outerwear. It should be comfortable but should also give you confidence," I said, "You should feel good and then you will look good."

"Hey guys, check out Cass!" called Lydia. We walked into the changing room.

"Oh, hello!" I said grinning.

"I have boobs!" said Cass amazed.

"Yes you do," said Lydia laughing.

"See what I mean, the right bra counts," I said.

"Ok, from now on I'll take your word for it," said Cass, "You gave me curves!"

"You always had curves. I just helped you dress them," I said.

After that we went from boutique to boutique. Lydia was very into flowing tops and floral patterns. Gwen loved her traditional dresses and sweet skirts. Cassidy was very much a girl from Texas as she ran to checked shirts and cowboy boots. Ron was very sporty in her choice.

So I started guiding them away from bad colours and ugly cuts. I stopped Gwen buying a dress that was backless, as I knew she'd never have the confidence to go without a bra. I encouraged Cass to buy a denim skirt and patterned crop that went well together.

We hopped from store to store, and I was not afraid to get the shopping assistants to help me when I was trying to persuade one of the girls to buy or not buy a particular item. I myself bought a few choice items, expanding my limited American wardrobe. I was used to far more choice back home.

Soon, we were weighted down by shopping bags.

"Ok, this has been so much fun," said Lydia as we were sat enjoying smoothies for our lunch.

"Oh yes, we have to do this often," agreed Cassidy

"Often? My bank account will start squeaking," said Ronnie.

"Ah, that is why girls struggle, and exactly why I have so many pairs of shoes," I said and Lydia laughed.

"I just feel guilty that Marley isn't here," said Gwen.

"Yeah," agreed Cassidy, "Why wouldn't she come?"

"She didn't say," said Gwen with a sigh.

"That's a shame, she might have enjoyed herself."

Undercover Thief

"Why does she keep herself to herself I wonder?" asked Lydia. Part of my wondered whether I should tell them all about what I had seen. The other half told me to keep my mouth shut.

Part of me was glad that she hadn't come, because she was up to something. And that meant I didn't trust her. If she was here, I would have been constantly watching her to make sure she didn't so anything stupid or dangerous. It would have made the day much less fun.

"We try to include her and she just sulks off by herself," said Ronnie, "I don't understand it."

"Perhaps she just isn't a people person," offered Gwen.

"Neither are any of us particularly," pointed out Cassidy.

"You guys are all lovely. I take some getting used to," I disagreed, "I think we should just let Marley be. She might be homesick or something."

"We could help her with that."

"I think, because she doesn't know us well, our help will be misinterpreted as nosiness," I said trying to dissuade Gwen and Cassidy from bringing it up.

"So you think we should just leave her be?"

"Yeah, be nice and keep inviting her, but don't push her. We can't force her to be our friend or to sit with us," I reasoned.

"Oh....ok," said Gwen.

"So, where after this Pam?" asked Lydia.

"Well, we've done clothes. Now it's time for hair and makeup," I said with a grin.

"Oh?"

"First, hair," I said, "We can all go and get our hair done. Then makeup."

"I like my hair," said Gwen putting her hand to her hair.

"Hon, don't do anything you don't want to do." I said, "but I always get my hair done at least once every eight weeks. It's a good idea to go to a good stylist who really knows what they're doing. You don't have to get it cut, just talk over getting it styled or something."

"So, where do you suggest for that?" asked Lydia looking at her luscious raven hair

"I was talking to one of the sales representatives in that boutique down by the fountain. Remember the one with those gorgeous fringe? It's so hard to get a fringe right, but I was impressed. So I asked her where she got them."

"Ok," said Cass, "sounds interesting."

Undercover Thief

So we headed down to get our hair done at the salon. I got my hair re-trimmed and styled. Ronnie had hers layered and blow-dried. Cassidy had some warm honey tones put in her hair. Lydia had a manicure instead of getting something done to her hair, as her hair was so lovely anyway there was nothing really that needed to be done. Gwen got hers styled and then decided she wanted a manicure too.

We weren't the only girls from the school in the salon; there were three others there as well, maybe two years above us. And they were talking happily while they got pedicures.

"Wow, I love this," said Gwen looking at her bouncy hair in the mirror. Her short hair now had a bit more volume and had a messy, fun look about it.

"I hate saying I told you so," I said with a sigh as my hair dresser finished blow drying my hair.

"You don't hate it at all," said Ronnie with a snort.

"Absolutely right my friend," I agreed grinning.

"Do you like it?" asked the stylist.

"Love it, really great. I was wondering what you thought about some low lights. I've been getting a lot more sun than usual here and my hair colour has lightened significantly," I said, "Do you think that adding some low-lights next time will make the colour return to what it was?"

"It should, but the lighter colour looks nice," said the stylist looking at my hair critically.

"It's redder than I'm used to."

"It's not noticeably red. Only in the sun," she said shaking her head, "and it's a very warm colour. Nice, I would kill for hair like that."

"Ok, thanks for the second opinion."

"No problem," she said smiling, "That's what I'm here for."

Then the door opened and in walked two boys, obviously older than us. They made a B-line for the other girls in the salon. I exchanged a look with Ronnie and wiggled my eyebrows as we all watched silently.

"Hey Chelsea," said one of the boys walking over to the blonde girl who was pulling on her shoes.

"Oh, hi Ben," she said blushing. Oh, she had it bad.

"I was wondering whether you wanted to go catch a movie."

"Now?"

"Sure, why not?" he asked shrugging his shoulders."

"Oh! Wow! Um, sure!" She said, "Give me a couple of minutes to finish up here."

Undercover Thief

"Cool, I'll wait for you at the movie theatre," he said with a grin and left.

And that's when Chelsea started to panic.

"No! No! No! What do I do? I'm not dressed for this!" She said turning to her friends, "what do I do?"

"Calm down, this is good Chels. He finally asked you out!"

"But I'm not dressed for a date!"

"Hair," I called over.

"What?" she asked looking at me. I walked over and took the clip out of her hair, tossing it at her friend.

"Shake your hair out," I instructed. After a moment of hesitation she flipped her hair forwards and ran her fingers through it and threw it back.

"Whenever in doubt, work the hair," I said smiling, "Shoe size?"

"Six."

"Ok, swap shoes with me," I said slipping off my heels. She hurried to do what I said, stowing her socks in her hand bag.

"Ok, get rid of the jacket," I said. She slipped it off.

"What if I get cold?"

"Then he gets to be a gentleman and offer you his jacket," I said.

"Oh! Nice," said one of her friends smiling.

"How much do you love Chelsea?" I asked her, tilting my head to one side.

"Why?"

"Swap earrings, better outfit," I said.

"Sure! No problem," she said. When that was done I pointed to one of the mirrors. Chelsea grinned.

"Wow! You're a miracle worker!" She said laughing, "you have turned my jeans and top into an evening outfit."

"Heels and hair, it's all about heels and hair," I laughed.

"Thanks. What's your name?"

"Pam. And keep the shoes; they look good on you."

"Thanks Pam," she said, "you're a life saver."

"They're Jimmy Choos, so no water," I warned, "and no problem. Enjoy your date."

"Do you know anything about dates?" she asked tentatively.

"Movie dates are easy, you watch the film and don't talk to each other until the walk home," I said, "so that's easy.

Undercover Thief

Now, if he buys tickets, you buy snacks. If you're buying your own everything then that's fine, but you mustn't let him pay for the whole evening. Equality remember. If you want a snack at the movies, the answer is mint chocolate."

"Mint chocolate?"

"Tastes good and keeps your breath fresh if he tries to kiss you. Gum is a not good because you might not have somewhere to get rid of it, and mints are too crunchy," I said.

"Wow, thanks, I'll remember that."

"No problem, enjoy your date," I said.

"What year are you in Pam?"

"First," I said.

"You're fourteen? How do you know so much about dating?"

"I've had a boyfriend before – we broke up three months ago. Nothing major, only two months long, but we dated for a bit."

"Well thanks. See you around Pam," said Chelsea as she and her friends left the salon.

"No problem. Bye!" I called.

"You're such a people person Pam," said Lydia almost envious.

"Yeah, you just walked up and started helping the third year like it was natural," added Cassidy almost in awe.

"Well it is, girls like us got to stick together," I said slipping her trainers into my bag and pulling on a pair of shoes I had bought earlier on that day instead.

"Normally the years don't mix all that much," said Ronnie.

"Why not?"

"I don't know, just the way it is."

"Well that sounds boring."

"No need to play into the click system," agreed Gwen.

"We need to break down those barriers," I said, "It's not healthy to think you can only talk to people in your own year. You are going to one day talk to people that are older than you and younger than you."

"Perhaps you should bring it up to one of the teachers," said Ronnie. I laughed.

"No one will listen to me."

"Mr Compton might, you're his favourite."

"That's because I'm doing third year work," I said shrugging, "and I can have a half decent argument with him."

"Your mum might not say no," said Lydia.

Undercover Thief

"No," I said flat out, "it's not happening."

"Alright, it was just a suggestion, you don't need to bite my head off."

"Sorry....I know you're right...."

"You said next stop was makeup, where are we going for that?"

Chapter Thirteen

The weeks blurred together after a while. Ronnie, Gwen and I had become fast friends.

They were wonderful friends really. They were fun to hang around with, and with them I could almost forget that I was a thief, or training to be a spy, or that my life was actually insane when I had to put it in words.

No, with them I felt like nothing more than a normal school girl, hanging out with a group of her good friends. I felt normal, which was something that had not been present in my life for a very, very long time. And the others in our year group were wonderful as well. Friday became mandatory poker night, and George had been surprisingly good at it from the word go. It was often him and I who would go head to head.

Marley still refused to take part in any of our year group games, and kept to herself. I didn't see her doing anything particularly suspicious after that. Whatever it was that she was trying to find, I had to assume she hadn't found it yet. Or I hoped so anyway.

Undercover Thief

I got two or three detentions a week, on average. And Miss Price was about to tear her hair out in frustration with me. She had started putting me down for double detentions, and it had no more effect. The teachers were used to seeing me in their detention, and I kind of think some of them enjoyed it. I know Mr Compton liked seeing me, and used the time to teach me more and more advanced syllabus – soon surpassing the third year syllabus and into the fourth year. Even when I didn't have a detention on Mondays, I went along anyway, because I liked it.

"Why don't you come to my classrooms on Saturday mornings," he said one Monday.

"What? Why?"

"Well, that's when I run a group in manipulation for the older years."

"There is a manipulation club?" I asked with a small laugh.

"Yeah, and you should come. I think you'd really like it."

"I'll consider it," I said.

I hadn't gone yet. Other things always came up. But I had every intention of going in the future. Sleep seemed to always be preferable to going to the club for some reason.

And before long, it was October 23rd. My birthday.

When I was at home, on my birthday, Micah wouldn't let me sleep in. He would come in early, and jump on my bed. Then he would drag all of us into the lounge where Jerry would have made breakfast, and Micah would be hyper. Then we'd sit there with cups of coffee and breakfast as I opened presents. Usually we'd go out for the day, go to a theme park or do something different. As a treat.

But I was sure that wasn't going to happen today.

My alarm clock went off as per usual. I groaned as I dragged my body out of bed. Monday....it could be worse. I went and got into the shower, the water forcing the last of the sleep from my eyes. I changed into skinny jeans, a white top and a leather jacket and pulled on my favourite ankle boots.

I opened the door and walked out.

"Answer your bloody laptop!" moaned Ronnie throwing a pillow at me. She was right. It was ringing. I went over and hit the green answer button.

"Happy Birthday!" shouted everyone. They were gathered around the laptop. I grinned.

"You guys!"

"Sorry we can't be with you Pammie," said Micah, "but we got you presents anyway. They're here for you when you come back. I'll go and get them."

Undercover Thief

"That's lovely. You didn't have to do that," I said as Micah disappeared off screen.

"Hey, it couldn't be your birthday if Micah didn't wake you up stupidly early," said Jerry and I laughed.

"Pam was already up, it was me you woke up early," grumbled Ronnie walking over, "So you must be the family Pam talks about."

"That's us!" said Leah, "who are you? Gwen or Ronnie?"

"Pam told you about me?"

"Of course I did!" I said.

"Pam told us everything about that place. All the people and the stuff. Sounds amazing to me. It's such a shame that all that tech is completely wasted on her," expanded Leah.

"Well, I'm the roommate Ronnie," she said throwing me a look, "and you aren't supposed to know about this place."

"What? Victoria? Pam told us the name and we did the digging ourselves," said Leah with a sniff, "It's sort of what we do. Still don't know exactly where it is."

"That's sort of the point," said Ronnie with a laugh.

"Micah, watch the coffee table!" Leah said, "back in a moment Pam."

"No worries," I said as she went to go help Micah.

"So what are you doing today?" asked Jerry.

"Oh, you know, nothing special," I said shrugging.

"Seriously? It's your birthday!" said Jerry, "you have to do something."

"I have school. You know what it's like here."

"It's your birthday!" crooned Ronnie, "You sly dog! You should have said!"

"I didn't see any point in telling you. Honestly not feeling in the birthday mood."

"We'll have a girls night tonight," said Ronnie, "and you will like it."

"After detention."

"You don't even have one yet. You want detention on your birthday?"

"I want to act like nothing is different," I said.

"Not going to happen!" said Ronnie walking into the bathroom.

"Sorry, did we just drop you in it?" asked Jerry.

"Kind of," I said with a laugh.

"Oops."

Undercover Thief

"No worries. I'm glad you called. I miss you guys so much."

"Yeah, we miss you too. The jobs aren't the same without you. Plus, without your genius, they are a little repetitive and dry."

"What can I say? I'm irreplaceable."

"One hundred percent," said Jerry grinning, "but I got a problem with this," he held up some blueprints and pointed to one section.

"What's the hitch?"

"The lasers are fine, and the alarm only goes off if both heat and motion sensors are tripped. However, to disengaged the lasers, I need to get through those, and I can't get through those until I disengage the lasers."

"Can you go in beforehand?"

"How will that help?"

"Hair spray," I said. Jerry hit his hand to his head.

"Of course, it creates a heat barrier. The heat sensors will be put down."

"And if it requires both of them, it doesn't matter that the motion detectors are still working."

"And that solved my problem. Thank you very, very much."

"Where and what?" I asked as I packed my bag.

"We're in Athens, you can probably tell."

"Tell me you've gone to that little café shop."

"No way. We need you here to do that."

"Tell you what, go, buy a big piece of cake and stick it in the freezer for me for when I get home this Christmas."

"You think you can get away?"

"I'm going to give it a go."

"Sweet."

"But don't tell Micah, just in case," I said.

"You got it," there was a knock at the door.

"Who is it?" I yelled.

"It's me!" called Gwen.

"Come on in Gwen," I said. Leah re-joined the conversation.

"Did you fix our little problem?" she asked as Gwen walked in.

"Ready to go Pam?" asked Gwen.

"Um, I might be late down," I said.

"This the infamous family?" asked Gwen.

Undercover Thief

"You must be Gwen. Love your hair," said Leah.

"Why thanks," said Gwen beaming ear to ear.

"Listen, Micah has a doctor's appointment in the morning, so we're going to hang up now. Sorry Pam."

"No, no, don't apologise. I totally get it," I said, "good luck for him."

"We'll keep our fingers cross. Bye Pam and have a great birthday," said Jerry who hung up.

"I like them," said Gwen, "and it's your birthday?"

"Ok, I really, really don't want to talk about it," I said picking up my bag from the side and closing my lap top.

"But you should have said!" Gwen pouted, "I would have got you a gift."

"Gwen, I don't need presents," I said smashing my fist on the bathroom door.

"What?" yelled Ronnie.

"We're going to breakfast. Meet you down there."

"Ok!"

"But you should get one on your birthday!" Gwen said unhappily.

"I love that you wanted to do that for me, but seriously, there is no need. I really don't want to celebrate it. Like at all."

"Why?" she asked as we headed down the stairs towards the hall.

"It doesn't feel like my birthday," I said shrugging, "You know, I'm not at home with everyone. We're not having a birthday morning."

"What's a birthday morning?" asked Gwen gently, slipping and arm through mine.

"Jerry would be cooking breakfast, Micah would me bouncing completely hyper for the entire day, and Leah would be snoozing with a blanket in the corner while I open presents they got me. You know? And we're not going anywhere special for the day. They would take me out on a trip somewhere. For Leah's birthday we did Harry Potter world. But today is just going to be a plain old ordinary school day. Yet another day that I'm not spending with some of the most important people in my life."

"Just because it's different doesn't mean that it can't be just as good," said Gwen pouting.

"I don't want it to be anything other than a normal day Gwen," I said walking through the doors to the breakfast hall. We grabbed our usual food and sat down.

Undercover Thief

"Ok, so you don't want presents and you don't want to celebrate, but that doesn't mean we can't hang out?" said Gwen.

"Sure we can hang out. Ronnie and I will even steal food from the kitchen; we can hang around in our room. But there is to be no mention of my birthday. By the by, how does Marley seem to you?"

I had asked this question every couple of days. I hadn't told them about what I heard. I had never seen anything similar again. And there was always the chance I had misheard and was over reacting. So I decided to let sleeping dogs lie. But that didn't mean I was giving up. I still had my eyes open. Gwen shared a room with her.

"Fine. Same as usual," said Gwen. She never asked why I was interested in Marley. For that I was thankful.

"Good to know."

"Father, incoming," she hissed as she picked up a jug of water and poured some for herself.

"Hi Pam," said my father walking over to where we were.

"You're back then," I said simply.

My father had come to me a few weeks before telling me that he would be gone on a mission for a few weeks. I don't know what exactly he'd been expecting. But I think the indifferent reaction that he got was definitely not it.

243

"Couldn't miss your birthday," said my father, giving me an awkward side hug.

"What are you doing here?" I asked brushing off his arm easily.

"Well, I came to see you. I got back late last night, and I would have come and seen you then but I didn't want to wake you."

"Good call," I said making myself a cup of tea.

"So, how does it feel to be fifteen?"

"Exactly that same as it did to be fourteen," I said rolling my eyes, "age is just a number."

"Now you can see fifteens at the cinema though."

"Right!" I said laughing, "because that's the meaning of life right there."

"It's not to be over looked."

"I could see a fifteen at the cinema before if I wanted anyway."

"Not legally."

"Oh, like it's a terrible crime," I said sniggering.

"So, you'll come over later this evening right?"

"What? You mean coming up to your rooms?"

"Yeah?"

Undercover Thief

"Why on earth would I do that?" I asked stunned, and my father couldn't completely keep the hurt off of his face.

"To celebrate your evening with us,"

"Pam doesn't want to celebrate," pouted Gwen. I threw her a dirty look and she went back to her porridge smiling.

"Why not?" asked my father, "kids normally like birthdays."

"Well, I'm not your average kid."

"But surely you want your presents," said my father with a chuckle. I frowned at him.

"Really? You got me presents?"

"That's what you do when your little girl turns fifteen."

"You haven't bought me presents since my ninth birthday," I said, "Sorry if I was not exactly expecting them."

"It just means we'll make this birthday a bit more special, being as it's the first one in a long time we've been together as a family," said my father.

"Listen, you don't have to do this. I'd really rather not do anything for my birthday."

"Oh come on, it will be fun. You, me and your mother. Just the three of us. I'm cooking."

"You cook?"

"I'm much better than your mother, I promise."

"So you're telling me she can't cook?"

"I'm a wonderful cook, your father is just trying to big himself up," said my mother walking over. I neatly dodged the kissed she tried to plant on my head. This was not an unusual occurrence. Outside of the classroom she tried to be all mum-like. But I wasn't having any of it.

"I'm not trying to big myself up; I'm a better cook than you are."

"Not true. Remember Monte Carlo?"

"That was a faulty gas line, not me."

"If you guys stop fighting about who is the better cook, I'll try it alright?" I said throwing up my hands as people started to look over and watch.

"Really? Oh excellent!" said my mother with a happy clap of her hands, "I'll make a chocolate cake and everything. You used to love the ones you had as a kid."

This was the first thing they had suggested that I had actually agreed to. I decided if I was in a bad mood, I might as well get it all over and done with on the same day. But apparently my mother was ecstatic.

"Nana made those with smarties in the middle. Where are you going to get smarties in America?"

Undercover Thief

"Ah, it's all about who you know," she said with a laugh, "Surely you know that by now poppet. So what time will we see you at? Six?"

"Make it half seven," I said turning back to my tea glumly, already not looking forwards to this, "I have to see Mr Compton first."

"You got it," said my mother smiling from ear to ear, "What do you like to eat?"

"Anything," I said, "Actually I lied; I don't eat mushrooms."

"Me either," said my father wrinkling his nose, "can't get over the idea I'm eating a fungus."

"No, it's not that. Long story short, I can't eat mushrooms because the taste makes me feel ill," I said, "and it's not pretty."

"Ok! No mushrooms. You got it darling," said my mother, "I'll see you in class later."

"Sure," I said as the two of them got up and moved away.

"Did you just say yes to something they wanted you to do?" asked Gwen with an open mouth.

"Well, it's my birthday, I should be trying new things," I said taking a bite out of my toast.

"Hey," said Ronnie coming and sitting down.

"Pam agreed to go to dinner with her folks," said Gwen.

"What! What happened to girl's night?"

"Ronnie! That is not the focus here!"

"Huh? Oh, right! You actually agreed to do something they wanted you to?" said Ronnie sitting forwards, "Are you feeling ok?"

"No, it's my birthday," I answered before taking a long draft of my tea.

"Seriously though Pam! Why did you suddenly say yes?" asked Gwen.

"And what took this long to make you say yes?" asked Ronnie. I paused, setting down my tea and looking at my hands.

"You want to know why I haven't said yes before," I almost whispered.

"Yeah," said Gwen gently, "because we worry about you and we want to understand."

"I know you do, I know.....but .....this is a huge deal for me," I said, "I mean, we're literally talking about the last six years of my life."

"We know," said Ronnie, "but you can trust us. We're your friends. We aren't going to tell anyone."

Undercover Thief

"I do trust you guys. I do. I don't think you'll use this against me."

"Then what?" asked Gwen. I tried to form the words.

"How about I tell you about me first," said Ronnie, "The reason I don't have a father is because mum doesn't know his name. There. I said it."

"Oh my goodness," I said sitting forwards, "you're serious?"

"Yep."

"And your mother just told you that?" asked Gwen.

"No. I put it together over the years. I knew I wasn't her ex-husband's child. My mum just told me that her and my father didn't have much in common so didn't stay together. She didn't want to put the idea in my head that I was unwanted. I know my mum loves me. I also know she wouldn't change anything about what she did.

"But who is your father?" I asked, "I mean what was his job, what does he look like? Where does he come from?"

"I don't know and I don't care," said Ronnie simply, "it's a bit like you with your family. My mum is all the family I need."

"Alright then," I said pushing the plate of toast towards her.

"Gwen?" prompted Ronnie helping herself.

"I used to be a twin," said Gwen. Our mouths fell open.

"Used to?" asked Ronnie tentatively.

"Yes. She got cancer. Didn't make it. I was five."

"Oh honey. I'm so sorry," I said taking her hand comfortingly.

"Oh, I barely remember to be honest. So I'm ok about it," said Gwen before taking a swig of her juice, "She was called Cleo."

"Wow, that's heavy," said Ronnie with a deep breath.

"My parents were really cut up about it. Still are. I have a few photos of her though."

"But you're ok? Right?" I asked worried for my friend.

"Oh please, yeah," said Gwen smiling at me to reassure me, "it's not inherited or anything. She just got unlucky."

"Wow," I said sitting back.

"Pam?" asked Ronnie.

"Ok, well.....you know how I haven't seen my parents in over six years?"

"Before they came home, yes," said Ronnie.

Undercover Thief

"Well.....they left me with my Nana when I was nine. And my Nana died shortly after they left. And they didn't come home. Nobody came to help me. I was on my own."

"What?" Ronnie gapped and Gwen dropped her spoonful of porridge onto the table with a clatter. I jumped and wiped porridge from my cheek with my sleeve.

"I was nine years old, and my nan died. It was quick, and it was painless so I guess that is something. I called so many times after she died, telling them that she had passed. But I never got through. It just went to answer phone. In the end I went and buried her anyway."

"What happened?"

"Nothing. I waited at home for someone to come. For them to come home. They didn't. And then the money ran out. I was nine years old, on my own, in London, without a penny. There was talk of me being put into care, but as soon as I realised that was on the cards I ghosted."

"What do you mean?"

"I disappeared, kept moving. Lived on the streets for bit. I literally vanished, long enough for the social workers to move on to the next case anyway, before I went home again."

"Oh wow," whispered Gwen.

"Mum and Dad abandoned me," I finished, shrugging one shoulder but it didn't fool them for a minute, "and......they haven't even said sorry."

"Oh Pammie," said Ronnie throwing an arm around me and squeezing my shoulders, "I'm so sorry to hear that."

"Hey, don't worry about it. I'm fine now. But you can understand why I'm not thrilled."

"That's an understatement, I'm angry on your behalf!" said Ronnie crossly.

"Oh no, don't be. I've moved on. Honestly! I have Jerry, and Leah and Micah. I'm happy."

"But what did you do?" asked Gwen, "For money? None of the four of you are old enough to work properly."

"Ah....."

"What? I thought we were past the hesitation," said Gwen frowning.

"I am....I'm not hesitating for that reason........"

"What is it? You don't want to tell us?" asked Ronnie.

"Let's just say what I did was....well......I don't think you would like me any more if you knew," I whispered.

"Did you kill someone?"

"NO!" I said instantly, kind of offended. Did I look like a killer?

Undercover Thief

"Then what? If no one died then I'm sure it's fine!"

"Listen, here is my deal to you. I am not going to tell you what I did. However, you are allowed to make three guesses. And I promise, if you're right, I'll tell you everything," I compromised.

Ronnie and Gwen exchanged a grin.

"OK, challenge accepted," said Gwen.

"And we don't have a time scale on this thing, so take as long as you want," I said.

"Don't worry. We will," said Ronnie, "I bet we can figure it out."

"Well my parents haven't yet and they've been trying for about four months now."

"Ten bucks says we figure it out before they do," Ronnie wiggled her eyebrows up and down.

"Alright. You're on," I said as we shook hands.

"Come on, we'll be late for class," said Gwen as the bell went.

"Manipulation....what a way to start a birthday."

Chapter Fourteen

That evening I walked into Manipulation detention at six o'clock as per usual on a Monday. There was already another kid there, doing some form of work with his head down. Occasionally I wasn't the only one there, but I was definitely about to set a record for the school.

"Hi Mr C," I said walking through the door.

"Hello Pam," said Mr Compton, "Happy Birthday."

"Have my parents been telling everyone?" I asked annoyed.

"Pretty much."

"Urgh!" I groaned collapsing into one of the desks.

"Aw, they're just being proud parents."

"I wish they would go back to ignoring me sometimes."

"Oh, did you actually get detention today?" he asked as he came over with a book for me to read.

Undercover Thief

"Actually no, surprisingly!" I said thinking about my day, "I wasn't really feeling myself."

"Ah, perhaps the birthday and added year have presented you with a new perspective on life."

"Probably not," I sniggered, "I think I deserved to get detention in French, but Madam was being nice to me."

"Why on earth are you here if you don't have detention?" asked the other kid.

"The alternative is dinner with my parents," I said with a shiver, "I'm beginning to regret the decision to go."

"Why? You're parents are lovely people," said Mr Compton. He handed me a book.

"We have our differences," I said wrinkling my nose.

"I don't see that many you know," said Mr Compton, "You and your mother are very similar."

"Oh don't say that, I'll burst into tears right here."

"Ok, please don't cry," he said joking with me, "but in all honesty, I don't see why you don't get one with them."

"It's a history thing."

"Think you can move past your history?"

"No," I said shortly.

"You haven't even tried."

255

"What do you think I'm doing in this place?" I asked looking at him, "If I wasn't trying to move past my past then I would have left ages ago. I've had the opportunities."

"So, if you dislike your parents so much and want to leave, why haven't you?"

"My parents would only try and track me down again, and I don't want to spend the rest of my life running."

"That is a very sensible decision," said Mr Compton smiling.

"Well, I do make them occasionally," I joked.

"You know, Pam, you could give your parents a chance to bridge the gap," said Mr Compton, "they are trying very hard you know."

"Mr Compton, thank you for trying to help, but I'd really rather that you didn't, at least not with this. It's a very, very painful subject for me."

"Ok, if you prefer."

"So, what have you got for me today?"

"So, this is some advanced psychology," said Mr Compton sitting on his desk, "And that is important. Understanding the different aspects of the mind is the key to a proper understanding of the fundamental nature of people."

"Ok," I said scanning the page quickly. Interesting.

"Now, a part of being good at manipulation is how to make someone feel something. Now, that can be love, anger or another emotion or it can be a physical feeling, you can make someone tired or more alert. It's about playing with the mind."

"Right."

"So, this is the science behind it," said Mr Compton, "how good is your biology?"

"Shocking," I said honestly.

"And your chemistry."

"Again, it's appalling."

"Ok, well, I'm not a science teacher, but I can cover the basics."

"Do I need to learn these experiments?" I asked pointing to a few of the pink boxes.

"Well, if you were going to take a third year test anytime soon, then yes. But you aren't."

"Right, ok."

"And to help with your essay structure, why don't you spend the hour writing me an essay on this," he said. I sighed.

"I hate essays."

"I know Pam, but practice makes perfect. Let's see if we can't give you the literacy skills to go with your brain. A large part of a spy's life is, unfortunately, paperwork."

"So what's that then? Like mission reports and stuff?"

"Much, much bigger," said Mr Compton with a laugh, "one of the reasons I got out of the life."

"And became a teacher? To do all that marking?"

"Would you believe, all eight years could give me something to mark at the same time and it's still less than what I would do when I was still an active agent."

"You're really not selling it to me Mr Compton," I said with a laugh as I wrote the title at the top of the page.

"Well I'm not here to sell it to you. You'll have enough of that the closer you get to graduating."

"Alright then," I said reading down the page. Before you knew it, the hour was up. I handed Mr Compton my half-finished essay. He scanned down it.

"Ok, well, the information is good. Do you understand all of it?"

"The science is a bit lost on me. Particularly the neurone stuff."

"Ok, well, we can go over that a bit more next time. The structure is good but your writing needs to flow a bit more. It's all over the place. Remember for each paragraph, point, evidence, explanation."

"Right."

"But this is much better than that first one you handed into me a few weeks ago."

"Really?"

"Why don't you finish it off and get it back to me once you've done. You can rewrite this so it flows a bit more," he said.

"I suck at this," I muttered.

"No, no, the information is all there," said Mr Compton, "and considering where you started, this is a massive improvement."

"Ok, thanks sir," I said shoving the paper in my bag as I got ready to go.

"I'll see you on Wednesday," he said.

"What are they doing?"

"Still working on reading a target."

"Really? How much haven't they covered about marks?" I asked.

Occasionally the language we used when talking about the same thing was different. He would call it one thing and I would call it another. But he never asked me more about it. And in our debates, we'd both picked up a bit of the other person's terminology.

"So much," said Mr Compton with a small smile, "most people struggle with the idea of manipulation."

"That's basically the core of being a spy though," I said sitting on the desk.

"I know," said Mr Compton, "I think it's the word, you know, it has bad connotations."

"Big word there Mr C."

"Ah, it means it's related to things. So manipulation is seen as bad."

"Oh, oh right. And yeah.....have you considered giving it another name?"

"And what would you call it?"

"Can I get back to you on that one?"

"Please, be my guest," he said with a chuckle, "now you have a dinner to get to."

"Damn, I was hoping I could claim I forgot about that."

"Oh no, you said you were going to go and you should go."

"Oh, I know. I'll keep my word," I said with a sigh.

Undercover Thief

"Good bye Pam," he said.

"Bye," I said as I left and walked down the empty corridors.

I looked at my iPod. It was a little past seven. I sighed. I had to go to dinner with my parents now. There was literally no choice in the matter. I had given my word. I was a thief with principles; my word had to have meaning.

I plugged in my iPod and walked up the stairs towards my mother's rooms. Students weren't allowed in the teacher's quarters without express permission from a teacher. So I didn't really know my way around. I walked along the corridor carefully, looking up and down.

It looked like any other corridor in the school. Only the doors had numbers and key cards. I walked further down. Then a door opened.

"You're not allowed up here Miss Torres," said Miss Alson walking down the corridor, "off you go."

"I'm supposed to meet my mum," I said with a sigh.

"Do you have that in writing?"

"No," I said shrugging.

"Then I'm going to have to ask you to leave."

"Really?" I asked brightening up. She eyed me for a moment.

"Why are you looking for your mother?"

"Dinner," I said looking at the floor and kicking it.

"I was under the impression you didn't get along."

"We don't," I confirmed.

"Well." she looked at me for a while and took a deep breath, seeming to come to a decision.

"Do you know which room is hers?" she asked.

"No," I admitted.

"That one," she said pointing.

I looked at the door, and forced my feet to move over in that direction. I raised my hand to knock and turned away, bending over my knees. I felt sick. Physically sick. Like I was cheating on Jerry, Leah and Micah. Like I was playing myself, it felt like I was running back to Mum and Dad, after everything they did. I should know better. I should know to steer clear.

"Come on Sklar, pull it together. You gave your word. You gave your word," I told myself, "and you're nothing without your word."

"Is everything alright?" asked Miss Alson who was watching, slightly concerned.

"Fine," I said standing up and pausing looking at the door.

"You know how to knock, don't you?" she said sarcastically.

Undercover Thief

"Of course," I said rolling my eyes, "but my family is a little bit more complicated than that."

"Miss Torres, I can't leave you up here unsupervised. So please knock on the door so I can go about my business," she said nodding. I took a deep breath and knock on the door three times.

A moment later the door was opened.

"Hi Pam, come on in," said my mother.

"Enjoy your evening Pamela," said Miss Alson.

"Thanks," I muttered as I stepped into the room. Why did I feel like I was walking into a trap, and I didn't have an escape route?

"How was school?" asked my mother brightly.

"Fine," I said looking around the room.

The kitchen, lounge, dining area was all one room. My dad was in the kitchen part, cooking something that smelled amazing. The walls were a faded blue, the curtains a pale yellow, and the whole place was cosy yet not expensive.

The sofas were mismatched and didn't fit the room. There were two doors made of the same colour wood as the rest of the building, but obviously everything else in here was more modern, one door was slightly ajar and I could see a descent sized bathroom.

"Hey Pam," said my father opening the oven and looking inside.

"Hi," I said.

"Well, you can put your bag down. Want something to drink?" asked my mother.

"What you got?" I asked slinging my bag on one of the sofas.

"Um, Lemonade, diet coke, juice," rattled off my mother. I just frowned at her and picked up an open bottle of red wine. I sniffed it and raised an eyebrow.

"Chianti, nice" I said, "What are we eating? If it's something with fish I'd prefer white."

"Pork," said my father.

"You drink wine?" asked my mother.

"Course I do. Love a good red," I said.

"You're underage," she said hesitantly.

"Are you going to arrest me?" I asked sceptically. Because it was drinking I was afraid of getting caught doing, I thought to myself sarcastically.

"Of course not poppet!"

"Then we don't have a problem," I said.

"Do you just drink wine?" asked my father.

Undercover Thief

"No, I'll drink whiskey, cider, beer, lager. Not a fan of shots though. To me that just seems to be drinking for the sake of getting drunk, and that just seems pointless to me."

"Have you ever been drunk?"

"Once, not an experience I intend to repeat," I said remembering it and smiling to myself at the memory. That had been an interesting night.

"Would you like a small glass?" offered my mother, "It would have to be the only one for the evening though. I'm not really comfortable giving you an alcoholic drink."

"Thanks," I said, sure I'd be able to slip myself more if I wanted to later.

"Here you go," said my mother handing me a glass and I poured myself the wine.

"So what are you doing in classes at the moment?" asked my dad. I shrugged.

"A lot of things, I do a lot of classes."

"Your mother tells me that you had a class with her today. What did you do in that?" he asked.

"Um, well I was planning my Christmas holiday. But I think I was supposed to be learning about hazard perception," I said.

"We were thinking about Christmas too," said my mother brightly, skipping over the fact I said I wasn't paying attention in her lessons.

"Oh?"

"We were thinking we could go skiing? Have you been before?"

"Skiing? No."

"I think you'll enjoy it," said my mother.

"Wait. Hang on, you want me to spend Christmas with you?"

"Of course! We're your parents," she said putting the water in front of me.

"Why? What were you planning?" asked my father.

"Well, I was going to go back to London," I said, "See my friends, apologise for disappearing like a ghost with no reason. Set my affairs in order. It'll probably take the whole two weeks."

"Right," said my father sharing a look with my mother, "and what affairs are those?"

"Oh, you know, business," I said vaguely.

"What kind of business?" asked my mother.

"Private business," I said firmly and took a sip of my wine.

"Ok," said my father. They exchanged another look.

"You'll like the Alps," said my mother.

"So what, are you saying I can't go home?" I asked.

"No, we're not saying that," said my father, "we're saying that the Alps will probably be more fun than London."

"Yeah, but I have to sort out a few things. That's the problem with you guys plucking me out of thin air off the street, nothing is sorted," I said.

"Well....we can spend one or two days in London beforehand I suppose," said my mother sipping her own wine.

"What?"

"Yes, we can go to London with you while you sort out things," said my father.

"This isn't happening," I muttered rubbing my eyes with both hands.

"Yes. It'll be a lovely chance to meet some of your friends," said my mother.

"You know what, the Alps sounds better," I said quickly, "I'm sure that a few phone calls can get the emergencies sorted out."

"No, no. Seeing your friends will be good for you," said my mother, "from school right?"

"Um..."

"You don't know them from school?"

"No."

"Then where?"

"Oh, around," I said scratching my head. I didn't want to lie to them, so indirectly answering was perhaps better.

"Like where?" asked my mother. They were pushing to find out more about what I did while they were away.

"Just around, never mind that," I said trying to side step it, "can I use the bathroom?"

"Sure, it's in there," said my mother pointing for me.

"Thanks," I said walking through into the bathroom. I didn't really need to go; I just wanted to do something to get away from the potentially dangerous conversation. I waited three minutes, flushed the toilet and washed my hands. Then I walked out to see a small pile of presents on the counter where I had been sat.

"Happy birthday poppet," said my mother brightly.

"You weren't kidding about presents," I said walking over.

"Of course I wasn't," said my father stirring a pot.

Undercover Thief

"I wasn't sure what you wanted," said my mother, "so, I had to guess."

"Ok," I said eyeing them, not eager to start taking gifts from them.

"Go on, open one," said my mother pushing.

I picked up one of them that was obviously some kind of clothing. At least I sort of knew what I was getting into there. I neatly unpackaged the paper, folding it and putting it to one side. It was a really nice shirt, made a very smooth silk, a blush colour.

"I thought it would go with your black jeans," said my mother.

"Thanks," She'd got the colour just right.

"I had to guess sizes, did I get it right?"

"Um, yeah, by the looks of it," I said nodding.

"Great! Open this one next," she said. Frowning I took the small black box from here and opened it warily. Inside was a locket.

"Do you like it?" asked my mother. I took it out of the box and held it up to the light. It was lovely, made of silver. Delicate, it wasn't a flashy statement piece.

"It's pretty," I agreed.

"We didn't know what photos you wanted to put inside so we just left it blank," said my father.

"Thanks, it's nice," I said putting it back in the box and snapping the lid shut.

"The rest of the gifts will have to wait ladies, as dinner is served," said my father pulling the pork out of the oven, "so if you would make your way over to the table." I waited for my mother to sit down first before picking the opposite seat.

"It looks wonderful Gordon," said my mother as she helped herself to green beans.

"Good," said my father smiling, "Help yourself Pam."

"Ok," I said putting some of the potatoes on my plate.

"So, Pam, do you like it here?" asked my father. I cleared my throat as I thought.

"Well....I like some of the people here," I said by way of answering.

"You made friends?"

"Yes."

"You're always with Ronnie and Gwendolyn. Are you getting close?" asked my mother.

"Yeah. Ronnie and Gwen are great," I said as I put some pork on my plate.

"Anything else? What's your favourite class? And you don't have to say mine," said my mother smiling.

Undercover Thief

"I like Manipulation. It's a bit basic at the moment so Mr Compton sets me different work to do while everyone else gets up to speed," I said.

"You're ahead in Manipulation? That's excellent Pammie," said my father.

"Anything else?" asked mum.

"PE is ok, but when you're partnered with Ronnie you end up on the floor a lot," I said shrugging.

"She's good at it is she?" asked my mother.

"Good? Yeah. But she's also insane," I said shaking my head, "That girl has way too much energy for her own good."

"That's nice that she's getting on so well. I know how Sally was worried that she wouldn't take to it very well."

"Why wouldn't she? She's lived here for a vast majority of her life. She knows how things work here," I said.

"Parents have a tendency towards paranoia," said my mother.

"Silly but true," agreed my father.

"Ok," I said taking a bite of my pork. Dad was a good cook.

"So Pam, what school did you go to back in London? We've been looking but can't find records," said my mother. I just looked up from my plate.

"Everything alright Pam?" asked my father.

"I didn't," I said quietly, giving them a glimpse at the truth. The atmosphere instantly plummeted.

"You didn't go to school?" asked my father, "Why not?"

"Why do you think?"

"That's illegal," said my mother.

"I was also living alone mum."

"So what did you do with your days?"

"Stuff."

"Stuff? That's not really a good enough answer Pam, considering you didn't go to school."

"It's the answer you're getting so tough," I shot back shortly.

"Pam, what did you do with your time if you didn't go to school?" asked my father, a warning in his voice.

"Or what? You'll send me to boarding school? Oh wait!" I said sarcastically.

"Pam! Tell us!" snapped my father hotly.

"You know what? If you wanted to know, you should have bloody been there," I snapped.

"We were working."

Undercover Thief

"Right, because that makes it all ok," I said sarcastically. I got up from the table, walking away and closing my eyes. I took two deep breaths to calm down before I did something stupid.

"Pam, please sit back down," said my mother. I needed to take two more deep breaths.

"This was a bad idea," I said going over to the sofa and getting my bag.

"Aw no Pam! Come on!" said my mother, "you've barely had anything to eat."

"I really shouldn't be here."

"Pam, please. This is stupid."

"Yeah it is," I said pulling open the door. My father was there and pushed it shut.

"Pam, leaving when a tricky topic of conversation comes up isn't going to fix anything."

"Perhaps I don't want to fix anything."

"That's very childish behaviour."

"You treat me like a child, so why can't I act like one?"

"Pamela, that's ridiculous."

"Really? Apparently I have to tell you absolutely everything that has ever happened in my life! That's what's ridiculous!"

"We're trying to protect you," he said.

"I didn't ask you to do that."

"You don't have to, it's our job."

"That's funny," I said with a dry laugh, "that's actually hilarious!"

"Pamela, why are you acting like this?"

"If you don't like the way I act then tough luck, you should have raised me," I snapped, "now please get out of my way, I have better things to do than sit here and spend what remains of my birthday having a pointless, roundabout argument with you." I forced the door open again and walked out.

"Pam! Pam!" my mother was following me.

"Can you just leave me alone?" I called back as I almost ran down the stairs.

"Pam, your father was just shocked! You can't drop something like you didn't go to school and expect us to be ok with it!" said my mother.

"Well, I don't care about your opinion on the matter," I said.

"Pam!"

"Just leave me alone."

"No! Never again, do you hear me?" she called and I froze, not turning to look at her.

"I'm not leaving you again!" she repeated.

"You shouldn't have left the first time," I said and continued moving.

She didn't follow me.

Chapter Fifteen

It was after PE that Friday. Ronnie and I were walking back up to our room early. Ronnie had managed to throw me into a rather large, muddy puddle and I was now dripping rank, brown water all along the corridors as my trainers squeaked.

Ronnie laughed as I finished a joke and punctuated it with throwing muddy water at her from my skin.

"I'm sorry, next time I will try to avoid dumping you in the puddle," she promised.

"That would be appreciated!" I said with a laugh, "I might never get the mud out of my clothes."

"Aw, and they were such nice shorts."

"Yeah, they were."

"We should go have a girl's trip again," said Ronnie.

"I could use a good manicure," I said nodding in agreement.

"Great, we should talk to the girls about it!"

Undercover Thief

"I'm sure they'll be up for it, it all depends how Cassidy feels about not going to badminton club."

"Who knew she was such a fan of badminton?"

"I know, right?"

Then I stopped. I heard something. I held up a hand to Ronnie and pressed a finger to my lips. She frowned and listened, then, she nodded. She heard it too. I bent down and slipped off my noisy shoes. Then Ronnie and I crept to the stairs.

It was the same alcove where Marley had been calling someone last time. I recognised her voice, even if I hadn't heard it that often.

"I'm close. I'm so close," she said quietly. Ronnie looked at me with wide eyes.

"Who is she talking to?" she whispered. I held up my hand to my ear in the shape of a phone. Ronnie shook her head. I nodded firmly and then pressed a finger to my lips.

"Be ready to go in a couple of weeks, it won't take me much more than that," said Marley to whoever was on the other end of her phone, "This will be done before Christmas."

I closed my eyes. It was almost November, so that didn't give us a long time scale.

"They're just for show....right?.......No! No I don't care about them! I'm not an amateur! But there are kids here!........they're my age!.........yes......I know.......ok......."

She was worried because there were 'kids' here. Her age.....what she was planning sounded dangerous. That wasn't a comforting thought at all.

"Yeah. I miss you too. I'll see you soon." She was ending the call. We needed to move, and quickly. I grabbed Ronnie hand and pulled her silently up the stairs and away from the small alcove. I snatched my shoes from where I had left them and we ran into our room.

"What was that?" demanded Ronnie as the door swung close, her eyes were still wide and she looked slightly pale.

"I don't know. It knew that she was planning something, but now I think it's dangerous," I said.

"You knew about that? You knew she was on the phone? And you didn't think to tell a teacher?" I just looked at her.

"Or me?"

"The first time I overheard her I didn't know what I was hearing. She could have been planning to bust out because she was homesick or something, like me. Only her mummy and daddy have given her a way to phone home."

"That was not a homesick call Pam!"

"I know that now! She's up to something now!" I said throwing my wet shoes into the shower, "The question is what."

"Yeah! That's one of the questions crossing my mind! So what? She pretended to be sick the last few days so she could make that call?" asked Ronnie.

I sat down on my desk chair and tried to think.

"No. She has pretended to be sick to get off lessons so she can take a look around. She's been sneaking around the school. She's looking for something."

"You know that? Why didn't you say something?"

"Because I only now have figured out that's what she was doing. If I wanted a look around, I would pretend to be sick as well."

"Then what is she trying to find?"

"I don't know, you'd have a better idea about that kind of thing than I would."

"Well....there is a lot of stuff here," said Ronnie, "a lot of classified, dangerous stuff."

"So the question is how are we supposed to figure out what it is?"

"We don't have to! We have to go to a teacher and report this!"

"We can't."

"Why not?"

"We don't know for certain that something is up!"

"Yeah we do!"

"We have no proof! What we heard? That's really sketchy Ronnie," I said, "if no one believes us, she'll know we're onto her and she'll be extra careful and then it will be twice as hard to catch her."

"Why wouldn't they believe us?"

"One word. Me!" I said simply. She sighed and flopped onto her bed.

"Yeah that makes sense. Damn your rebellious streak sometimes Pam."

"Keeps things more fun," I said with a snort.

"So what do we do?"

"We need to know more about Marley," I said, "We need to know where she is at all times, and we need to know what it is that she's after."

"So what? You want someone to always be with her?"

"That won't work."

"So what else can we do?"

Undercover Thief

"We could bug her," I said my eyes lighting up at the idea, "put a trace on her shoe or clothes or something."

"And where are we going to get bugs?" Ronnie paused and then broke into a wicked grin.

"Gwen," she said, coming to the answer all on her own. I nodded.

"Of course, Gwen. She also has the perfect cover. She has a reason to be in her room, to ask how she is."

"To accidentally go through a draw or two," said Ronnie catching on, "She is perfect." Then I sighed, seeing the flaw in our plan.

"Except she can't act for toffee."

"She doesn't need to," said Ronnie tapping her chin with a pink nail (painted by me last night) "she just has to monitor the bugs. We can do the rest."

"But we'll still have to tell her."

"Well of course we do. We have no secrets from our best friend," said Ronnie.

The bell went for lunch.

"Ok. You need to shower, and then we'll talk to Gwen and let her into this," said Ronnie.

"I almost feel guilty about it," I said as I grabbed new clothes.

"I don't. She's training to be a spy, we had to corrupt her perfectly innocent view of the world at some point," said Ronnie. I let off a short laughed and almost ran for the shower.

If there was a record for the quickest shower in the world, I bet I broke that record. It was the fastest I had ever moved, I was pretty sure. Once I was changed, Ronnie threw me my bag and we hurried down the stairs towards the main hall.

We spotted Gwen at our usual table by the window, already with a plate of pasta in front of her, a thick computer text book in her hands that she was holding so close that her nose was almost touching the page. We hurried over and sat down.

"Hey guys, don't you want food?" she asked noticing our empty hands.

"Gwen, we have a problem," said Ronnie quietly as we both sank down into our seats.

"What kind of problem?"

"Marley."

"What?" She looked confused, "did you have a fight or something?"

"No, we just saw Marley *on the phone*," said Ronnie. Gwen's mouth fell open.

"Not possible," said Gwen quietly.

"I get internet connection, you think she can't get phone signal?" I whispered looking around me to make sure no one could hear me.

"But how? Who to?"

"We don't know."

"But.....I'm confused......Pam has the internet. So what does it matter if Marley has a phone?" asked Gwen.

"The phone itself isn't the problem. It's the conversation she was having," I said, "She isn't using it to stay in contact with her family like I am Gwen, she's using to because she's working a job."

"A job?"

"A mission," said Ronnie, who was used to translating my thief jargon, though she didn't know that's what she was doing, "she has a mission and it's not a good one."

"What is it?"

"We don't know, we only heard one half of the conversation, but she was reminding whoever it was that there were kids in the building."

"That's not good," said Gwen swallowing.

"We know that!"

"It sounds dangerous!"

"We know that too!"

"When is this going to happen?"

"Before Christmas."

"Why?"

"We don't know."

"Wow....ok....we need to tell someone."

"We can't Gwen, we have no proof," said Ronnie.

"We're thinking that, since you're so good with computers and stuff, maybe you could help us out."

"What do you mean?"

"She wants us to bug Marley," said Ronnie.

"What? We can't do that! What if we're wrong?"

"Gwen, what if we're not?" I said.

"There are things here Gwen, prototypes for new weapons, secret files, chemical formulae, in the wrong hand they could hurt a lot of people," said Ronnie.

"You think Marley would do something like that? She's only fourteen, like us!"

"It doesn't matter what age she is Gwen. You can do maths, science and work a computer better than most sixty year olds. At this stage Gwen, age doesn't matter," I said firmly.

Undercover Thief

"Are you sure?"

"Yes. Someone our age is certainly capable of doing something like this."

"But if no one else has picked it up, are you sure of what you heard?"

"Positive," said Ronnie. Gwen took a deep breath.

"I can't believe this. Alright, I'm in," she said nodding.

"Excellent," said Ronnie.

"But, how can I run it from my room. I'll get caught," said Gwen.

"I think I might have the answer to that one," said Ronnie. Gwen and I exchanged a look.

"Oh?" we asked.

"Follow me," she said getting up. We threw our bags over our shoulders and headed out of the hall.

"Pam!" I turned around to see my mother walking towards me.

"Mum, listen, now is not a good time," I said trying to brush her off and move on.

"You got five detentions in one week? Five!"

"Mum, I've got to go," I said rolling my eyes, "can we do this later?"

"No we can't!"

"Mum, I'm leaving. I'll talk to you later, alright?"

"Sorry Mrs Torres, we're kind of in a rush. I lost my homework. I can't find it anywhere," said Ronnie lying smoothly, "The girls promised to help me re-write it. Come on, we're running out of time." Ronnie grabbed my hand and pulled me along.

"Thank you," I said once we were out of the hall.

"Don't sweat it," she said as we ran up the stairs. She went up and up and we followed. She stopped on one of the floors and walked down the corridor.

"Where are we going Ron?" I asked.

"It's a surprise," she said grinning, "I found this years ago."

"Found what?" I asked as we stopped by an old grandfather clock. She reached behind it and then there was a small clinking sound. A wooden panel popped out of the wall a little bit.

Gwen's mouth and mine fell open.

"Secret passages? In the school?" I grinned, "Oh nice! This is like Hogwarts."

"What's that?" asked Ronnie, innocently, then sniggered at the look I gave her, "I'm kidding. I've read Harry Potter."

Undercover Thief

"Thank goodness, because I would have given up right then and there," I said.

"They're not really like secret passages. This is just an old house, and really big old houses often had separate corridors and things for the servants to get about without the rich owners being disturbed. But when they converted this place into a school they boarded up all the old passages and...well...they kind of forgot about them."

"But you knew where they are?"

"Oh yes. After you," she said and we all entered the dark passage. It was a bit like a tunnel, and I walked along, pulling my iPod out of my pocket to use as a torch. There were candles on the walls that had long been abandoned.

Then the corridor split into two.

"Which way?" I asked.

"Right," said Ronnie, "but keep your voice down here because we're just over the teacher's lounge."

"Oh wow!" whispered Gwen as we slowly climbed steadily upwards, "this is so cool!"

"I know all of the corridors, I've been exploring ever since I learned about this little beauty. Another time, I will show them all to you just in case you ever need them. But, this is how I steal food from the kitchen," she said, "there is a door that opens out behind one of the counters, so you have to jump that, but that's the only problem with it."

"Ok, next time I am coming with you," I whispered grinning.

"Deal!" Ronnie said, "two of us can carry more. We're almost there," she said.

"Ok, this is amazing," said Gwen – still obsessing about the fact that we were in an abandoned servant's corridor.

"I completely agree," I said looking around.

The corridor was old and covered in dust and cobwebs. It was dark and pokey, but I could have spent hours in here mapping it all and learning where all the tunnels lead. I could completely see a young, bored Ronnie who had been kicked out of middle school spending her days in here, learning all about the tunnels.

"Ok, we're almost there," said Ronnie as I came to a door.

I turned the rusted handle and walked through. We were in a circular room, in one of the corners of the school, up by the roof. I could tell, because there was a small, dirty window that looked out over the front of the school – almost hidden from view by the front of the house due to the way the roof sloped down. It was framed by thick, old red velvet curtains that were filled with dust. Despite that, and the fact it was a cloudy day the room was still filled with light and I could turn off the torch on my iPod. There was a bare thread rug on the floor, but that was the only furnishing in the place. It was completely empty.

Undercover Thief

"What do you think?" asked Ronnie wiggling her eyebrows up and down.

"I love it!" I said walking around the space, looking up at the large wooden ceiling above us and around. Oh, what I would do with this space.

"The old servant's wing has been converted into loft space, all but this room. This room was forgotten about, like the corridors behind the walls. I mean, technically people know about them but no one ever thinks about them. No security or anything. Complete privacy."

"Can I get electricity up here? My laptop needs charge," said Gwen, immediately getting down to business.

"I don't know. I guess you can cut through the plasterboard to find the mains and set up what you want," said Ronnie. Gwen immediately went over to the walls and started having a look.

"It needs a clean," I said, "but we can do that,"

"So, do we have our HQ?" asked Ronnie, sitting down on the floor.

"Oh yeah," I said grinning, "We definitely have our HQ. It could use a few things though, a few improvements,"

"Like what?" asked Ronnie.

"Well for starters, it doesn't have a kettle," I said and she burst out laughing.

Chapter Sixteen

About a week later, HQ was looking great. It was a Saturday evening, and Ronnie, Gwen and I now came up here to hang out all the time. It had taken a ridiculous amount of cleaning to get the smell of dust out of the air (never thought I would be sneaking around the school with mops in my hands).

Gwen had managed to set the place up with plug sockets and even a few electric lamps for lighting. Ronnie and I had managed, over the last few days, to get our hands on the items that we needed. Ronnie had been amazing at finding things in storage for us to use. They had all been put there because they had broken in some way, but they weren't all that hard to fix.

It was fun, the girls didn't really care that we were breaking the rules. We weren't going to tell anyone about this place after all. It was our secret. We had a desk in the corner where both my laptop and Gwen's were set up. I had managed to get a hold of two additional tables and about five stools. We didn't really need five stools, but you never knew when that might come in handy.

Undercover Thief

Gwen was sat at the table, messing about with wires. Ronnie was supposed to be doing her homework, but I had kind of derailed her by starting card tricks. So far I had taken fifteen dollars from her with a simple three-card-monty.

"How do you do that?" she said throwing her pen at me in amazement.

"Ok, look, this time it'll be easy. I'll bend the corner up for you," I said, "find the lady," I started moving the cards again, she pointed to the card and I turned it over.

"No! No way! How did you do that!" she said. I laughed.

"Sleight of hand."

"Show me!"

"But that would ruin the magic!"

"It isn't magic!" she said, "I want to learn."

"Ok, ok, here, take three cards from the deck," I said, "and I'll show you."

"Isn't that a confidence trick?" asked Gwen.

"I think so," I said knowing full well it was, "but it's a good way to get money off drunken guys in a pub. My friends taught me."

"Do you know other card tricks?" Ronnie asked as I showed her the hand movements that went with what I did in slow motion.

"Oh yeah," I said with a laugh, "see, I can make the card jump from the packet, like this."

"You're always playing with cards," agreed Gwen, "And you always carry a deck."

"Of course I do, never know when a spontaneous game of poker will break out," I said with a wink. Ronnie laughed.

"Do you cheat at poker?" asked Gwen.

"I know how to, but I don't with you guys," I said showing Ronnie a few more card tricks I knew how to do.

"How would we know?" Ronnie asked as she picked a card from my deck.

"You're just going to have to trust me. Ok, that's your card. Pick another card for our bullet card. I'm going to do a trick called the card gun," I said as she took a second card and held it up.

"OK, now replace your chosen card into the pack somewhere," I said and shuffled the pack, controlling her card so it was at the top.

"Now, I'm just going to make a gun," I said taking a third of the pack and farrowing it in.

"So, what's supposed to happen?" asked Gwen watching now.

Undercover Thief

"It's going to find her card. Her card should shoot out of the gun," I said, "so, I'm going to push this card in the bottom of the gun like I would if it was a magazine in a real gun, and your card should fly out the top. Try to catch it, ok?"

"Right," said Ronnie grinning.

"Ok, bang," I said smashing the card in as hers sailed into her hand.

"No way! That was so cool!" said Ronnie holding up her card.

"Why thank you," I said laughing as I shuffled the cards again. I made the cards fly from one hand to another and got them to flip as well.

"You are going to teach me!" said Ronnie.

"Guys! Guys look at this!"

"What Gwen?" I asked as we walked over to her computer, I was still pinning cards in my hands.

There was a video feed from the bedroom. Gwen had stuck a camera in the room to watch everything. Marley was talking to my mother. Gwen turned up the sound.

"Come on, surprise test," said my mother.

"Damn!" said Ronnie, "we've got to go! Come on!"

We all grabbed our bags and ran to get out. If my mother couldn't find us, she would get suspicious..

"Cards Pam!" whispered Gwen.

"What? There's nothing wrong with owning a pack of cards!" I protested snapping them out instantly into a fan and turning them over.

"Girls!" called out my mother as we walked down the stairs, "surprise test."

"What? It isn't even class time!" I protested.

"Yeah, this happens," said Ronnie, "teachers can just come and give us a test."

"What!" Gwen gasped, her face falling, "I haven't studied!"

"No, not that kind of test Gwen. Come with me," said my mother with a knowing smile. I didn't like the look of that smile.

"Then what kind of test?" I muttered to Ronnie.

"Hey Pam, why have you got a pack of cards?" Lydia asked as she and Cassidy bounced over to us.

"Hey, pick a card. I just blew Ronnie's mind with a card trick," I said grinning.

"Time for that later girls. You have a test right now," said my mother as we followed her down the stairs.

"Oh fine," I muttered doing one last trick and putting them into my bag.

Undercover Thief

"Pam! Pam!" I turned around to see three girls walking my way. I realised one of the girls was Chelsea.

After I had helped her out with that emergency date a while back, she and I had spoken a couple of times, mainly about boys but about other things too. We'd become quite good friends over time, she helped me out with a lot of my law homework.

"Oh, hey," I greeted.

"I have another date again tomorrow and I could really use your help with an outfit. You're like a fashion guru you know."

"Oh hey, no problem," I said grinning, "it'll probably be cold so you should wear the black jeans."

"So that's what I was thinking, but I've worn that before."

"He's a boy, they really don't register clothing on that level," I said shaking my head.

"Could you come and have a look now?"

"Chelsea, I'm very sorry but my daughter and her year group have a test right now," said my mother cutting in.

"Oh...." Said Chelsea disappointed, "after?"

"Sure thing Chels," I said.

"Great, I'll see you then. Good luck!" she called as she walked away with a wave.

"Thanks!"

"Come along Pam, we don't need any more distractions," said my mother with a gentle push.

"What? I was helping out a friend," I muttered kind of annoyed.

"How do you know her? I thought years didn't ordinarily mix," she said.

"I'm extraordinary," I said and Ronnie laughed.

"So, my test is practical as well as theoretical," said my mother deciding to move on as we walked down a corridor into a part of the school I hadn't been into before. Then it was down some stairs and into the basement. She walked over to the first door, throwing it wide.

"In you go," she said. We walked inside. Instantly my eyes spotted the cameras, the motion detectors, and the potential for a laser grid.

"What is it?" asked Ian.

"Your test," said my mother simple, "When I close this door, you have an hour. You have to spend an hour in here and not get caught. Or you can leave through that door over there."

"What?" squeaked Gwen. My mind was already working, racing and planning through what I was going to do. I immediately turned my back on my mother, blocking her out and looking around, clocking everything I could.

Undercover Thief

"If you get caught, it's game over, you fail the test."

"What happens if we fail?" asked Cassidy.

"We'll just see about that," she said, "your test starts in two minutes. Get ready and good luck." She closed the door.

"Damn! Oh damn!" Lydia was jigging up and down with nervous adrenalin, "what do we do?"

"Hide," I said looking at them as I pulled something out of my pocket. It looked like a simple yoyo. It wasn't. It was long, super strong fibre attached to a magnet. I was so glad I had thought to bring my coat. It had a few of my toys in it.

"What are you going to do Pam?" asked Ronnie as I began swinging the yoyo.

"Trust me, I'm going to get us through that door," I said throwing the yoyo up and catching it on the metal beams up on the room, "All the cameras are facing downwards, so I have to get above them." I started to shimmy my way up. I climbed to the top, crouching on the beam on the ceiling.

I crawled along and took reflective tape out of my pocket. I went over to the nearest heat sensor and covered it up.

"What are you doing?" hissed Ronnie.

"Getting us out of here," I said, "are you coming?" Ronnie shimmied up the cable after me.

"What are the rest of you doing?" I yelled at them "hide!" They all dived for cover behind an assortment of boxes, pillars and junk that had been left in the room by my mother for the task. I rolled my eyes. Some of them only just made it as the lasers turned on.

"Ok, what now?" asked Ronnie. I tore off a piece of tape and threw it to her.

"Tape it over these like this," I said pointing to the one I had just done.

"Why?"

"It stops it detecting heat signatures," I said, "which means that we won't get caught that way."

"And you just happen to carry this stuff with you?" she asked.

"Yes," I said, "I'm always prepared."

"Bad luck Mr Demarin," came my mother's voice over the speakers, "you've been caught already." I looked down and saw they were all hiding, but part of Adam's knee could be seen poking out from behind the destroyed sofa. Adam sighed and sat down on the floor.

"Come on, no one else is going to fail this test," I said to Ronnie quietly. She and I went around coving up the heat sensors. It didn't take very long at all.

Undercover Thief

"Ok, what now?" asked Ronnie. I took the yoyo and started to swing it throwing it up onto the roof above where it connected with a small click. I tugged on it to make sure it was stable and turned back to give her a grin.

"Don't follow me," I said. Then I jumped. Lydia gave a small scream of alarm as I swung across the room to the next beam, which was running across the control panel on the wall.

"Pam! Are you crazy!" yelled Ronnie, "If you fall you could kill yourself!"

"Don't you dare kill yourself for a damn test Pam!" hissed Gwen.

"Relax guys, I won't fall. I've done way riskier stuff with this little thing," I said, "and you don't need to be quiet guys, there aren't any noise detectors, which there totally should be if it was to be a proper test."

"Please, just don't do that again," begged Ronnie.

"No promises love," I said with a laugh, tying the yoyo tight around the beam, "I need you to get to that motion sensor over there. There is the one covering this floor here. Now, when I say so, I need you to give the red wire a nudge."

"The red one," she repeated as she crawled along the beam to the motion sensor I had pointed at.

"Yes. I need you to pull it out and put it back within two seconds," I said.

"You're mad!"

"Just do it!" I said, "on my mark. Three. Two. One. Now!" I jumped, grabbing the rope on my way down, stopping me from hitting the floor and at least breaking bones. I froze still, back to the room. There was no alarm. The trip had made the cameras freeze for a moment – long enough for me to slide behind a convenient wardrobe and get to work.

"It worked," shouted Ronnie amazed.

"I'm going to have a heart attack Pammie!" yelled Cassidy, "stop doing crazy stuff."

"Aw, but that's no fun!" I said grinning. I slowly opened the security panel, searching for the right wire before plugging my iPod into the system.

"What is taking so long?" asked Ronnie.

"Calm down!" I said, "this sort of thing takes time! Precision."

"So what is the plan?"

"OK, my iPod contains a minor hack. Just a small one, but it's enough to stop the motion sensors, freeze the cameras and cut off the lasers," I said, "And from there we can all get out."

Undercover Thief

""You're a bloody genius!" called Trevor.

"I know!" I said with a laugh, "Ok, you can come out of hiding when the lasers freeze. You have all of two minutes to get through the door over there before the system reboots. In three, two, one!"

Everyone hesitantly came out of their hiding spots. But now wasn't the time for hesitant

"Move you idiots!" I called.

I tugged on the yoyo and pulled it down and threw it up to Ronnie so she could climb down. I grabbed Gwen's hand and pulled her along with me. She was clumsy, but we made it to the door with fourteen seconds to spare. Everyone one else was coming. Lydia got through the door. Then Peter. Lucas. Ian. Gavin. Cassidy. Ronnie. Marley. Then the lasers started moving again.

I closed my eyes as George got hit by the lasers coming back on.

"You're out Mr Montgomery," said my mother's voice over the speakers. Allister had managed to jump into a hiding place. Ronnie tossed the yoyo back to be, grinning from ear to ear.

"We did it! Pam, that was just incredible! Reckless and completely stupid but incredible!" said Lydia hugging me tight.

"We've still got a man inside," I said, "We've got to go back."

"How?" asked Peter immediately up for it.

"As Pam has demonstrated, the roof is unprotected," said Marley, "But with a system like this, you can't pull a trip like that again. It will trigger the alarm. He had his chance and blew it."

"I am not leaving a man behind," I said acidly to her, "We're a team. It's time we start acting like one."

"You're going to have to lead him out over the supports in the ceiling," said Ronnie.

"How do we get him up to the ceiling?" asked Gwen.

I paced a little bit as I thought.

"Just sit tight in there buddy, we're coming for you," called Gavin.

"Thanks guys!" said Allister.

"George, would you move away from the door, thanks," I said absentmindedly, "sorry you didn't get out."

"No problem," said George.

"You can't use people who have already failed to help you," said my mother's voice over the speaker.

"Figured as much!" I shouted back, "not helping!" Then Marley cleared her throat and pointed to a box on the wall.

"That any help?" she asked. And I was struck with inspiration.

"Oh, this might just work," I said dancing over to it, "ok. And you said there was no reason for me to have cards." I pulled out my pack and pulling out the joker. I folded it and then handed it to Peter.

"Ok," I said as I used a penny I had in my pocket to unscrew the covering and had a look at the wiring.

"Peter, take a look at this. You see that there?" I said pointing.

"Yep."

"When I say, I need you to push that card in, and pull it out after exactly five seconds."

"Ok," he said nodding.

"Ok, this is going to have to be very, very quick," I said loosening up by jumping up and down. I took a deep breath to prepare.

"What is?"

"Allister! Get Ready! I'm coming!" I shouted through the still open door, "We're going to have twenty seconds to get out ok. So you are going to have to move like you're about to be hit by an avalanche, but move carefully, do you think you can do that?"

"Sure," he squeaked, "I'll try."

"I will refrain from the urge to quote Yoda at this point," I said, "Ok, Ronnie, see that wire just inside the door?"

"Yeah."

"When I say, you need to rip it out, at the same time at Peter uses that card I gave him," I said pointing to Peter who nodded.

"But that will cause the whole system to go into lock down," said Marley.

"After a twenty second window. Like I said, I have to be quick."

"And it's only the motion sensors, not the lasers," said Marley.

"I know," I said, "ready Ronnie?"

"Yep."

"That's crazy," said Marley.

"Might just work though," I said with a wink.

"Ok, ready everyone?"

"Yeah," they all chorused.

Undercover Thief

"Gwen time us.....ok...now!" I threw the yoyo up and started climbing. I ran along the beam to where Allister was and threw the rope down to him. Gwen counted out loud, everyone was nervously shifting from foot to foot.

"Climb! We have twelve seconds!" I yelled. He climbed up and scooted along the beam. Six seconds left. He slipped to the floor and I followed, throwing myself through the door, it clipped my legs as I rolled onto the floor next to Allister. The alarm sounded.

Allister and I started laughing where we lay on the floor.

"WOOOO!" yelled Allister in celebration.

"That was amazing!" said Ian. We were all laughing. And then they started cheering and whooping.

"Nice one Pam!" said Gavin helping me to my feet.

"Why thank you," I said with a mock curtsey to their cheers.

"That was insane! So bloody insane!" said Cass hugging me and jumping up and down.

"We did it!" Peter cheered tossing my card back at me.

"Ah, card tricks, I told you they were important Gwen," I said grinning.

"Shame that Adam and George failed," said Gwen.

"I expected you all the fail." We turned to see my mother stood there.

"If you expected us to fail, why did you set the test?" asked Gwen confused.

"I wanted to see what I was working with before I started practical work," she said, "field trips and the like. I wanted to see how people's minds worked. How you handled failure."

"We didn't fail," said Ronnie putting her arm around me and squeezing my shoulders, "We're a resourceful bunch."

"Yes, you have surprised me," she said, her eyes resting on me.

"What can I say? I'm just one of those girls," I said, "always got something up my sleeve."

"Indeed you have. May I see the tape you used to cover the heat sensors?"

"It's just reflective duct tape," I said spinning the small roll around my finger, "It's not the best stuff in the world, but it works just fine for a system like that,"

"And your little rope thing?"

"Oh this!" I said holding up my yoyo, "now this is one of my favourite toys,"

"Where did you get them?"

Undercover Thief

"A friend," I said mysteriously.

"And you happen to carry them with you?"

"Actually, yes," I said, "at all time."

"Why?"

"Never know when your teacher is going to set a surprise test," I said. My class laughed as I made the joke. My mother didn't look all that amused.

"You went back for Allister? Why?" asked my mother.

"Never leave a man behind," I answered.

"He wasn't in any real danger."

"I know," I said, "it's the principle of it though. I'd like to think if the situation was reversed, Allister would have come for me."

"That's a bit of a gamble."

"It was the right thing to do," I said. My mother simply smiled.

"Yes. It was. Like I said, you surprised me."

"Well, I keep telling you, you don't know me that well," I said pocketing my tape and yoyo and spinning on my heels to walk away, "Come on guys. We should celebrate in the common room."

They cheered and followed.

Chapter Seventeen

The next day, I walked into HQ. Ronnie and Gwen were already there. Ronnie was by the window and Gwen was watching the camera feed we had in the bedrooms.

"I have something important to say!" said Ronnie instantly.

"Oh dear, if it's a break up I think we should keep this reasonable for the kid," I said pointing to Gwen.

"Hey!" said Gwen half offended half giggling.

"We think we know what you did," said Ronnie, "to get money."

"Oh. Ok," I said not exactly thrilled. I walked over and sat down on one of the stools at the table.

"Let's hear your theory," I said preparing myself.

"First, we have a few things we wanted to say," said Gwen drifting over.

"Ok."

Undercover Thief

"First of all, don't hate us if we're wrong."

"And second of all?"

"If we're right, we don't think any less of you," said Ronnie hurriedly.

"Ok. Hit me with it," I said holding my breath.

"We think...." began Gwen taking a deep breath.

"That?" I pressed.

"You were a thief," finished Ronnie. I nodded for a little while.

They'd guessed it. Damn. I looked up at them. I should say no. I should laugh and tell them to keep guessing.

But I didn't.

I took out my wallet and held up two five dollar notes for Ronnie.

"Well done," I said, "you got it." Ronnie grinned taking the money from me. Gwen beamed from ear to ear.

"I knew it!" said Gwen, "how could we be wrong?"

"How did you figure it out?" I asked soberly.

"Yesterday," said Gwen, "no way does a normal girl know that kind of thing!"

"So you were a thief? Hit anywhere cool? Anything I might have heard about? Anything in the news?" asked Ronnie. I laughed nervously.

"You're seriously ok with it?" I asked, a little stunned they weren't suddenly starting to hide their valuables.

"Yeah, of course. I mean, you were stealing in order to have money to eat," said Ronnie, "how can we begrudge you that?"

"And we're guessing your whole family are thieves as well," said Gwen.

"We are," I agreed nodding.

"Ok, I want to know everything!" said Ronnie.

"You want to know how to be a thief?"

"Yeah! I want to know everything that you've done!"

"Wow, that's a lot of jobs."

"What have you stolen? Anything in the news?"

"A couple," I admitted with a laugh and Ronnie howled a little and leant forwards, eager for the story.

"Start at the beginning," she instructed.

"Ok, so you know the money ran out. That's when I started to steal. Small things at first, just food and water and things. I almost died not eating before I plucked up the courage to do it. I almost froze to death at night. London is really cold in the winter."

"Is that how you met your family?"

"Yes," I said.

So I told them everything. I told them how, when Micah needed medical treatment, we had had to step up to bigger jobs, which is how we became proper professional thieves not just pick pockets and street con men.

I didn't tell them that Micah was blind. I felt that was something that they didn't need to know. That was Micah's information to share not mine.

I told them about how we struggled but then thrived, and that we were actually amateurs compared to some groups out there.

When they asked for specifics, I gave them to them. I told them all the tales they could possibly want. I told them about when we cased the Louvre, when we conned a Tory minister, when we convinced an entire church congregation that there had been a chemical spill. All of it.

And they got more and more into it.

They didn't care that I was a thief. They didn't hate me because of it.

I wondered what I had done to deserve good friends like them.

"If we could go straight, we would," I said, "but none of us are old enough for legitimate jobs. Jerry has an apprenticeship lined up for next September. We're hoping that, coupled with Leah's hacking skills will be enough to tick them over. We've saved up a lot of money for Micah's health."

It was such a relief to tell them.

"Ok, so you actually convinced this man that he was going to go to jail?" said Ronnie with a laugh. She rolled around on the floor gasping for breath, after I told them one of my more hilarious tricks.

"We had to!" I said, "It as the only way to get the money."

"Oh, that is genius," said Gwen laughing, wiping a tear from her eyes. Then she threw a cursory glance at her computer and then she went over.

"Everything alright hon?" I asked. We were sat on the floor.

"My room is empty," said Gwen, "we should go now."

"What?" I asked confused.

"To have a look in their room for any proof Marley is up to something," said Ronnie.

"Oh, ok," I said, "Are you certain Gwen."

Undercover Thief

"Dead sure."

We left the HQ and headed straight to her room. Marley liked to hang out in the bedroom, and not the common room. She was always there when we weren't in classes. Which had made searching difficult.

We went along to the room and went inside. Gwen was on look out by the door.

"Right Ron, be methodical," I said. I went over to the bed, crouching down and pulling out her suitcases and started searching through. Ronnie was flicking through the draws in her desk.

"So, how much do you make? On average?" asked Ronnie.

"We only do it when we need it Ron."

"I know that, but how much?"

"I have a fair amount in the bank," I admitted.

"How much is a fair amount?"

"Think high," I said simply.

"And how much do get for each of your jobs?"

"It varies from job to job. We're normally happy with a profit of about twenty thousand for a con. Slightly less when we're working a commissioned steal. It depends what it is – we once stole a Raphael from Prague, that earned us a lot more than a mere twenty thousand," I said.

"So that is how you are ahead in manipulation. Because you run so many cons," said Ronnie, "That makes sense. It's such an odd subject to be ahead in."

"Literally lived and breathed it for a large portion of my life," I said, "ok, the cases are clear."

"So is the desk," said Ronnie.

"Wardrobe?" offered Gwen. Ronnie and I went over to her wardrobe and started searching through the draws.

"Are you going to tell you parents?" asked Ronnie tentatively.

"And how do you think they'd take that?" I asked.

"They're your parents, and despite what you think Pam, they do love you."

"Ron, I know that in their weird, super controlling way they do love me. But they would only take that badly."

"But now you can go straight," said Ronnie, "this is your shot."

"But what about Micah?"

"They're handling it ok without you right? And you said that the cost of that was actually coming down. If you have a high amount of money saved up...."

"What about food and things Ron?"

Undercover Thief

"You want to go straight right? Why not go straight here? You won't get anything like this again."

"I know," I said with a sigh, "and I wish I could come here properly, you know. But I just feel like I'm abandoning them by doing that."

"You're not," said Ronnie, "to be fair, if Leah is as good as you say, she could probably get in here when she's old enough."

"And what? Leave Micah to Jerry on his own?"

"I didn't think of that."

"See. Not easy," I replied.

"Ok, this is clean," said Ronnie.

"Ok, so if the phone isn't in here, and it isn't in the alcove, where is it?" asked Gwen.

"Are we missing something?" asked Ronnie.

"I don't know. Perhaps it's in plain sight, or somewhere else. I mean, if you were going to hide something that you didn't want linked back to you, you wouldn't hide it in your room right?"

"Right. So it's not here,"

"No," I said.

"Hi Marley!" said Gwen loudly. I straightened the bed sheet quickly. Ronnie grabbed one of Gwen's many folders from the desk.

"Found it!" she called loudly.

"Oh well done," I said, "Where was it?"

"It slipped down the back," said Ronnie handing it to Gwen.

"Thank you guys," said Gwen trying to play along. She was such a bad liar.

"Hey Marley. See you in class," I said as we left.

"That was close," said Ronnie.

"Could have been closer."

"How?"

"She could have caught us."

Chapter Eighteen

Another week went by. The Christmas exams weren't far away at all now. Barely a week. Gwen was always panicking about them, gripping her set of flash cards like they were a life preserver and carrying them everywhere we went.

The whole class was headed to the science labs for the last lesson of the day. Gwen was babbling on about her own experiment she was running with George and Adam. Apparently, they had made something. I wasn't sure what, because neither Ronnie nor I could decipher the science babble into English.

We walked in and sat at the desks.

"Ok, so, today class, we will be doing a reflux reaction. We will be making aspirin from willow bark. Procedures are on the desk," said Mr Finch, "you'll need lab coats, gloves and goggles. Hair tied back ladies and gents with long hair. Off you go."

I pulled my hair onto the top of my head while Ronnie got a sheet with the experiment on.

"Ok, so we need to crush the willow with a mortar and pestle and put in a pear shaped flask with sulphuric six acid and potassium manganite seven solution."

"I can cut up the bark if you get the acid," I said taking the fresh twigs and stripping the bark.

"Sounds good to me. Oh! Goggles," she said passing me a pair. I put them over my eyes and worked, cutting up the bark first and then crushing it.

"Ok, apparently we need to set up a reflex condenser," said Ronnie showing me the diagram.

"Ok, and that means what exactly?"

"Old fall back?" she asked pointing to where Gwen was doing an experiment with Marley. Marley was just watching bored. I nodded.

"Copy Gwen," I agreed.

"Where are the Bunsen burners again?"

"In the cupboard to the left," I said pointing. I carefully added the willow bark to the pear shaped glass and Ronnie and I set up the equipment.

"Is this right?" asked Ronnie. We looked around.

"Everyone else is doing it like this. We need to run water through it though," I said connecting one rubber tube to the tap.

"Ok. So, let's steal some fire from someone," said Ronnie. She grabbed a splint and borrowed a flame from someone else's Bunsen burner. Soon our reaction was bubbling away. We turned back to the experiment sheet.

"Ok, so how long do we do this for?" I asked.

"Fifteen minutes."

"And what then?"

"Then...not entirely sure if I'm honest," said Ronnie wrinkling her nose, "it says we're supposed to use a dropper pipette to transferred one centimetre cubed of solution to-"

"Ron! Pam!" yelled Gwen. We span around to see the reaction we were stood next to that belonged to Lydia and Cassidy. The mixture of purple acid shot up their condensing tube and squirted out of the top. I dived for their gas tap, turning off the fuel to the Bunsen burner at source. The hot acid stopped spitting everywhere. I went straight to the sink to wash the acid off my skin. Thankfully I had halted the unfolding disaster in its early stages and only a little bit had splashed on me, but it did leave horrid brown stains.

"Miss Torres!" Mr Finch yelled angrily, "that was extremely dangerous!"

"I had to stop the acid going everywhere!"

"No! To leave your experiment unattended like that! You should have been watching it!" he shouted, "Look! There is acid everywhere! Have you seen what you've done?"

"Sir, that wasn't their-," began Cassidy but I put a hand up to stop her. No point both of us going down with the sinking ship.

"You are right, Sir. It's my fault. I should have been watching my experiment," I said.

"You could have caused some serious injury! These acids are corrosive and highly flammable! I am astounded by you! Go to the headmistress's office! How thoughtless can one person?"

"It was an accident sir."

"I highly doubt it! You have a reputation for being deliberately subversive. Come here!" he yelled going to the desk and writing furiously on a piece of paper. Then he handed it to me, "Go to Miss Price's office immediately. And take your bag with you! I don't want to see you again today!"

"Yes sir," I said with a sigh, throwing my goggles and lab coat onto the side. I grabbed my bag from under the desk while everyone was watched in stunned silence.

"Go!" he screamed, when I didn't move fast enough. I kicked the door closed behind me as I went and trudged the familiar path up to the headmistress' office.

I sighed as I saw the big brown door in front of me. Time for another round. I knocked on it.

"Enter," I opened. She looked up and sighed.

Undercover Thief

"What did you do this time?"

"Wasn't watching an experiment," I said walking over and handed her the piece of paper. She unfolded it and looked down at it. Her mouth fell open.

"You filled the room with boiling hot acid!" she said.

"It was an accident," I said.

"Really? I might believe you if you weren't up here so much!" she snapped.

"Wait, I may have an attitude problem but I wouldn't intentionally put anyone in harm's way!"

"And I'm just supposed to believe that! Sit down Miss Torres, I think you and I need to have a little chat!" she shouted. I sighed and sat down, letting my bag slide off my shoulder. Time for another one of our 'chats'. The one sided sort, basically her just yelling at me.

"How could you do this? How? This was so, so incredibly dangerous!"

"It was an accident!"

"You know, I don't understand you," she said standing up, apparently deaf to what I had just said, "Children your age would kill to come here. They would do any and everything to receive an education like this. Something you are throwing it away!"

"I'm not like other children my age!"

321

"You're right! You're much, much more irresponsible! You are a silly, compulsive, foolish, irresponsible girl! You are so full of yourself that you don't stop and look at the other people you are hurting around you! I don't understand it! I don't think I will ever understand it!"

"Good thing you don't have to."

"Miss Torres! Do you think I have time for you? Do you think I enjoy you being here? You are, without a doubt the most difficult student I have ever had the misfortune to walk through my school!"

I didn't move, blink or react in any way. So she just kept rampaging.

"You almost hurt someone today!"

"That was an accident!"

"How can I believe you Miss Torres?" she shouted.

"I've never lied to you."

"But how can I trust that? I almost think you like being in trouble! That you are doing it deliberately! I can't fathom why!"

"Really? You can think of nothing?"

"If it's to do with the methods used to get you here then you need to grow up! The truth of the situation is that you are a child and your parents asked for my help."

Undercover Thief

"Which you didn't have to give."

"Is it that? Is that why you are constantly here! Why you are constantly in trouble?"

"No."

"Then what! Is there a reason?"

"I don't like being told what to do."

"You are a child! You are told what is best for you."

"And you know what is best for me?"

"Yes!"

"I highly doubt that."

"You see! That! That is incredibly rude! I am at my limit with you Miss Torres. At first I hoped that my Ronnie could install some sense in you, but now I want her as far away from you as humanly possible!"

"Then send me away! Move my room! Give me detention for the next seven years!"

"You are a stupid, unintelligent girl!" she shouted, "yes you have brains and you have talent but you waste them! You waste them out of spite! And I can't understand why! Why would you do such a thing?"

"Well why don't you tell me?" I yelled standing up, "Seeing as you have me all figured out?"

"Do not speak to me in that tone!"

"Why not! You're just as human as I am! I have free will! I will speak to you how I like."

"How dare you!"

"Watch me." I hissed.

"You are nothing like your parents! I really thought that you could just be acting up while you settled in! But you've been here almost nine weeks now and you are still acting like a spoiled toddler who was told no!"

"Well maybe that's all I am. A spoiled toddler!"

"I wouldn't be surprised! I am sick and tired of dealing with you! I have tried being nice. I have tried leaving you alone. But apparently none of those things are going to work! So, this time it isn't going to be a detention! It is going to be isolation for the rest of the day!"

"Isolation? So I sit on my own all day? Fine by me!" I snapped.

"You know, you act so above it all Miss Torres, above everyone here. But you are nothing! You're not above anyone! You are a worthless, good for nothing girl!"

"And that's fine by me," I said picking up my bag and making to walk out the door.

Undercover Thief

"There is no place for you in my school Miss Torres! You do not belong here!" I paused at the door. I looked back to where she stood, red faced and leaning against the desk.

Then I turned and walked away.

She was right.

Chapter Nineteen

"Ok, so when you put an alkene in bromine water, it goes colourless?" asked Ronnie as we headed down to dinner the next day.

The day in isolation had seemed to go on for hours and hours. I missed Ronnie and Gwen. I had gotten all my homework done, and the work set by my teachers. Finally, at five, Ronnie and Gwen had come up to see me so we could go down to dinner together.

"Yes, because the double bond breaks and the bromine becomes attached instead. It's an example of an electrophilic addition reaction," said Gwen nodding.

"Ok," said Ronnie sitting down. I took some bread from the centre of the table.

"Hey guys," said Peter.

"Hey man, how you doing?" asked Ronnie.

"Good thanks. How was isolation Pam?"

"I don't recommend it," I said, "but it isn't the worst thing I've done by far."

Undercover Thief

"Hey, if you want to copy my notes you can," he said.

"Thanks," I said.

"I've photocopied all your homework assignments," said Gwen, "and put them on your desk along with the date they're due."

"Thanks Gwen," I said with a laugh.

"You're welcome," she said beaming, not getting my sarcasm.

"Hey Pam," said Cass, "do you want my muffin?"

"No thanks. And you don't need to keep doing nice things for me," I said, "seriously."

"You should have let us own up to what we did," said Lydia for the hundredth time.

"Nah, there's no point. The teachers all hate me as it is, no point having them think less of you," I replied yet again, "don't worry about it."

"I still can't believe my mom gave you isolation," said Ronnie glumly.

"Hey, it wasn't like you gave it to me," I said.

"So, what did you do?" asked Gavin.

"Would you believe I actually did some work?"

"You what? Are you feeling ok?" asked Ian joking, putting a hand on my forehead as if testing my temperature.

"I know right, I must not be well. Anyone up for a card trick?" I asked.

"Oh sure," said Adam grinning.

"Ok, so this one is really cool," I said, "It took me ages to get right. Pick a card."

"Ok."

"Pamela!" yelled my mother bursting into the hall like a fire storm.

"If you still wanted to do something nice for me Cass, you can make them disappear," I muttered quietly turning around to look at my mother. She, Miss Price, my father, and several teachers were marching my way.

"Holy cow, your mom is scary," whispered Gavin.

"What the hell is this?" she shouted, throwing a piece of paper into my hands making the cards spill over the floor. I frowned, turning the paper the right way up and looked at it. It was an account. My account. In an off shore bank. For four hundred thousand pounds.

"What the hell are you doing digging into my finances? Why are you snooping?" I shouted angrily. Ronnie took the paper from me and ogled at the number on the page and showed to Gwen who gasped.

Undercover Thief

"It's not snooping, you're our child! Where on this earth did you get that kind of money!" shouted my mother, "Huh? I have had enough of your evasive attitude! Just tell us."

"Where I got it is my business! You have no right to investigate my private business!"

"How does a fourteen year old girl get her hands on four hundred thousand pounds? And what on earth does she intend to do with it?"

"It's not for me!" I said, "I'm holding it for someone?"

"What? Like your forger friend?" asked my father disparagingly.

"My brother!"

"You don't have a brother!" shouted my mother, "that family isn't real! They're using you!"

"They're more real than you are!"

"Pam! This is not a joke! Why are you in possession of this much money and who for? People with this kind of money can be dangerous!"

"It's none of your business!"

"Yes it is!" my father roared, "For once you are going to answer a question that is asked of you and you are going to do it now!"

I glared at them as they waited for my response. I folded my arms and looked at them calmly.

"No," I said simply.

There was a long pause. The entire place had gone silent. Everyone was watching the heated exchange. The teachers had started to ferry students out but continued to ear wig on the conversation, clearly interested.

"What did you just say to us?"

"I said no."

"Pamela! So help me!" shouted my mother exploding with anger, "what the hell am I going to do with you? You are a stubborn, thoughtless girl! Do you have any idea what this means?"

"There is nothing illegal about having four hundred thousand pounds."

"Pamela! You didn't get this money from us? How did you get it?"

"I earned it."

"Not legally! Pamela! You are going to tell us everything, from start to finish. What the hell are you messed up in? What were you doing in London while you should have been at school?"

I just looked at them.

"Pam! Tell us now!"

Undercover Thief

I said nothing.

"You stupid girl!" shouted my father, "Don't you see we're trying to help you?"

"I didn't ask for your help."

"You think that this other family love you Pam? Let me tell you something. They don't love you!" shouted my mother, "not like we do. Not like we care."

I just stared at them and refrained from hitting her in the face. How dare she talk about my family like that? How dare she start screaming at me in front of my new friends and class mates! I was so upset that I was literally shaking with rage.

"Pamela! What the hell have we done to deserve this attitude from you huh? What the hell did we do?"

"YOU ABANDONDED ME TO DIE!" I screamed at them.

They actually took a few steps back.

"You abandoned me!" I repeated, loudly, "On my own! I was nine years old! And I had nobody!" I pulled out my iPod, "You want to look at a bloody bank statement? Here is a freaking bank statement. That's your bank account! The one you left with Nana and me so she could look after us. Take a good look!" I thrust it into their hands.

"That number there is zero! Do you see it? It hasn't changed in the last six years! It's empty! Empty for the last six years! You left me alone, in the middle of London, with no money! None at all! I couldn't afford heating; I couldn't even afford to eat! How was I supposed to go to school? I was being home schooled remember? The tutors left when the money stopped. You need a 'responsible adult' to sign you into a proper school, something I didn't have. Anyway I had more pressing things to do with my time like trying to ring through to you!

"I lost count of all the times I called you! The nights after nights I spent crying myself to sleep. The times I talked myself hoarse wishing on every single star in the sky that you would come home and make the pain of hunger in my stomach go away! Have you ever been that hungry? So hungry that the pain in your stomach stops you sleeping? I prayed that you would come and help me!

"But you didn't come! Nobody came! I finally realised there was no one coming to save me! So, when you finally show your faces again, after I had managed to fix my life so that I was happy, you want to know why I'm not jumping up and down with joy and kissing your feet? After what you did to me, after the way you abandoned me you're lucky you get a single word out of me!

"So you don't get to tell me that what I do is wrong! You don't get to tell me that I'm stupid, or that I'm stubborn! Call me thoughtless all you like because you know what? I learnt every ounce of that from you! If you don't like who I am, then tough luck, it's your fault! Because the way I grew up, the way I survived on my own, who I am and the people I met, it's all your fault!"

Undercover Thief

"You don't get to tell me that you care about me! You don't get to make judgements about the people that I have come to love! Because the reason that I even met them is your fault! When I was starving on the street, they gave me food when they barely had any of their own! When I was cold, they gave me a hug to try and warm me up, because they were cold too! When I was feeling alone and upset, they let me live with them so I didn't have to be alone anymore! Every single time I have ever needed someone, they were there! Never, once, have they ever failed me! They were there and you weren't! They did it because they love me! Because we are a family, and that is all that a family is! People that look out for each other. You weren't there!"

I furiously wiped the stream of wet tears falling down my cheeks away with me sleeve in a futile attempt. More tears replaced them instantly.

"Oh Pam," stammered my mother through tears of her own, a hand over her mouth in her grief, "We had no idea that the money had run out!"

"It was your job to know!" I said quietly, "It was your job to know what was happening! You were supposed to look after me but all you've ever done is let me down!"

"Pam, we're so, so sorry," said my father, his voice was strained, his own cheeks looked wet and his face was ashen, "We're here now! I promise, I swear it to you, it will never, ever happen again. I won't let it."

"People don't change," I said, sniffing, just looking at him with raw emotion on my face, "People never change. If they let you down once, they'll do it again."

"No Pam, no, please don't say that. We're here now. We can look after you again, like we're supposed to," whispered my mother thought her tears.

"That ship has sailed! Six years ago! I have my own life now! My own family! People that do the job you were supposed to do, and they did it without being asked. They just did it. Because they care about me! They can tell you what I got for my thirteenth birthday, they know the date I got the chicken pox, and they can even tell you why I won't go near a strawberry ice-cream even if you paid me! They know me! Everything about me! And they care!"

"We care too Pam. We do," sobbed my mother.

"You don't get it do you? I don't want you anymore!" I shouted, punctuated with ripping sobs of pain as I finally voiced my pent up anger and fear and hurt.

And with that, I pushed through the crowd of teachers that had gathered around the table where my entire class sat in the otherwise empty main hall, and ran away.

"Pam! Pammie!" yelled Ronnie and Gwen scrambling to their feet and running after me.

I didn't stop running, as I ran all the way up to our room. I threw open the door, standing in the room, not sure what to do now. My brain wasn't really working. Ronnie was only moments behind me.

"Oh my goodness Pammie," she said hugging me as I dissolved further into tears. Gwen came in slightly behind and out of breath, and hugged me too. I fell to the floor as my knees gave way and I cried like I have never cried before.

"That was brutal," whispered Gwen gently, "I'm so sorry."

"They needed to know. I had to tell them," I sobbed, "I couldn't keep it in anymore."

"We know Pam, we know," said Ronnie, "you're right. They needed to know."

"This looks like we need the big guns Ronnie. None of the frozen yoghurt, ice-cream all the way," said Gwen.

"You got it," she said getting up and running off. Gwen just let me cry myself out on her shoulder. She sat me, with my back against my bed and handed me a box of tissues.

"I'll be back in a moment," she said and went over to my desk while I dried my eyes. I sniffed and took it deep ragged breaths. I had told them. I had told them everything. I had done it. And now that I had told them, I had permission to cry.

Cry over everything that I had ever done, cry over everything that had happened to me. Everything that I had been holding back for all those years, the anger and the sadness and the fear, it was all coming out at once in one ugly explosion of emotion.

Then Gwen came back with my laptop. On it was Jerry and Leah, looking at me worried. Gwen sat with me and hugged me again while I spoke with Jerry and Leah.

"Hey there Pam, Gwen says you had a major fight with your parents," said Leah gently. I nodded and burst into even more tears.

"Oh Pammie," sighed Jerry, I knew he wanted nothing more than to reach through the screen and make whatever was hurting me stop, "This is a good thing."

"Good? How is it a good thing?"

"They need to know what they did. They deserve to know how much pain and suffering they caused you."

"Yeah honey, this is good. Keeping all that bottled up for much longer was going to kill you, I'm pretty sure." said Leah.

"But I don't care," I sobbed, "I don't care about them! I'm over it! Why am I crying again?"

"Because Pammie, when you tell yourself you don't care, when you *have* to tell yourself that you don't care, it's a lie," said Leah, "and you're the best liar I know. You can even lie to yourself and believe it."

"They were looking into my accounts," I babbled through my sobs, "they found all the money I have saved."

"I'll move that right away honey," said Leah pulling over her tablet.

"Is that what sparked this thing off?" asked Jerry.

"They wanted to know where I got it."

"How much is in that account anyway?" asked Leah.

"Couple of hundred thousand."

"Oh, so it's your savings account," said Leah pursing her lips, "yeah, that would spark a few questions."

"Did you tell them?" asked Jerry.

"No! They have badges. They would put me in prison."

"I don't think they would Pam," said Jerry, "they love you."

"Love? They don't love me," I blanched at the very idea. Love? Me! Impossible.

"Yes, they do. You told us they didn't know your grandmother died. Did they know the money was gone?" that was when Ronnie came back, panting a little. Her hands were filled with two tubs of ice cream and three spoons.

"So, I have cookie crumble and mint chocolate," she said passing me a tub with a spoon.

"Pam, did they know about the money running out?" asked Jerry again.

"No."

"So, maybe they did care. But they didn't know they needed to be home. They didn't know that you needed them."

"Like that's an excuse!"

"It's not one. You're right Pam. You shouldn't have to tell them that they were needed, not when you're nine years old and in that kind of situation," said Leah, agreeing, "But Pam, you have parents that love you. We don't have that."

"We have us! We have our family!" I sniffed, "we're a family."

"And we'll never stop being your family. You're just including a few more people. Give your parents a break. You know, now this is out in the open, this is a chance to heal this chasm wide divide between the three of you."

"They want me to never talk to you again," I said.

"They don't know us," said Jerry shrugging, "and we know that you'll never turn your back on us. You're a Sklar, even if you don't have our blood."

"Yeah Pammie, besides if you don't talk to us we'll come down to that school and knock on the front door. You know us," said Leah trying to make a joke. I chuckled slightly through my tears, because that was exactly the kind of thing that they would do.

"That's another thing Pam," sighed Jerry, "we think that you should stay at the school."

"What?" I whispered, not quite able to believe he had said the words.

"The opportunity you have there...it's incredible. Pam, you shouldn't throw that away. Think about what it could mean in the future."

"But what about you guys? I don't want to leave you."

"You're not going to leave us Pammie," soothed Leah, "But think about it, you have a way to go straight and in a way that is completely your style. You might never have this opportunity again. And it's good for you. In the future, it could be good for all of us."

"You know that you always have us. We're right here for you, as always," said Jerry.

"Thank you," I sniffed, "I...I'll think about it."

"Of course, it's your decision and we'll back you whatever you decide to do. We still have your birthday presents here. You can open them when you see us at Christmas."

"Yeah. Yeah, I'll come home and see you at Christmas," I promised, thinking about how I would ditch my parents at the airport if I had to.

"Ok. Chin up," said Leah. I nodded and gave a meek smile.

"I love you guys," I said.

"And we love you," said Jerry. Then the call ended.

"Feel better?" asked Ronnie. I nodded.

"I love you guys too," I said hugging them. Ronnie laughed and Gwen nodded.

"We've got your back. Forever."

***

We spent the rest of the evening eating ice cream and talking. They didn't talk about my parents. They steered clear of the topic. They talked about how one girl in the year above had had a really bad nose job. How two boys in their final year had accidentally managed to knock each other out in PE. Girl talk.

And eventually I had crashed out on the bed and Gwen had gone back to her room. It was the middle of the night. I woke up when I heard the door opening. I didn't move. I didn't turn around. Ronnie did however.

"Mrs Torres?" She asked rubbing her eyes.

"Sorry to wake you Ronnie. Go back to sleep."

"Yeah. That's going to happen!" said Ronnie sarcastically and sitting up in her bed, "what are you doing here?"

"I just....needed to see her. Check she was ok."

"She's not," said Ronnie simply.

"I know. And it's our fault."

"It is," said Ronnie.

"You must think I'm an awful person Ronnie. Her father and I, we're undercover in Pakistan. And then our job suddenly turned into something so much bigger. We couldn't leave it. And we had no communication with the outside world. I would have gone insane if Gordon wasn't there with me......but I never intended to hurt my daughter. Not in any way shape or form."

"I don't think badly of you Mrs Torres, if you're worried about that. This is just a really sucky situation. And Pam's right, it was your job to know. But you didn't and you had no way of knowing what had happened. You didn't know you were needed at home."

"She hates me....doesn't she?"

"No," said Ronnie, "If she hated you, you wouldn't need to ask me. She's not exactly subtle. She's blunt as a sledgehammer. But, I find it rather refreshing. She says things how they are, always honest to the point of brutality."

"Yes, I've noticed that."

"I have a theory about that. I think one of the reasons is because she's afraid, subconsciously, that things won't actually be what they appear. I think it's one of the reason she's trying to push you away. She thinks you'll leave her again."

"Never," she almost growled, "never again."

"I know it's not my place Mrs Torres, but........Pam has told me rather a lot.....and I mean a lot. And, some of the stuff....there is serious stuff in her past. She's overcome loads."

"I don't suppose I can bribe you into telling me what they are?"

"Not a chance. No way am I giving up my girl."

"I knew I always liked you Ronnie."

"My point is that you can't change what happened. The events in your life are what shapes you as a person. And there have been a few....defining moments in Pam life. But....and I know I am asking for a detention.....you keep doing this."

"Doing what?"

"She's grown up without someone looking over her shoulder and guiding her. And you're a little bit.......restricting. Trying to control what she does, acting angry or upset when she does something different. You are trying to change who she is fundamentally. She is who she is. She's unique...you can't talk to her and deal with her like you would a normal person – she hasn't had that upbringing. You need to approach her with an open mind."

"I didn't want that life for her! I didn't want her to think she didn't have love in her life. I'm terrified that something terrible has happened to her."

"Hope you don't mind me saying, but that is not the way it looks to us. What were you expecting to come home to after six years exactly?"

"Ronnie....is she safe?"

"You can see her."

"No. I mean....was she safe. These people she knew back in London. You know who they are?"

"Oh yeah, Mrs Torres. And she's right, they do love her. They're really nice people, just like Pam. We spent the evening with them on video phone-don't ask how. They were trying to cheer Pammie up and get her to stop crying."

"Are they good people?"

"Yeah Mrs Torres. They are, the same way Pammie is. They spent the entire time trying to convince Pam it was finally time to forgive you and try to heal the break between you. They want her to be healthy and happy. They want nothing more than that."

"I feel like a monster. I saw that money and panicked. Where does a girl her age come by that kind of money? Surely not any legitimate job!"

"Mrs Torres, what jobs are there for nine year old girls?" reasoned Ronnie gently.

"You're right. Of course she got it illegally."

"You're not a monster. Only human. And we can't do it all. We like to think we can, but the truth is we can't. When we slip up, we have to accept it and try to fix it."

"Pammie doesn't want to fix it."

"Yes she does. But every time you have a conversation with her you are too quick to judge. Tell me, have you ever stopped and just tried to accept? Ok. She's not perfect. But do you know what I see when I look at her? I see freedom, I see kindness, I see goodness. She has such a big heart. I see some fierce loyalty – I've never seen someone so willing to fight in the corner of someone she loves. I see someone who's been hurt and is afraid of getting hurt again. Someone who it intelligent enough to question why things are the way they are. I see someone who never, ever takes things at face value. She sees the world in a completely new light, and it's fun and happy......"

"I've never seen that."

"You never tried. Fundamentally, she'd a wonderful person. And once you realise that, the rest doesn't matter so much."

"When did you become so wise then?"

"Well, you taught me how to observe the world. I'm merely stating what I see."

"Thank you Ronnie. You can go back to sleep. I'll go now."

"See you Mrs Torres. Whatever you do, don't give up."

"Thank you Ronnie. Now I believe you have a double history class in the morning. You'll need your energy," she said and left.

Chapter Twenty

The next morning I woke up and I was groggy. I felt exhausted and completely dehydrated. I had a head ache that could split wood. I groaned and got up switching off my alarm.

"Hey," said Ronnie.

"Ow," I complained.

"Need some pain killers?" She asked. I nodded as she went to her draw and found some.

"You slept in your clothes," she said.

"Oops."

"Your mother came by while you were asleep," said Ronnie handing me the paracetamol.

"I know," I said.

"You do? You didn't say anything."

"I had nothing to say."

Undercover Thief

"You ok?"

"Yeah. I'm good," I said with a small smile.

I swallowed the pills and drained a glass of water before climbing into the shower. The hot water helped relax my aching muscles. I didn't want to leave, but I snapped off the water and climbed out, wrapping a towel around me.

I picked out my usual, black jeans, ankle boots, leather jacket. I pulled my hair into a pony tail and sat down to try and cover up the bags under my eyes with makeup. Normally I didn't bother, but today I decided, I could use it.

"I'm so hungry!" said Ronnie.

"After all the ice cream we ate last night?" I asked astonished.

"Ice cream isn't food! It's like a snack! And I'm craving waffles!"

"Craving? Oh dear. We should go and feed you then," I said linking my arms through hers. I slipped my bag over my shoulder and we hurried off downstairs. Gwen caught up with us on the way down.

"Hello!" she said, "so, I don't think I can eat a single thing for breakfast!"

"Madness!" said Ronnie.

"Just because I actually have a limit of food I can eat? Not all of us have hollow legs!" said Gwen. I laughed.

"But you're too skinny," said Ronnie poking at Gwen's ribs.

"I'm perfectly fine," said Gwen unimpressed by the poking and trying to dodge. So Ronnie chased her. Gwen squealed as she ran, trying to bat away Ronnie's prodding fingers.

"No!" she squealed as she ran past Mr Compton on the stairs almost knocking his folder from his hands.

"This is not a playground ladies!" called Mr Compton.

"Sorry sir," they replied in unison. Then Mr Compton nodded absentmindedly and moved on. Gwen jabbed a finger in Ronnie's ribs as pay back. Ronnie slapped her hand away just in time as Mr Compton stopped and turned back around just as I reached the bottom of the stairs.

"Ah! Miss Torres, I have that essay you wrote to return to you," he said opening his brief case.

"Oh?" I asked, and then cleared my throat as it was thick.

"Very, very impressive work, Miss Torres. I think you have writing essays cracked," he said producing it and handing it back to me.

"Oh! Thanks," I said looking over my work and liking the large amount of red ticks and the positive comments I saw scrawled on it.

Undercover Thief

"As always, such a unique angle to take on it. I never thought about it like that. I swear I'm going to have to make a folder of all your essays and keep them. I hope you don't mind?"

"No. If you think they're that good!" I said with a laugh as I took my essay back, "it's just how I thought about the question."

"I like your idea there, manipulating your way into someone's office. You make it sound easy, and it sounds like you have had experience."

"I know people who do that sort of thing," I said with a shrug. Ronnie and Gwen grinned and glanced at each other.

"Well, they sound like interesting people."

"I don't know any other kind," I answered. He laughed.

"Of course you don't," said Mr Compton with a chuckle, "I still haven't seen you at Manipulation Club."

"Maybe after Christmas....if I'm still here," I said shrugging, "I'm not doing so well in my other subjects and.....well.....I'll probably fail some of the end of year exams and then I'll be out."

"Oh! Surely not!" said Mr Compton frowning, "what subjects?"

"Science," I admitted, "Law....always had a problem with law."

"Hmmm.....well, do your best. I will keep my fingers cross then," said Mr Compton walking away.

"Ok. When did you start doing extra work?" asked Gwen taking the essay from my hands and reading it.

"In detention," I said.

"You sly dog!" Ronnie nudged me as we went over to a table.

"Not really. It's just some extra reading."

"This is third year stuff!" Gwen said, her eyes glued to the page.

"So I'm told. And how do you know the third year syllabus?" I asked pouring myself a cup of tea while Ronnie vanished off to get a cooked breakfast from the hatch. I stuck to my usual three pieces of toast.

"I looked ahead, I like being prepared," she said handing it back.

"Finished memorising it?" I asked putting it away.

"Oh please, photographic memory or not, I don't need to memorise your essay."

"Won't stop you trying," said Adam coming over with George and sitting next to us with plates piled high with food.

Undercover Thief

"So, you guys ready for our pop quiz in history?" George asked. I groaned and stole one of the five hash browns from his plate. He gave me a grumpy look.

"No! I didn't revise at all last night!" Gwen said, "I've only spent time over the weekend and the night before last and-"

"Gwen! You've done more than the rest of us! I'm probably going to have to wing most of it," I said.

"But we are so close to the Christmas exams!"

"I haven't even started thinking about those yet."

"Don't worry! We can do some work together, I'm sure, get you up to speed. We can get a revision timetable made for you and I can help you and-"

"Whoa Gwen, allow the girl to breath," said Ronnie coming back over, "Pam can do what she wants. Revise or not revise."

"OK, so, who do you think will come out top?" We all just looked at Gwen.

"What!" She protested.

"I'm not even going to answer that question," I said, "except to say that if we have a PE exam, bagsy I get to partner Gwen!"

"Hey!"

"No offence love, but if I'm paired with you I'll look so much better than I actually am."

"Just because you say the words 'no offence', doesn't mean no offence is taken."

"Gwen, we love you," said Ronnie, "But your hand eye coordination is exactly zero."

"Um....ok...yeah....that's true."

"But you can hack a NASA satellite. So, you know, don't worry about it," I said tearing my toast in half and taking a bite.

"Speaking of exams, has anyone got a clue what economics is going to be on?" asked Peter.

"Greece," said Ronnie, "I mean, what else would it be on at the moment?"

"Ronnie's right," said Adam, "I'd put money on it."

"You'd put money on anything," said Gavin sitting down.

"Yeah Adam, you don't have much attachment to your dollars," said Trevor sitting with him.

"Well, that narrows down what we have to revise," nodded Peter.

"Well, it didn't take rocket science to figure it out," said George.

Undercover Thief

"I know, I can do rocket science," muttered Peter.

"You might be the only one," I said with a sigh.

"Aw Pam, you'll do fine," said Ronnie, "don't be so glum."

"If you paid a little bit more attention in class you'd probably find it easier," said Lydia.

"I know, I dug my own hole and now I have to sit in it and all."

"What?" asked Lydia laughing, "I've heard the 'made my own bed' expression but a hole?"

"Not heard it before?"

"No!"

"Um, Pam," said Ronnie clearing her throat.

"What?" I asked.

"Incoming," she whispered and my mood instantly hit the floor.

"Hi Pam," that was my father's voice. And my mother was probably with him. I set down my piece of toast and turned to look at them.

"What?"

"Can we have a word in private?"

"Oh, so now you want to talk privately? You weren't so concerned with private last night," I sniffed.

"You're right. We're sorry. We were in the wrong and we shouldn't have done that," said my father, "We let our fear rule our actions. We didn't think it through."

"Please? We just want to talk," said my mother.

"......alright then," I muttered with a sigh, getting up.

"I'll save you some food," reassured Ronnie.

"Ta," I said as I left to go with them. We walked outside of the hall into the empty corridor.

"Pam, we realised that we may have been acting....rather hastily considering what happened," said my mother, "considering the.....complexity of the situation."

"Listen, you can stop. I'm over it. Honestly, I'm fine now. We can go our separate ways and forget all of this happened," I said turning to go back to the hall.

"No! Pammie," she said grabbing my arm, "we desperately want to.....repair this. We want to fix this family. We want to be the parents you deserve. We want to know you," said my mother.

"We realise that we haven't been fair. We realise why you have a lot of justified resentment towards us. But we want to try to move past that, be a proper family again," said my father.

Undercover Thief

"I'm not really traditional family material," I muttered, "I'm a bit broken."

"Pam, we want you," said my mother, "we don't want anyone else, we want you. And if you're broken, let us help to put you back together. Please?"

"Listen, guys, you don't have to pretend for me," I said.

"We're not pretending," said my father, "We want to take care of you. Look after you."

"I....I just...."

"I have to go on a mission in a few days," said my father, "So your mother and I wanted to take you out on Saturday. What do you think? The three of us can go to town and spend some quality time together."

"Last time that ended badly," I said.

"This time it won't. We'll do our absolute best to be understanding," said my mother with an earnest nod. The words that Jerry and Leah had said drifted back to me. I did have parents. They were trying to make amends.

I would follow my family's advice. They'd never lead me astray before.

"Alright, Saturday," I said, "I'll be down here at ten."

"Excellent! We'll see you then poppet," said my father as I turned and walked away. I went back over to the table and sat down.

"How did it go?" Asked Ronnie.

"I think I just got myself into a family outing," I said shaking my head.

"That's good!" said Gwen, "you'll enjoy yourself."

"Just keep in mind, murder is bad," said Ronnie.

"Her parents are the Torres. I'd like to see Pam try," said Peter with a laugh.

"I did hit my father around the face one," I said.

"On purpose?"

"No. I accidentally hit someone around the face," I said sarcastically rolling my eyes, "I'm not Gwen!"

"Hey!"

"That should be a class saying!" Ronnie teased.

"No!" Gwen protested.

"I'm not Gwen. I like it!"

***

Undercover Thief

Saturday came around way too quickly for my liking. I had called Jerry and told them this was what I was doing. And they all said I was doing the right thing. They were wonderfully supportive. So were Gwen and Ronnie.

It was a chilly November morning, as I walked down the stairs to where my parents were already waiting. They smiled as I came into view.

"Hi darling, ready to go?" asked my mother. I nodded, shoving my hands into my pockets, just for something to do.

"Shall we go to the car?" suggested my father.

I followed them out, down the steps to where there was a car waiting.

"So, what do you want to do? We can go bowling, get something to eat?" said my mother as I got into the car.

"Don't mind."

"Why don't we go to the park? Just go for a walk," suggested my father.

"That sounds nice? Pam?"

"Yeah. Sure."

"Excellent." The car pulled away from the school and soon we were speeding down open roads towards the town.

I knew the moment we were out of range of the scramblers because my phone went absolutely crazy.

"Forty one missed calls!" I gasped groaning.

"Is that bad?" asked my mother.

"I was expecting it to be worse," I admitted scrolling through the list of people I had missed contact from. Most was from friends. Most had tried about five times each. I sent them all apology texts. There were a few unknowns. They were probably clients.

"Pam?" asked my mother hesitantly.

"Yeah?" I asked looking up.

"Is everything ok?" she asked.

"Oh yeah, mind if I make a small call?" I asked as I was dialling the number.

"Um, guess not," she replied looking to my father.

"Thanks," I said hitting call and holding the phone to my ear. Milo picked up.

"My my, is that my Pammie?"

"Hey Milo, it's a long time since I heard your voice. How's business your end?"

"I'm good. It's you I'm worried about kid."

"Me? Don't worry about me Milo, I'm fine."

"Really? I heard you were kidnapped by your parents and they'd taken you across the Atlantic."

Undercover Thief

"They did," I said rolling my eyes, "long story. You need to stop sending business my way. Send it to Jerry. I'm out of play for a little while."

"For how long?"

"Don't know. It's beginning to look longer than I was first thinking."

"Hang on, you found a way to go straight didn't you? I know that what you kids have been wanting to do."

"I'm not sure yet," I said honestly, "but I need you to direct business to Jerry."

"I don't have his number."

"I'll send him by tomorrow. I know they have an opening about now."

"I have a client that's eager to acquire a painting."

"How much are they offering?"

"One hundred and fifty?"

"And our price is two hundred thousand."

"As per usual, pushing the boat out. I'll let them know."

"What are we dealing with?"

"Private collection. In Manchester."

"Do I need to be concerned?"

"No. This is an easy job. I bet I could case the place myself. Hence I sent them your way."

"Thanks. Let Jerry know I've called and made the deal."

"Will do."

"Excellent. Always a pleasure working with you."

"And you kid."

"Until the next time," I said and hung up.

"Um Pam?" I looked to see my mother.

"Yeah?"

"Two hundred thousand? Pounds?" she asked hesitantly.

"Well, I didn't make four hundred thousand pounds in six years at a pound a go," I said. She bit her lip.

"Ok, so tell us more about yourself," said my father, "what kind of music do you like listening to?"

"Well.....anything really. If it has a good beat behind it."

"Anything in particular?"

"Well, I went to a Muse concert. That was cool. And a Paramore concert. Jerry got me the tickets for my birthday last year," I said as we got to the town. I was texting Jerry, letting him know about my conversation with Milo.

"That's sounds fun," said my father, "so would you say you're a fan?"

"Of Paramore? For certain. But I like all kinds of music," I said as he found somewhere to park. We got out of the car and I followed their lead towards the park.

"That's lovely. Do you play?"

"No. Don't have the time for that," I said with a laugh.

"Why not?"

"Working. Always working," I said, "had to put food on the table somehow."

"But you couldn't always be working."

"Well, if I wasn't working I was learning languages or reading. Learning things for the next job....I'd have loved to learn music but I just.....well there are never enough hours in the day."

"Now that we can agree with," said my mother.

"Plus, TV is really good now."

"That is true," said my father nodding, "what do you watch?"

"I have missed watching Doctor Who actually," I said, "I am pretty sure at Christmas all I'm going to be doing is sitting on the couch with Netflix and a big bowl of popcorn."

"I've missed almost all of the new series on the TV. Are they good?"

"I'm a David Tenant girl, but I did enjoy Matt Smith too," I said with a laugh.

"Isn't there a new one?"

"Capaldi? Not sure. Haven't seen enough of him yet."

"I think it'll be nice to have an older doctor. Like before, in the original series," said my father, "I remember watching those when I was a kid."

"I've never watched Doctor Who," said my mother, "what is it?"

"Did she just say that?" I teased, "and you married her?"

My father laughed, but my mother didn't look amused so he hurried to placate her.

"It's about a thousand year old alien that travels through space and time in a police box from the nineteen sixties," said my father. The look on my mother's face was priceless.

Undercover Thief

"I guess when you explain it like that, it's a bit mad," said my father with a chuckle.

"It sounds mad," said my mother, "you're not normally into that kind of sci-fi thing Gordon."

"Well, Doctor Who is the exception. It's a part of being British," said my father, "ah, here we go. The park."

We walked into the park. There were children playing, people walking, enjoying the morning. There was a lazy little river running through the centre. Joggers, who looked determined to keep running, even if they had to run over small children. A typical park.

"It's lovely," said my mother who pulled on her leather gloves to keep her fingers warm. It was a very cold morning.

"Yeah," I said wishing I had thought to bring a coat with me, thankful I was wearing a woolly hat. A football strayed over, followed by a very red and out of breath little boy. I kicked it up, caught it, and threw it back.

"Thanks!" he called running off.

"What's that?" I asked. They followed my gaze.

"It looks like a fair," said my mother, "Shall we go and take a look?"

"Oh they're all tricks," I said with a laugh, "want to go and break a few?"

"Sure," said my father with a laugh.

We walked over. There was live music playing, kids with parents running around, groups of friends with big sticks of candy floss. It was all very cliché.

"Knock down all the bottles and get a prize!" called a vendor who picked me out of the crowd. I smiled and pulled on my purse.

"How much?" I asked.

"A dollar."

"Oh. I only have sterling," I said, "sorry. I lost all my US currency in poker on Friday."

"You play poker?" asked my mother.

"Yeah, I taught the guys in my year to play, and Friday is poker night."

"You taught them to gamble?"

"No, I taught them how to card count first," I said, "poker just sort of...happened."

"I'm afraid I only take US currency," said the stall owner.

"I got it Pam," said my father pulling out his own wallet, "swap you."

"Current exchange rate is about one to one point five," I said handing him a tenner. He handed me back fifteen.

"And you just have that off the top of your head?"

"I take economics at school remember," I said setting down a dollar on the table. I picked up three of the balls.

"So, know how to beat this game?" asked my mother. The vendor heard that and did not look pleased.

"Sure do. They're weighted at the bottom," I said, and threw the ball at the pyramid of bottles, three on the bottom row. I hit the middle of the three. The rest of the bottles came crashing down, except the other two which were holding up the tower. I threw again. One more bottle to go. I threw again. I hit.

"See," I said.

"Well, the little lady is quite the throw," said the vendor annoyed, "pick a prize."

"That one," I said pointing to a toy cat thing that wasn't huge. He handed it to me and we walked away.

"Do you know tricks for all of them?" asked my father.

"No," I said, "like that one. You just have to be a damn good shot." I pointed to a stall where you had to hit the moving bunnies and ducks with huge guns.

"Well, let's give it a go," said my father walking over.

"Ok, I get the feeling you guys are good shots, but I haven't held a gun in my life. Let alone fired one or hit a moving target," I said as we went over.

"I'll give you a quick lesson now if you want," he offered.

"I don't like guns," I said, "steer well clear of them. Nasty things."

"Yeah, they are. But incredibly useful when someone is firing at you," said my mother as we got to the stall.

"When do you start guns? Third year?" asked my father looking to my mother for confirmation. She nodded. My father picked up the huge gun and raised it to eye level.

"I haven't held something like this for ages," he said. I rolled my eyes.

"Just take the shot dad," I said.

"Alright, alright," he said. He hit five out of five bulls-eyes.

"Pick a prize sir," said the vendor, looking annoyed. Huh. Annoying these small time, almost legal, con artists was fun.

"That one," said my father pointing to the huge white fluffy bear.

Undercover Thief

"Um no, we cannot fit that in the car, and could you imagine getting that up to the school?" said my mother.

"Ok, which one do you want?" asked my father.

"The watch?" offered my mother.

"It's a dud," I said, "it'll be a five pound thing at Asda dressed up to look like it's worth more."

"Well then, that," said my father pointing at a five dollar voucher. He took it and we walked off.

"Let me guess, the expiration date is next week," I said. He turned it over and started reading.

"Well, I'll buy a coffee with it now then."

We spent about an hour walking around the fair, playing the different games and looking at all the stools. We stopped by the live music. It wasn't at all bad. I watched while my father went to buy a coffee for himself and mum. Then I heard crying. I looked around to see a little girl in tears because she hadn't won a prize.

I walked over and crouched down.

"Hey. I have a small problem I think you can help me with. See, I can't keep this because I have to go back to school soon. Do you think you can look after it for me?" I asked handing it to her. The little girl grinned wide and cuddled the grubby toy cat close. Her mother smiled and mouth thank you. I turned and walked back to where my parents were watching the group that were playing.

"That was a nice thing you did," said my mother without looking at me.

"What? Oh. Well, I didn't really want it," I said shrugging.

"Ok," she said with a small smile.

"Sure you don't want anything Pam?" asked my father.

"Dead sure," I said, "although I could use finding somewhere to change up my cash."

"Um, well, I don't know where you could do that. The bank?"

"Mind if we head up that way?"

"No, let's go," said my mother.

"I have a few questions," I said, "and you can say nothing if you want."

"Alright, what is it poppet?"

"First one, why Victoria? Why not the King George?"

"That's a very simple answer," said my mother smiling, "I chose the Victoria because that's where I was trained and that's where Sally was headmistress and they had a job opening."

"Would you have preferred one of the other two?" asked my father.

Undercover Thief

"Well, I was just wondering why I wasn't at the King George, in Britain. Why fly me all the way to America, but I guess that's a fair reason," I said.

"Any more questions?" asked my mother.

"This one might be a bit obvious but where were you for six years?"

"Ah! That!" said my father, exchanging a look with my mother. They seemed to have an entire conversation in a look. That was annoying.

"We're not really supposed to tell you much," said my mother apologetically, "need to know basis."

"I'm your daughter," I reminded them.

"National security poppet," said my father shrugging.

"Ok, well, can I know a country?"

"We were in Pakistan," said my mother, "We didn't mean to be away for as long as we were. It was only supposed to be a couple of weeks."

"And weeks turned into years?"

"It was a lot more complicated than we had believed before," said my father, "I...it got a lot deeper and a lot more dangerous and we got sucked into it."

"Oh....okay."

"Yeah?"

"I guess."

"I would have given anything to come back Pammie," said my mother putting a hand on my arm, "but there were a lot of lives at stake."

"Including ours," added my father. I nodded and kicked the floor.

"Never been to Pakistan," I said lightly.

"I'm put off ever going back," said my father with a laugh.

"Any more questions dear?" asked my mother.

"Can we go somewhere a little warmer? I'm getting a bit cold," I said.

"Sure, let's go into town. Maybe we'll see something else we can do."

"Cool," I said shrugging.

Chapter Twenty One

I was slowly beginning to warm up. We walked into the town. We had spent a lot of time shopping, looking at things. Mum had decided to buy me a coat, because I didn't think to bring one with me.

"You know," said my father, "we still have your birthday presents that you never opened."

"Really?" I asked with a small laugh, "I would have thought you'd just charity shop those."

"No! Never. They're yours," said my mother.

We were sat down outside a café in the centre of the town, eating a lunch. Now that I had a coat, it was ok to sit outside and watch the normal people walking past. It was almost comical that they didn't spot the two superspy parents and their criminal daughter.

"Well, thanks," I said with a laugh as I popped another chip into my mouth and chewed.

"So, is school getting any easier for you?"

"A bit. Gwen and Ron have been really big helps. Actually, I should probably get them something as a thank you for that. They've helped me catch up and get into the swing of things I guess."

"That's really nice of them," said my mother, "Ronnie and Gwen are great girls. Really talented."

"Gwen almost killed herself with a paper clip once," I said giving my mother an odd look, "the girl is a danger magnet. She can turn the tiniest thing into a deadly weapon for her own destruction."

My father burst out laughing at that and my mother's mouth turned up in a smile.

"Yes....I had noticed that she was a little clumsy."

"Little? I'm thinking we need a new word to describe Gwe-"

I stopped in what I was saying at my eye caught something. It was a man, a homeless man. He was sat under a bus stop; someone had just thrown him a dirty look, and kicked his bag away.

I sighed, remembering when I had been on the street. He must be freezing, and hungry. Today was so cold. My mother had bought me a coat....his coat had holes in it.

"Pam? Is everything ok?" asked my mother gently.

"Can....can you guys give me twenty minutes? I'll be right back," I said getting up.

Undercover Thief

"Sure poppet," said my mother.

I turned and walked straight into the first supermarket that I saw. I grabbed a bag, and walked through, grabbing things off the shelves like a disposable razors and shaving cream. I got him some new, smart looking clothes as well.

I filled the bag up with essentials and went to the till to pay for them all. The woman gave me an odd look, but said nothing as I produced my credit card to pay on.

Then I took the bag, disposing of the price labels, before throwing it over my shoulder. I moved to the cash point outside, and took out two thousand dollars in cash, ignoring the price it would take to exchange the money.

I turned around, in search of the homeless man and spotted him. He hadn't moved far, just outside the bus stop now. People were ignoring him as they walked past.

I hopped over the road, heading straight for him. He looked stunned when I stopped in front of him and sat down.

"Hi," I said putting the bag down.

"Hi," he said cautiously.

"What's your name?" I asked.

"Liam," he said.

"Hi Liam, I'm Pam," I said.

"Well Pam, it's nice to meet you. Why are you sat down talking to a beggar like me?"

"Because, I'd like to know you," I said shrugging, "tell me about yourself."

"What do you want to know?"

"Why don't we start with what happened to bring you here?"

"I....I...couldn't get a job. Lost my home, all my money, nowhere to go. The usual story."

"No family?"

"I couldn't be a burden," he said looking at his hands embarrassed, "I shouldn't be telling you all this kid."

"Hey, don't worry about it. I've been where you are," I said, "what did you used to do?"

"I used to be a dancer, professionally. I've danced in some really big shows too," he said grinning.

"Seriously? That's cool,"

"Yeah, oh, it was amazing. The audiences used to cheer out and clap when I finished dancing. I was even on broad way you know."

"That's seriously sweet. What happened?"

"I broke my leg by falling down the stairs. End of my career. You can't dance with a broken leg."

Undercover Thief

"Did you try to get back in to it?"

"Of course I did. Nothing stuck. My leg was never quite the same after that."

"That's such a shame."

"Yeah, well that's life kid."

"I've got something for you."

"You what kid?" he asked confused.

"This is for you," I said handing him the bag, "it has clothes, toiletries, a little bit of food. Stuff to help you clean up and start fresh."

"Wh- thanks kid but I can't accept this from you,"

"That's not all Liam. Here, this is for you too." I handed him a thick envelope from my pocket. There's two thousand dollars, cash in this. You should be able to use it to rent a place to live for a while. You'll have a home and it'll make applying for jobs easier. It's a vicious circle when you're on the streets. You can't get a job because you have no address, but you can't get an address till you have a job to earn the money to pay the rent. This should give you a head start."

"Listen kid, this is wonderful but I can't take this money from you."

"Please, I want you too," I said, "I want to help."

"But.....kid, this has to be your life savings in your hand."

"I promise you, it isn't."

"But kid, I can't take this from you."

"Yes you can. Because in a minute I'm going to get up and leave this bag here. Either you can take it and do something with it, or some lucky sucker can come across it and gain two thousand dollars."

"You can't be serious."

"Deadly," I said putting the money in the top of the bag and zipping it up.

"Why?" he asked.

"Like I said, I've been where you've been. The beggar on the street. No one looks at you. No one wants to meet your eyes."

"You're alright now though?"

"Yeah, I dug my way out, with a helping hand from someone. So I want to help others do it too. People like you and me who just got unlucky. So here," I said pushing the bag towards him, "Here's the shovel you need to start digging your way out."

"I.....I don't know what to say."

"Just promise me that you'll try," I said, "promise me that you'll look after yourself, get off the streets for good.

Undercover Thief

And, if one day you're in a position to do the same for another, that you'll take it."

"You got it kid. I promise," said the man getting up and offering me his hand, "Thank you."

"No sweat. Nice to meet you Liam," I shook his hand and headed back over to the restaurant.

"And you too. Pam right?"

"You bet," I called over my shoulder.

"You're one amazing kid Pam," he called, "I won't ever forget you Pam."

"Thanks Liam," I said as I walked back over to where my parents were sat.

"What was all that?" asked my mother.

"Just giving someone a shovel," I said sitting back down, "We were talking about Gwen. I think what we need to do is ring up the publishers of the Oxford dictionaries, or whatever the equivalent is over here, and just-"

"You gave him a shovel?" asked my father interrupting me, kind of confused, "I don't get it."

"No, not a literal shovel dad," I answered with a laugh, "I gave him some money and some material things to help get him off the street."

"Pam, that's very sweet of you, but a little naïve," said my mother, "He'll probably just use the money on drugs or alcohol."

"I never did," I said, "besides, I spoke to him. He used to be a dancer, used to perform on broad way."

"He did?"

"Yeah, broke his leg and was down on his luck. I looked at him; he didn't look like he was using drugs. He just looked a little scrappy, nothing a hot shower and a decent meal couldn't fix. I know what people on drugs look like. He looked relatively healthy, just a bit dirty."

"He could have been dangerous Pam."

"I can look after myself mum. Liam is a good man who fell on hard times. He just needed a hand back up."

"And that's very nice, what you did for him," said my mother, "but not everyone is like that Pammie. Have you done that before?"

"A couple of times," I said shrugging, "You saw the money I'm holding; I'm not really light for cash."

"Are you telling me none of the homeless people you've met were drug users?"

"Some were, in which case I gave him the location of a soup kitchen and the number of a rehab place that takes people for free," I said.

"Pam, what you did for him was lovely. But it was also very dangerous."

"Was it? You were right here," I pointed out, "and I might just have saved his life, I might just have helped him turn his entire life around."

"Pammie....I'm proud of you," said my mother patting my hand, "but....not everyone will be like that. Some people are just....bad."

"Why are you always so prepared for people to be bad?" I asked frowning, "Some people are good mum."

"And there are those that are bad. And bad people do bad things."

"Not everyone doing a bad thing is a bad person."

My mother looked at my father who smiled.

"You know, you may just be right about that," said my father to me, "have you ever done a bad thing?"

"Depends on your definition of bad."

"Broken the law?"

"Yes," I said simply, "Do you think I'm a bad person?"

"No."

"That proves my point. I'm not bad, just imperfect like the rest of us."

Chapter Twenty-Two

I groaned and stretched out. We had gotten back that Saturday late, and I had missed the school dinner. So my parents had cooked a meal in my mother's room, and we stayed up just talking. It was good. I didn't think I would actually enjoy myself. But I had.

I had gotten to know my parents a lot better. I could see the regret in their eyes, see the truth when they apologised for being away. They were sorry, and that was what mattered. They had made a mistake, and they wanted to be forgiven.

So I forgave them because one day I was hoping they might forgive me. I knew my secret life would one day come out, and when that happened, I would have to run for the hills. I hoped they would forgive me for disappearing on them.

I realised I was on a couch, and someone had put a blanket over me. I opened my eyes and sat up. I was still in my mother's apartment. I must have fallen asleep here. Oops.

Undercover Thief

"Morning Pam," came my father's voice. I looked up, blinking a few times to see him sat at the counter, a cup of coffee in his hands and a paper in the other. There was a packed bag on the stool next to him.

"You're off again?"

"Yep."

"Where you heading?" I asked sitting up and running my hands through my hair.

"San Francisco."

"Oh, lovely beach."

"I don't think I'll have time to visit the beach Pam."

"Well, if you find yourself with time to kill, be sure to visit. It's nice."

"I'll bear that in mind," he said with a chuckle.

"What time is it?"

"Just past half nine."

"Damn!" I muttered getting up, "I promise Ronnie we'd revise together."

"You're revising now?"

"Don't push it dad," I said grabbing my shoes from the floor and yanking them onto my feet.

"Ok, ok, I'm sorry. Just a question."

"I got to go, chuck me my purse," I said pointing to where it was just beside him.

"Sure," he said picking it up and tossing it over to me easily.

"Thanks Dad. See you," I said, "stay safe."

"You too," he said as I made it to the door and opened it. I paused and smiled at him.

"Tell mum I said bye."

"Will do," he said with a wave.

Then I left. I walked quickly down the almost empty halls towards the accommodation and the room Ronnie and I shared. Most of the students like to sleep in on Sunday, most of the clubs were in the afternoon. There were a few early birds heading down for a cooked breakfast already.

When I got back to my room, Ronnie was still fast asleep. It was unfair how even asleep she was stunningly pretty. I snuck inside and hopped in the shower, needing to change after I had slept in my clothes. I redressed in fresh clothes and left the bathroom, ready for the day.

Ronnie was sat on her bed, arms folded, waiting for me to come out.

"So?" she asked expectantly. I took a deep breath and nodded slowly.

"Not bad."

Undercover Thief

"Not bad?" she pushed.

"I kind of......had fun."

"That's good!" Ronnie said happily, "that's really good Pammie!"

"Yeah, well, maybe Jerry and Leah were right," I said shrugging, "Perhaps it's time I moved on."

"Good!" she said grinning, "I'm glad to see you and your parents are making headway at last."

"What's this?" I asked going over to my desk and seeing a bunch of papers that weren't mine.

"A revision timetable, courtesy of Gwen," she said. She pointed to her desk, "I got one too."

"She realises that normal human beings require time to eat and sleep right?" I gawked as I read through her jam packed timetable.

"I did mention it to her. But when I brought it up she said, and I quote, 'you can eat and read at the same time' and she also said 'there is enough time to sleep when we're dead,'" Ronnie sighed. I sniggered.

"Oh that girl is something weird," I said with a laugh, "genius but weird."

"She has a point though. The exams are a grand total of one week away," said Ronnie with a sigh, "I should have been revising more than I have."

"I'm such a bad influence."

"Yeah, you are! But it's not your fault. I should know better."

"I might revise too....I don't really want to fail."

"So you'll revise with me?"

"Yeah!"

"Ok! Great!" she said perking up at the idea.

"Great! I've got a study buddy!" I said grinning.

"Ok, so we should probably start with our worst subject, as we've got a lot of time right now."

"But.....that means history," I pointed out and our faces were twin masks of horror at the idea.

"We can start with something else," she hinted.

"How about tech?"

"I'm not in the mood for tech right now. How about science," she offered as an alternative.

"Only if you go and steal some teabags from the kitchen so I can have a cuppa."

"Done!"

***

Undercover Thief

That next week, I didn't get a single detention. I still went to Mr Compton's detention slot though, to read over the manipulation material. I was enjoying the higher year's work, and it was nice take a break from revising for science, and other exams I was pretty sure I was going to fail.

The revision bug had hit everyone, and even I had gone down with it. It was nuts! Lydia was on about six cups of coffee a day, Peter was always carrying flash cards with notes on them, muttering to himself as he constantly tested himself. Ian had recorded the entire history course onto his iPod to listen to it while he slept.

I was a little freaked out by just how obsessed they were by these exams. It even cut poker night short, which was something that everyone looked forward too.

I wanted to pass everything sure, but a simple pass was good enough for me. The others were all competing to be top. I didn't need to be top. I still didn't know if I wanted to be a spy. The money situation at home hadn't changed. But Jerry and Leah assured me it was getting a lot easier. But I had decided to keep my options open.

The first exam to come up was Manipulation, after my mother's little surprise text. Apparently we could relax about Operation Studies, apparently that was the only test we were going to get for it before Christmas. Not all of us were convinced however, preferring to be prepared.

Everyone had been revising like mad for Manipulation, except me of course. I knew memorising wouldn't help anything if it was a practical exam, and if it was written, I knew all the stuff I would need.

When we walked into the class room that morning for the test, I could see that some people had barely slept all night. That couldn't be good for them, they needed to take the stress off themselves a little bit.

"Ok, so this is a practical exam," said Mr Compton, "your job is to figure out the name of the person in the interrogation room when I show you through."

"First name? Last name?" asked Gwen immediately, clawing for more detail about what was coming her way.

"Go for what you can," said Mr Compton, "I'll be interested in technique remember, so don't be disheartened if you get nothing. Just show me you have learnt something. Up first is Mr Alderson." Peter swallowed, stood up and walked into the next room.

He did look like he was about to faint.

"Oh no, oh no!" panicked Gwen, her nose almost clued to her open text book. Ronnie was flipping through mind maps she had drawn up about practical exam techniques. I sat on the desk, cross legged, playing with a pack of cards.

"Gwen, I swear if you don't shut up I will gag you," groaned Ronnie rubbing her eyes.

"I'm so nervous," wailed Gwen, wringing her hands frantically.

"Don't be," I laughed, "It's just one little test."

"How can I not be nervous?" she practically growled.

"You're taking this way to seriously Gwen. Just do what I do. Take two deep breaths and remind yourself it's not the end of the world."

Gwen took two deep breaths and shook her head frantically.

"Not working!" she squeaked.

"Close your eyes," I instructed, "breathe with me. In." she sucked in a breath.

"And let it out.....and in.......and out......and in......and out. There is no stress about this Gwen.....in.......out......no stress.......in.....out."

"OK. I do feel better," she said opening her eyes.

"Atta girl," I said with a small chuckle, still playing with my cards.

"It's easy for you to be calm," said Ronnie, "You know you'll pass this exam well."

"Nah, I don't. I have no idea what I'm facing once I get in there," I said, "but I can't change anything about it."

"But you have had a hell of a lot of practice," whispered Ronnie, lowering her voice so only the three of us could here.

"True," I admitted nodding, "however, I think I'll be like Gwen before the tech exam."

"You and me both," said Ronnie.

"I'd rather be sitting a tech exam right now," mumbled Gwen.

"That makes one of us," I snorted, "start breathing Gwen, I can see the panic is just about eating you up again."

Each test took a long time. It varied from ten minutes to half an hour. We didn't see people after their test. Mr Compton called us in one by one. Next went Marley, then Adam, then Cassidy, then Ian, George, Lucas, and Gwen. The room was almost empty now. Lydia was pacing and whispering to herself.

"I'm next," said Ronnie with a shaking breath.

"Remember, if you don't like the game, change the rules," I said.

"Is that a thief saying?"

"More of a con," I said with a conspiratorial wink as Mr Compton walked into the room.

"Miss Price, your turn."

Undercover Thief

Then a small seed of doubt took seat in me. I knew it was ridiculous, but it didn't help all I had to talk to was Lydia who was talking to herself like a mad person, and Trevor and Allister who were looking so nervous one word from me to break the silence might make them expire.

I shook off my doubt and went back to playing with my cards for something to do. Doing card tricks always calmed me down. Fifteen minutes later it was Lydia's turn. I was left with Trevor Willis and Allister Wale. I was next. Seventeen minutes and thirty seconds later Mr Compton walked in.

"Pam," he said brightly, holding a hand out for the next room. I jumped off the desk and followed in through into a new room.

"So, we want the name of this lady," said Mr Compton. We were the other side of some one-way glass. I looked her up and down and started to come up with a plan or attack.

"Ok," I said, taking a hair bobble from my pocket and a few pins, pulling my hair up into a professional if simple looking bun, "and she knows why she's here?"

"Yes. She's been instructed that you will want to know her name."

"And she knows not to tell me."

"Exactly."

"And has everyone had a different person to interrogate or has everyone passed been tested with her?"

"No, everyone has had someone different. She's not gone through this before," He said as I took off my leather jacket and threw it onto the side. I was glad I was wearing black jeans today that weren't ripped.

"Can I borrow that?" I asked.

"This?" he asked holding up his folder, "um, sure."

"Great," I said taking out my earrings. I opened my purse and took out a mirror and miniature make up bag. Eye liner, mascara and a quick slick of lipstick later and I looked significantly older than I was. An adult. Perfect.

"Time starts when you open the door," said Mr Compton. I went to the door, closing my eyes and pulling on the new persona I needed to have for this. My eyes snapped open and my mouth curled into a confident smile.

"Show time," I said with a grin and walked into the room.

"Hello," I said walking over to the table and holding my hand out for her to shake, "I'm Miss Mathews, one of the members of staff here. I just have a few last minute questions and wanted to run a few things by you before we send in our candidate. She's not dangerous, just has a bad attitude. It's part of our security procedure to warn you, you understand?"

Undercover Thief

"Oh, ok."

"Great. Well, first, I want to thank you for coming in for this," I said sitting down and putting my file on the table, "this can be quite an unusual experience. Is this your first time with us?"

"Yes," she said smiling.

"How are you finding it?" I asked folding my hands over the folder and crossing my legs.

"The people have been really lovely. I mean, it's been great," she said nodding.

"Excellent. That's perfect. Just what we wanted to hear," I said, "we see public relations as a very important part of what we do here."

"I'm glad I could give positive feedback."

"Now, you've already been prepped by my colleague, but there are a few more pieces of information I need to give you. Like a little crash course of things she may try if you will."

"Oh, alright."

"So you know that she is after your name."

"Yes, and I'm not supposed to give it to her."

"Right. So she may try things like enquiring after hobbies, school career, life."

"How so?"

"Um… she may ask if you have a partner," I said, "do you have a partner?"

"Yes, I'm married."

"So she could ask after his name and occupation and things like that," I said.

"Oh. I see."

"Relax. It's not a problem if you do let it slip. Whether she actually gets your name or not is not what this is about."

"Oh, ok."

"But you must have a conversation with her. You can't just sit there and refuse to say anything. She may have a bad attitude but she is still just a kid," I said. She smiled and nodded.

"Thanks."

"She might also try threats. Now, that would never, ever be allowed to be put into action of course. But please remember, if you feel at all uncomfortable you are perfectly within your right to leave the room."

"Ok, I'll remember that."

"Are there any more questions miss…." I looked in the file flicking through the paperwork in front of me pretending to look for a name.

Undercover Thief

"Delefy," she said.

"Sorry?" I said looking up.

"Delefy. I'm Miss Abigail Delefy," she repeated.

The door opened.

"Very good Pam," said Mr Compton walking in, "very good indeed."

"Why thank you," I said with a bright grin, handing his folder back to him.

"I'm sorry....I don't understand," said Abigail frowning at our exchange.

"Oh, I'm sorry. I was lying through my teeth. I'm the difficult candidate," I explained. She opened her mouth to say something and then laughed.

"Oh, now I feel like an idiot."

"No, no, don't. You were amazing," I soothed, "seriously."

"Me? I genuinely thought you were someone who worked here!" she said standing up, "you don't look fourteen."

"I'm actually fifteen, and make up and heels help," I allowed her.

"Well, this was a very interesting experience," she was still laughing to herself.

"Yes, through there if you will Miss Delefy," said Mr Compton. She left with a small wave.

"Very, very well done," rewarded Mr Compton with a small laugh, "I had no idea of your game play before you were going in. How did you decide on this?"

"Well, she was expecting to be questioned by a teenager, not adult. So I played the part," I shrugged.

"Well, I think that might just be a new school record for a first year Manipulation exam," said Mr Compton, "full marks."

"Thank you sir," I beamed at him.

"Go on. The others have been moaning about some PE exam this afternoon. I suppose you'll want to go and prepare for that.

"Yeah. It sounds like it's going to be painful," I groaned and he gave a small chuckle.

"Off you go, and good luck."

Chapter Twenty-Three

I choked back my laughter.

"Oh, and it was so cool when Peter did that flip! Did you know he could do that?" asked Ronnie animatedly.

"No, it was awesome," I agreed.

The three of us were sat on an old carpet in our HQ, eating food we'd stolen from the kitchen. Lemonade, crisps, popcorn and cookies. Ronnie licked her fingers clean and jumped off the window sill. It was a week and a half since the Manipulation exam. I threw popcorn at Ronnie as she started walking over, and she caught it in her mouth.

"Woooo! Yeah!" she called. Gwen had sound proofed this place just before the exams, so now this was officially our hang out. Ronnie started doing a victory dance.

"You promised to teach me how to pick a lock," said Ronnie sitting down, "Like on a safe and things. So come on, teach me."

"You guys realise we still have a lot of exams left to go right?" piped up Gwen, who was, even now, lying with an open textbook in front of her.

"Oh, none of the important ones," scoffed Ronnie sitting down on the floor next to her.

"Not important? They're languages!"

"Pam already speaks like what? One hundred?" joked Ronnie looking at me. I laughed.

"Yeah, something like that. What do you guys think if I take up Albanian?"

"Really? You? You're going to take up an extra class?" asked Gwen, a little bit disbelieving.

"Why not? It's extra credit for a couple of hours a week. Besides it's a language, they're easy to learn."

"For you maybe," said Ronnie, "the rest of us have trouble with that kind of thing."

"Yeah, most people prefer to learn things in the language they already speak," said Gwen.

"Hon, if you are referring to your knack for science or tech, you're still abnormal," said Ronnie lying flat on the floor.

"Not true!" Gwen protested.

"Yes it is," I said, "and I'm pretty sure you are the only one who knew what an N.M.R machine was."

"George knew."

"No, George guessed and got ridiculously lucky," said Ronnie pulling an Italian book in front of her.

"You guys are boring," I said going over to the window and looking out.

"Here, read this," said Ronnie throwing a book at me. It was Jane Austen, translated into Italian.

"Seriously? Why do you even have this?"

"Apparently last year the extract was from that," said Ronnie, "so enjoy."

"Will do. I'm a Mr Darcy fan," I said opening the book.

Then the lights went out.

"Gwen, what did you do?" I teased out of the black.

"Hey!"

"Is it just us?" asked Ronnie. Gwen crawled over to her computer and started wiggling the mouse.

"No....not just us," muttered Gwen frowning, "It's the entire school."

"Impossible, backup generators would have kicked in by now," I said walking over and folding myself onto the floor next to her.

"Is it a black out?"

"With backup generators all failing too?" asked Ronnie.

"An exam of some kind maybe?" offered Gwen, "they said expect disruptions."

"At the dead of night?" I asked.

"Yeah, that's not unusual for the higher years," said Ronnie.

"What? That's going to suck!" I muttered.

Ronnie was rummaging around in a draw in the desk we had moved up here and put back together. She drew something out and switched it on. A torch.

"Well, some light, thank goodness," said Gwen, "I thought all we'd have was the light from the laptop."

"Guys....the security system here is a Malikam Mark 6," I said, suddenly freezing.

"Ok, we don't speak thief," said Ronnie.

"What's that noise?" asked Gwen. Ronnie and I exchanged a look and ran to the tiny window, switching off the torch so there was no chance we wouldn't be seen.

We watched in horror as we saw huge black vans charging up the long drive towards the school. They were non-descript with lots of big men with even bigger guns.

Undercover Thief

"Oh no," squeaked Gwen alarmed.

"How did they get the power down?" hissed Ronnie appalled and anxious.

"I don't know. But I'm sure as hell going to find out," I said pulling my hair into a tight pony tail. It was time to go to work.

"What are you going to do?"

"Well, who do we know that's been creeping around the school with an ulterior motive?"

"Marley," hissed Ronnie, "I'm going to kill her!"

"Not until after I've questioned her Ronnie," I said, "and then she's all yours. Gwen, find her."

"Hang on guys, shouldn't we just wait for the teachers to fix it. They are way more experienced," said Gwen.

"Gwen....they can't," I said.

"What do you mean?" asked Ronnie.

"The security system here is a Malikam Mark 6," I said, "The power goes and the whole place goes into automatic lock down. That means that every single door gets locked and is bolted with titanium bolts. Everyone inside a room will be locked inside with no way out."

"Except us," Ronnie caught up quickly, "Because we aren't in a room."

"Exactly," I said, "but they want to get into a specific room, which is why they brought that." I pointed to a group of men carrying in a huge piece of complicated looking laser equipment.

"What are they after?"

"I don't know, but I bet Marley does," I said.

"Ok Pam, what's the plan?" asked Ronnie ready to jump into action.

"Wait!" said Gwen running over to the desk. Then she scampered back and handed over tiny listening devises.

"You have coms!" said Ronnie. I shoved one into my ear.

"Gwen, you are golden!" I said.

"I know. I was messing around, trying to get them to be more effective. And they are. All you need to do is whisper and we'll all hear it."

"Perfect," I grinned.

"Got anything else up that sleeve of yours?" asked Ronnie.

"Sorry. I'll get more stuff for the next time," said Gwen.

"Next time?" Ronnie muttered, "I hope not."

"Ok," I said, "Gwen, I want you to stick here. Can you get into the security feed?"

"Won't it be down? It's a black out."

"No, it's on a separate system to locks and lights."

"Oh, well, ok," she said going over to her computer. There was a lot of technical typing done before there were images on her screen. I handed her my laptop.

"Ok, we're going to talk to you through these. Use this if you have too," I said. She nodded.

"Ok."

"Gwen, I want you to be our eyes and ears. You have our backs."

"Ok," she said nodding, brushing a stray piece of hair out of her eyes.

"So, what do you need?" asked Ronnie folding her arms, she meant business.

"I need an outfit," I said tapping my fingers together as I came up with a plan.

"What kind?"

"I was thinking something black....with a mask," I said pointing out of the window towards where men were pouring into the building. She gave me a wicked grin.

"I think you'd look great in that."

Together, she and I ran for the door that lead to the old servants corridor and then slowly we snuck out into the corridor. We hid behind a pillar, there was no one around.

"Come on," whispered Ronnie and we crept over to the stairs. We dived for cover as some people walked up, heading further and further deeper into the building. They were heading to the accommodation area.

Not good.

"Ok, where are they going?" I whispered.

"I have no idea. But I don't like it," said Ronnie, "They have big guns."

"Yeah, they do," I whispered.

"Ok, there is a woman about your height coming up the stairs alone, Pam," came Gwen's voice in our ears.

"Perfect. Ronnie," I said letting her go.

I watched as our target moved up the stairs. Ronnie crept up behind her. I winced as Ronnie took her down. That was going to hurt when she woke up. We grabbed her and dragged her away, so no one would see.

"I'm glad that you like me, because being your enemy does not look fun," said Gwen. I started changing. I pulled on the suit over my ordinary clothes, and then the mask.

"Ok, how do I look?" I asked standing up.

"Like one of them," said Ronnie nodding.

"Ok, go back, and take her with you. Make sure she isn't a problem," I said, "When I get Marley, I'll bring her here, then I want you to help me get her to the HQ."

"No problem," said Ronnie nodding.

"Good luck," said Gwen.

"Thanks girls. See you in a bit," I said and walked down the stairs, holding the gun how I had seen the others doing it. I had to hope that the way I held it didn't show my complete inexperience with this kind of a weapon.

"Ok, I've found her," said Gwen as I reached the bottom of the stairs, "She's in the hall outside the computing labs. She's just sitting there."

I headed over that way immediately, walking confidently down the corridor in plain view of the other guards. No one questioned me as I passed. Manipulation rule number 1; act confident and people will think you belong.

"Ok, there are five guards by the entrance to computer room seven. Something big is going on in there," I whispered, "people are yelling. And there are more all along the corridor."

"How many?"

"I've seen at least twenty so far."

"Oh man," said Ronnie, "Not good."

"Thanks Ronnie. Great confidence boost there," I muttered. Then I saw Marley. She was sat, staring at the floor. She seemed very, very pale. I walked over.

"You're to come with me," I said pulling on a perfect Russian accent. She just looked at me blankly for a moment before nodding.

"Ok," she said. I walked her up the stairs.

"Where are we going?" she asked.

"This way," I said.

"Why?"

"Because I was told to," I said. She sighed and looked at her hands. She seemed troubled. Did she regret what she had done? Did she regret helping them?

SMACK!

Marley fell to the floor unconscious.

"Hey Pam," said Ronnie grinning.

"That was a little pre-emptive," I said gesturing to her unconscious body, "We're not even on the right floor. What if someone sees us carrying her?"

"Yeah, but it made me feel a whole lot better. Anyway there is a hidden door to the corridor's just there," she said gesturing to what looked like a normal wall to me.

Undercover Thief

"Alright," I surrendered. We grabbed her and pulled her into the servant's tunnel, each of us had and arm.

"So, what now?"

"Tie her to a chair," I said as we got back to HQ. Ronnie pulled her over to a chair as I stripped out of my guard clothes. I saw the guard we'd taken them from wasn't here.

"Um? Where is our other friend?"

"I stuck her in the girl's bathroom," said Ronnie.

"Oh.....ok," I said, guessing with the way Ronnie punched that it didn't really matter. She would be out for a long time.

We used spare cables Gwen had to tie Marley down and dragged the chair to face the wall, so she had no idea where she was.

"So how do we wake her?" asked Ronnie. I picked up a lemonade bottle.

"Like this," I said and emptied it over her head.

Chapter Twenty Four

She gasped, floundering under the sticky lemonade, and looked at us, blinking sharply as the lemonade stung her eyes. She moved her hands, realised they were tied securely and tried jerking to get herself free.

"Help! Help!" she screamed.

"Go on, yell," said Ronnie, "no one can hear you scream, it's a sound-proofed room."

"How dare you! How dare you! Do you know who I am? Do you know who you're dealing with?"

"Actually, I do," said Ronnie standing square in front of her menacingly, "You are a traitor."

"Oh! We're playing the name calling came are we?" she asked with a sick little laugh. I could see Ronnie was about to knock her out again, so I neatly put an arm around her shoulders and gave Marley a short, unimpressed smile.

"Ok Marley, you know Ronnie runs on a short fuse. Antagonising her isn't sensible. So, why don't we start with some basic questions? One, why are you here?" I asked. She just glared at me.

"Ok, let's try this again," I said, "Marley, who is running the operation?"

"My father," she announced proudly.

"Ok, who is he?"

She stayed quiet, not saying a word.

"Can I hit her again?" asked Ronnie.

"No!" I said, "Marley, are you happy? Are you happy that you endangered the lives of everyone in this building? There are good people in here. Your teachers, your friends? Innocent children? They were people you could count on if you needed them. Are you happy that you have endangered all of their lives?"

"I haven't done that."

"I'm afraid you have Marley. The muscles behind all these guns have itchy trigger fingers," I said.

"Well, you're all government anyway! Why should I care?" I could tell the pain behind that statement wasn't her own, but someone else. Probably this father of hers.

"These are kids your age Marley. We are your friends. You know us," I said.

"You are not my friends! Anyway why do you even care?" spat Marley, "Once my father's work is done, you can do what you want to! You can go home! Everyone knows that's the only thing you've wanted to do since you stepped foot in the place!"

"That's true," I said slowly, standing back and pretending to take that in like it was a new idea, "I do want to go back to London. That is a very, very good point."

"Pammie?" hissed Ronnie in protest.

"Well, I am obviously not going to get home any other way, I've tried," I argued.

"No Pam!" gasped Gwen, they were both completely fooled. I felt evil for tricking them, even for a short time.

"Marley, what's your father hoping to do exactly?" I asked with idle curiosity, tapping my fingers together.

"He's going to bring it all down Pam," said Marley, speaking encouragingly to me. She believed I was the one that was going to break, that I was the weakest link in the chain here.

"Bring what down, exactly?"

"CIA, MI6, FBI, everything. All files these days are on computers. And he's going to release them all onto the internet. No more secrets. Everyone will know the truth. And then they'll all come crashing down."

"I see. Simple but effective," I nodded, carefully hiding my horror behind an appreciative mask.

"No one will chase you Pam. No one will have the time in the mess that's left. You and I, people like us can just slip away."

"People like us?"

"We both know what you are Pam."

"We do?"

"You're a grifter. And you're a damn good one," she said, and she meant it when she said it. I pressed my lips together and changed my stance. I was dealing with someone from my world.

It was time for a different approach. I smiled widely

"How could you tell?" I asked surprised.

"I'm Marley *Brittle*," she said.

I hit my hand to my head, feeling very stupid.

"You're a Brittle? As in a *Brittle*? Seriously, you're Jimmy Brittle's daughter, aka Jimmy the hover? No way!" I exclaimed.

"That's daddy!" she said proudly, "And he'd be happy to take you under his wing, if I asked him too. He'd teach you everything there is about being in a thieving family Pam, if you want. You and I, we could be friends. You do want to leave this place as much as I do, don't you? You could be a member of a proper *thieving family*."

"I'd like that more than anything," I said, "So what's the game plan here? You do know you have little more than twenty five minutes before FBI turn up don't you?"

"Pam!" protested Ronnie angrily.

"Shut up Ronnie, the professionals are talking!" I snapped and Marley cracked an evil smile.

"Don't need that long. The hack should be done in fifteen."

"Ten is enough for your exit?"

"Hell yeah. Me and dad get out, everyone else goes down."

"So the muscle is your scape goat. So, you can swing me out too?"

"You betcha. Of course, you would have to tie up....loose ends," she said gesturing towards Ronnie. Ronnie glared at me and changed her stance ready to fight me. I turned to Marley and leaned closer.

"Gwen, find that hack," I said calmly and watched as Marley's face fell.

"You were faking?" gasped Gwen in relief and fanning her face with her hand.

"Of course I was faking. Thanks for the belief in me, you guys," I said kind of hurt as Gwen began typing on the computer frantically.

"Aw, I'm sorry Pammie," apologised a chagrined Ronnie.

"Humph!"

"You're an idiot Pam!" snapped Marley, "You'll never be anything now! You can't be anything here, you're just a grifter, and without my father's help that's all you'll ever be!"

"Honey, you're right," I said turning to look at her, "I'm a grifter. But I'm not a killer. And what you're doing today, that is going to get some people killed. Perhaps not directly, but it sure as hell will indirectly."

"Idiot!" she spat.

"Me? I'm an idiot? You're the idiot! You're an awful grift by the way. We knew you were up to something weeks ago. Your dad should be cringing in embarrassment."

"Ok. I can't get onto the server because the power is down," said Gwen with a little annoyed scream.

"Where do you need to get to?" Asked Ronnie.

"Computer suite," said Gwen.

"No can do," I shut that idea down fast.

"What? There has to be a way!" Gwen said, "You always have a way!"

"Some places are just too risky Gwen," I said, "We're not doing it, not risking you like that. What do you need, like directly and we'll try working around that?"

"I need a computer directly linked to the server."

"My mum," clicked Ronnie instantly, "her computer is directly linked to the server."

"Ok. So we get to your mum's office," I said. I pressed my fingers together thinking.

"Pam?"

"Just coming up with a game plan Gwen. Ok, pack everything you need up," I instructed. She nodded and started throwing things in a rucksack.

"We won't have access to security videos up there," added Gwen as she started packing.

"I'll get that, don't worry about that," I muttered as I thought.

"What about her?" asked Ronnie with a voice of steel, throwing her chin in Marley's direction, who couldn't see us. She was trying to turn her head to look around the room, but couldn't.

"All yours," I said patting her back. Ronnie went over and punched her straight in the face. Marley was out cold. Gwen and I exchanged a look, both of us wanting to shake that one off ourselves.

Damn, Ronnie could be scary.

"Let's go," said Ronnie brushing off her hands. I went over to the corner and pulled out my own pack back.

Undercover Thief

"What is that?" Asked Ronnie.

"Some stuff," I said throwing out the clothes and money. My equipment was all there.

"Let go. Time is wasting!" said Ronnie.

"Go!" I said and we left running. We got to the door, leading out onto the main corridor of the school.

"Ok Ron, quickest way to you mum's office," I whispered.

"Follow me." We ran through the corridors.

There was barely any one up here, so it was easy to dart about unseen. Ronnie in front. I was behind, making sure Gwen didn't do anything stupid like trip up or lose us. We got there without much hassle.

"What now? You said something about titanium bolts!" hissed Gwen.

"I know!" I whispered back, "give me some room to work!" I pulled off my backpack and took out a small knife and started cutting through the plaster on the wall. I needed to cut off quite a square before I came to the wire cage I wanted.

"Bingo," I muttered. I took out my roll of tools and selected two of my picks.

"When I say," I said fiddling, "get inside. Because when I let this go the door will slide back shut. And fast." They nodded. Gwen got my backpack for me.

"Ok. Go," I said. The door slid open. They ran in. I threw myself at the door, rolling inside just as it closed.

"Ronnie!"

"Mum!"

"Ow!" I complained, flexing my wrist where I landed on it awkwardly, "Gwen, stop standing around and get on that computer!"

"Pam!" I looked up to see there were four people in the room, other than the three of us. Miss Price, my mother, Mr Compton and Mr Berry.

"Pammie, are you alright?" gasped my mother rushing over and hugging me.

"Fine Mum, sorry, time for hugs later," I said pushing her off gently. I took my knife again and started tapping on the wall behind Miss Price's desk, ear on the plaster, listening.

"What is going on?" demanded Miss Price.

I found what I was listening for. I stabbed the plaster and began cutting around the metal box, clawing away the covering with my fingers and knife. I let the debris fall to the floor.

Undercover Thief

"What are you doing Pam?" squeaked Miss Price, "This is my office."

"I need to get at the wires," I said, "I need to get into the security feed."

"Miss Torres, you're failing my class. How do you know where those wires are and how do you plan to get them?" Asked Mr Berry folding his arms, waiting for me to be stumped.

I opened my bag and pulled out a blow torch and some glasses.

"That should answer your question," I said pulling on the goggles, firing up the torch and starting to cut through the metal.

"Ok. Stop! What is going on out there?" said Miss Price again.

"Bad people are hacking the servers to try and get into the intelligence database and dump everything on the Internet," said Ronnie.

"How do you know that?"

"Marley was a part of it. And we questioned her," said Ronnie.

"Marley? Why? Such a quiet girl."

"It's the quiet ones you need to watch," I said, "can't believe I didn't see it before."

"None of us did darling," said my mother.

"No! You have an excuse. I don't have one. I should have recognised her surname. I should have made the connection. A Brittle!" I said shaking my head.

"Ok. Still confused!" Mr Compton said, "How did you get through a door that Ch – I mean Mr Berry said was rigged."

"It's impossible!" sputtered Mr Berry.

"Not impossible," I said, "I just did it."

"Ok, I can't get on it," said Gwen slamming her fist into the computer table.

"Use the back door," I said.

"What back door?"

"Leah discovered this little beauty a few weeks ago," I said with a laugh, "she sent it over to me because she thought I might find it useful."

I began to type on the computer, going through the small amount of code I could remember. Everyone crowded around to watch. Thirty five seconds later.

"I'm in," I said handing it back to Gwen.

"That was beautiful!" exclaimed Gwen.

"How did you learn that?" asked Mr Berry, scratching his balding head.

"Good question," I answered taking off my glasses and rummaging in my bag, "Ronnie, my computer?"

"Hold up! Hold up! How do you know how to do all of this?" asked Mr Compton.

"Because I've got past a Malikam Mark 6 before," I said, "the system is a nasty one but there are a few quirks you can take advantage of if you know how."

"And how have you come across it before?" asked Miss Price.

"Because I'm a thief."

"A what?" shrieked Mum. Everyone jumped. I rubbed my ears which were ringing.

"Wow mum, want to try that again? I think a few dogs in Norway didn't hear you," I said shaking my head and Mr Compton laughed.

"A thief! That's it? That's all it is? You're only a thief?" asked my mother, relief evident in her voice.

"I had my money on drug dealing," said Mr Compton shaking his head.

"Thank you very much Mr C. One, drug dealers are horrible people, violent, unreliable and likely to double cross you. Steer well clear. Two, there is no 'only' about my operations. I'm in for big pay offs, not small change. Three, Ronnie, my laptop needs to be put on please. Four, you had money on it?" I asked setting up the last boxes while Ronnie set up my laptop.

"Yeah. Teachers have to take their fun where they can," said Mr Compton.

"I refrained from betting, if that makes you feel any better," said Mr Berry.

"I was backing gang connections," said Miss Price.

"All their theories filled me with horror. If I had known you were just a thief I would have a few less grey hairs!" said my mother running her hand through her hair.

"There's no 'just' about it! She's broken into the Louvre!" Ronnie said grinning.

"Ron!" I said, "Not now, let's save Western Civilisation first. Then you can boast about my illegal activities!"

"Right, you got it Pam."

"I can't take down the hack," said Gwen.

"Let's see," said Mr Berry. He looked over the code.

"Someone is actively writing it. They'd have to. The security protocol adapts to any hack," he said.

"Can you slow it down?" I asked of him. Mr Berry looked at me a little surprised and then nodded.

"Yes."

Undercover Thief

"Good. Gwen, help," I said tapping my fingers together as I thought, "Ok. Let's do a variation on itsy-bitsy spider and Tweedle Dum and Tweedle Dee – traditional cons – don't ask. Ronnie, I need you and my mum to go and restore the power. There is a six second time frame where there is pitch-black and we're going to need it. Computers are unaffected unfortunately. Everyone needs to stay by my count, I will walk you through it. Gwen, you get their doors. My Compton, sit here, you are on watch duty. Call out strays and heads up. Miss Price, you're with me."

"Whoa, whoa, Pammie," said my mother coming over and brushing my hair with her hands, "what you've done is amazing. Really amazing! I'm so proud of you. But why don't you let the professionals take over from her?"

"Ok," I snapped angrily, "What's your plan?"

"Excuse me?"

"I'm assuming you have a plan then. Without all of the stuff we've done," I said gesturing to the computers and things.

"We'll think of something Pammie."

"We have to slow them down long enough for the FBI to get here in eighteen minutes and the hack will be done in eight! You need me. Because that man in there is Jimmy the Hover. He's the leader of the Brittle family!"

"What does that mean?" Miss Price asked.

"There are six major thieving families in the Underground," I said, "Brittle, Bellman, Santoro, Montenegro, Morgan and DiMargino. My family name is becoming recognised in the Underground, now, so I can use that. But, you need my information! I know that I don't belong here; I know I'm not one of you! But right now you don't need one of you. You need one of me. And I have a plan."

"She's right Isabell," said Miss Price.

"Sally, you're not serious."

"We don't have time to argue, and we don't have a better plan! She has one! She's got this far, why can't she get all the way?"

"She's fourteen."

"Miss Price, we're taking the vents. Ronnie, go. Gwen, doors," I said standing on the desk and pulling the cover of the vent.

"Ok everyone, listen up. Here is the plan."

Chapter Twenty-Five

I silently dropped out of the vent behind two guards not looking in my direction. I leaned against the wall, and watched for a moment before clearing my throat.

"If it isn't Jimmy the Hover. You know, I thought you might hire better thugs," I said easily.

He span around, seeing me in an instant.

"How the hell did you get in here?" he spat.

"It's sort of what I do. Sorry, I'm such and admirer of your work. And when I found out that you're in the building, I just had to come and introduce myself. I had to meet the man behind the legend. I loved your Sidney job! Did you really cross dress and was there really a kangaroo?"

"What? Who the hell are you?"

"Pamela Sklar. Oh put the guns down boys, I'm a member of the Underground too," I said waving my fingers.

"Sklar," he said slowly, "I've heard that name. Where did I hear that name?"

"Peru? One and a half years ago?" I offered. His eyebrows shot up.

"You were on the Peru job?"

"Honey, I ran the Peru job," I said with a confident little laugh. I walked forwards and held out a hand for him. He shook it.

"How on earth did the girl who ran Peru end up here?"

"Oh. I got screwed over by my aunt," I said with a sigh, "it was this place or prison. I made my choice easily enough."

"Understandably."

"Listen, let's get straight to it, I'm assuming you have an exit strategy."

"Of course."

"Got room for an extra man?" He paused and nodded.

"Alright," he said, "if you tell me how you did Peru." I smiled.

"Deal. The trick was cling film and a ball-point pen." I meandered over to the other side of the room.

"Ready," said Ronnie in my ear.

"Really? Oh wait -that makes sense!" Jimmy said laughing he pointed at me, "nice spot kid. That's a really nice spot!"

"Why thank you," I said smiling, giving a small little bow.

"Four minutes Pam," said Gwen.

"Stick with me kid," he said, "you got potential. How old were you when you ran that? Thirteen?"

"Fourteen," I lied.

"Oh, so you're in the year above my girl. Marley? Heard of her?"

"Nah, I tend to keep my head down around the others, don't want to get sucked in," I said, hoping up daintily onto the table and tapping the metal of a computer with my fingers.

"Ok, Ronnie is set. Thirty second timer," said Gwen. I flicked my eyes up to the vent. Miss Price was waiting and watching.

"Ah, well, she's here. Got the inside for me."

"I figured this had to be an inside job. I figured one of the techs. But a student? Got potential then?"

"Not really!" he said with a snort, "more her mother's child than mine. She'd make a fine forger though!"

"Well, we do need forgers," I said with a wry smile, leaning easily on the table.

"Now!" said Gwen. The emergency lights snapped off as the power started being restored.

One Mississippi, two Mississippi, three Mississippi, four Mississippi, five Mississippi, six Mississippi.

The power was restored, the lights back on. My eyes flicked back up to the vents. Miss Price was gone. Good.

"They've restored power," said Jimmy. He turned to the guards.

"Find whoever it is and get rid of them!" My heart almost stopped. Mum. Ronnie. I took a breath. They'd be fine. Mum and Ron were good. He turned to his hacker.

"How close?"

"Almost there. Two minutes or so-No!" The screen went blank.

"What happened?" Jimmy roared.

"The computer? It's unresponsive!"

"What?"

"It's shut down!"

"What how?"

"You were unplugged," I said pointing to Miss Price who was stood up and swinging the socket from one hand, the only guard in the room was on the floor, unconscious. I could see where Ronnie got her moves from. Ouch.

"You! You did this!" He said pointing to me.

"Yeah. I kind of did," I agreed.

"You didn't do Peru!"

"Yes I did," I said, "oh, and I was twelve. I'm such a fan of your work! Not so much this piece, I'll admit. What was your secret to the-"

"Pam, we don't converse with the people trying to destroy us," said Miss Price loudly.

"Right you are, sorry Miss Price," I said swinging my legs as I sat on the table, inspecting my fingernails.

"You little rat!" spat Jimmy at me.

"You know. People like you give honest thieves like me a bad name," I said brushing imaginary lint off of my jumper.

"You're a grass!" His shouted.

"You broke the rules!" I shouted back, "no one innocent dies! That's the first rule of the Underground! And you broke it! You almost brought an entire government to it's knees!"

"It's corrupt!"

"That's how people like you and me survive! We can survive the way it is now! You would have destroyed all of that!" Sirens. I could hear the noise of the cavalry coming to the school. We were saved.

"Times up Hover," I said. He grabbed me, drew a gun from his belt and shoved it under my chin.

"Pam!" Shouted Miss Price worried.

Oh no, that wasn't in my plan.

"Pammie!" squeaked Gwen over the comms units.

"What's going on?" demanded Ronnie and Gwen started to fill her in.

"One step agent, and she dies," hissed Jimmy digging the gun deeper into my skin. Oh no. Oh no. Not good!

"Let her go Jimmy," said Miss Price, her face an unreadable mask.

"No way, she's my ticket out of here."

"And what about your daughter?"

"Bring her to me, and I won't blow off this one's stupid bobble head," snarled Jimmy.

"I don't know where you daughter is!" said Miss Price.

"You must know where she is! She isn't outside!"

"Help is on the way Pam! Sit tight!" Gwen said in my ear.

"No. I don't! Let the child go Jimmy!"

"No! The girl who ran Peru isn't any old child! I bet that her family will pay to have her back!"

CRACK! The door smashed opened and there stood my mother.

"Get your hands off my daughter!" she shouted and there was a huge bang. The bullet sprung from her gun and into his neck. A knock out dart.

Right on mum!

"Pam, are you alright?" gasped my mother running forwards and gripping me in her arms.

"Yes mum, I'm fine. Thanks for that," I said wrapping my arms around her and hugging her back.

"Any time darling," she said softly, kissing the top of my head, "but please try not to let it happen again."

"You got it."

Chapter Twenty-Six

Ronnie, Gwen and I were sat on the stairs, watching as officials walked around all over the place sorting things out. I passed Ronnie the bag of crisps we had nicked from the kitchen. Marley was led past in handcuffs.

"Ooh, that's going to bruise," said Gwen with a wince.

"She annoyed me," said Ronnie. I laughed.

"She deserves it," I agreed, "but that is going to sting for a while."

"Good," muttered Ronnie and I snorted. My very violent but at the same time very loyal best friend.

There was a moment of silence between the three of us. I guess there was really nothing that needed to be said.

"I hope we get extra credit for this," said Gwen eventually.

"Oh you will," said Miss Alson walking past us down the stairs, "shouldn't you go to bed? Don't you have exams tomorrow?"

Undercover Thief

"You're kidding me? Exams? We still have to sit those?" I groaned and collapsed against the stairs as she walked past.

"Life doesn't stop," said Ronnie with a sigh.

"Afraid so Miss Torres. And considering your history, I expect you to pass my law exam with flying colours."

"What? I ignore and laugh in the face of the law! I don't know it!" I moaned.

"We have to be questioned Miss. We can't go to bed," said Gwen. Miss Alson nodded.

"I see. Well, enjoy," she said as she was spoken to by another Fed.

"Italian exams are not my idea of fun," I muttered.

"Oh be quiet. You'd pass in your sleep," said Ronnie.

"Pass me the crisps," I said holding out my hand for them, "I'm going to drown my sorrows in fried potatoes."

"So, now your mother knows," said Gwen after another long pause. I nodded slowly.

"Now she knows," I agreed.

"Now everyone here know."

"Yup, they know."

"What are you going to do?" asked Ronnie.

"I....I honestly don't know," I said biting on a crisp.

"Are you going to stick around?" this seemed the key question.

"I....I just don't know," I said with a sigh, "In an odd way I'd miss this place. I'd certainly miss you guys."

"We'd miss you too," gasped Ronnie instantly, grabbing my hands and squeezing.

"So much. It won't be the same without you!" Gwen said.

"Problem is. Now they know what I am...." I sighed and looked down at my shoes.

"You won't go to prison or anything will you?" Gwen asked tentatively.

"What for? Prove I did something," I said.

"You said so?"

"And that's it. Something I might have said in an emergency? Won't stand up in court," I scoffed, throwing the packet of crisps back at Gwen.

"That's good to know," smiled Ronnie.

"Yeah. I don't like jumpsuits," I said and they a laughed.

"Hello girls," said Miss Price coming and joining us on the stairs.

"Hey mum. Finished talking to officials?"

"Not even close," she said with a groan, "but it's your turn. Agent Simpson wants a word. And you know the drill."

"Oh yay," muttered Ronnie getting up, "this is so not what I want to do."

"Ron, do me a favor and don't mention the Louvre," I said and she grinned at me.

"Sure thing."

"Or any of her other illegal activities," said Miss Price.

"You got it. I won't mention a thing."

"I think I'm going to get some water. These crisps have made my mouth dry," said Gwen getting up. I stayed sat on the stairs. Miss Price walked over and sat next to me.

"You know, that was really impressive what you did tonight. There were flaws room for improvement of course. But it was impressive none the less. You assessed the situation, made a good plan on your feet. You acted quickly, but had still thought through the variables......you remained calm even when there was that hitch in the middle."

"Hitch? You mean when I almost got my head blown off. But yes. Let's call it a hitch," I agreed. She smiled and nodded.

"Like I said. Room for improvement. This isn't a museum or some place to rob. What we do is dangerous."

"You think being a thief isn't? Let me tell you, some guard dogs are pure nasty."

"Pam....you saved us today. Perhaps your mum and I would have thought of something. Before you came in, the two of us were about to hop into the vents ourselves. I'm sure we could have done something.....but if it weren't for you, my daughter and Gwen...I think we could have had a disaster on our hands. That's no small feat. And not everyone can do it."

"Like you said, you would have been fine," I said inspecting my nail paint which had a small chip on the thumb, "besides, that is just what my life is. Thinking on my feet. I've been doing it since I was nine. It's....what I do."

"You have a rare talent Pam. You're very good. You think differently about situations. Your plan....it was unusual and it was good. Unplugging the computer, I didn't think of that."

"The easiest solution is often the best."

"Which you thought of because you were a thief."

I looked down at my hands.

"I am a thief," I corrected quietly.

"I'm sorry."

"For what?"

"For acting the way I did that day I gave you isolation. I....I thought you were acting the way you were out of spite for you parents. But it wasn't. Not all of it anyway. And I should have spotted it. You felt you didn't belong, and I only made it worse."

"Don't worry about it, because you were right. I have no place here. I'm not one of you."

"And that's what you were trying to show me, to show all of us. You were trying to get me to give up and kick you out."

"There had to be times I was close," I asked looking at her, offering her the crisp packet. She laughed and took a few crisps.

"More than a few. My friendship with your mother was the only thing keeping you here at times," she said.

"Damn it. I told you my mother wrecks all my plans," I joked. She laughed. There was a small content little pause.

"I was wrong you know," she said.

"About what?"

"You do belong here," she said, "tonight proved it."

"Just because one arrow met it's mark doesn't mean the rest of them will," I said.

"Sounds like a quote."

"More like a saying," I said, "it means several things. But mainly it means don't leave anything up to chance."

"And what are you trying to say?"

"I'm a thief," I said, "I made one good move. Only one. It doesn't mean I can change what I am. And what I am is self-centered. I have questionable morals. You don't need people like that playing your game. I've been playing the old one for too long."

"You do belong here Pam," she said gently, "Perhaps you aren't one of us at the moment. You have a long way to go. But you could be. You have the potential to be something great."

"You…..you think I could be something?" I asked quietly, not quite believing what I heard, "be something more?"

"Yes, I do."

"No one……" I didn't know what to say, looking down at my shoes and resting my chin on my knees.

"No one what?" pressed Miss Price.

"Are you saying I still have a place here?" I asked deciding not to follow down that train of thought, "Even though I've broken the law?"

"Says who?" she asked, "there isn't even a case against you."

Undercover Thief

"You seem certain."

"Your mother and I have been trying to discover anything about your past for the last five or six months Pamela, and we've drawn blanks! No one will look as hard as we did, and any case with your name on it would have been flagged up to us."

"Well, that's reassuring," I said with a grin.

"Now, I'm not going to convince you that you have to stay Pam," said Miss Price, "and I know in all this confusion you've probably thought of about one hundred ways in which you could get clean away. But this is where you belong.....if you want it."

Then she got up and went back to the agents who were documenting everything that happened here today.

"Me?" I muttered to myself, "working for the law and not against it? That will be the day."

I leant back against the step and grinned to myself realizing that that was exactly what I was doing, what I had done this evening.

I looked around at the school I knew so well now, a place that finally was beginning to feel a little bit like a home rather than a prison. I smiled. Perhaps I did belong here after all.

Author's Note

I would just like to thank you for reading Undercover Thief. I had so much fun writing it. Please, if you enjoyed reading this, leave a review at your favourite online retailer such as Amazon and please recommend Undercover Thief to your friends.

I welcome contact from my readers. You can like my Facebook page www.facebook.com/htkingbooks and follow me on twitter @htkingbooks. You can also go to my website where I will post updates on upcoming books and developments and you can check out my blog! You can also sign up to my e-mail list to receive notifications about new releases.

Parties interested in my work in a business sense, please visit my website in order to send an e-mail to me directly. I am more than happy to receive your contact and answer any and all questions you may have.

Please visit me at;

www.htking.co.uk

~ H. T. King

Printed in Great Britain
by Amazon